The Cosy Travelling Christmas Shop

Lilac Mills lives on a Welsh mountain with her very patient husband and incredibly sweet dog, where she grows veggies (if the slugs don't get them), bakes (badly) and loves making things out of glitter and glue (a mess, usually). She's been an avid reader ever since she got her hands on a copy of *Noddy Goes to Toytown* when she was five, and she once tried to read everything in her local library starting with A and working her way through the alphabet. She loves long, hot summer days and cold winter ones snuggled in front of the fire, but whatever the weather she's usually writing or thinking about writing, with heartwarming romance and happy-ever-afters always on her mind.

Also by Lilac Mills

A Very Lucky Christmas
Sunshine at Cherry Tree Farm
Summer on the Turquoise Coast
Love in the City by the Sea
The Cosy Travelling Christmas Shop

Tanglewood Village series

The Tanglewood Tea Shop
The Tanglewood Flower Shop
The Tanglewood Wedding Shop

Island Romance

Sunrise on the Coast
Holiday in the Hills
Sunset on the Square

Applewell Village

Waste Not, Want Not in Applewell
Make Do and Mend in Applewell
A Stitch in Time in Applewell

LILAC MILLS

The Cosy Travelling Christmas Shop

CANELO

First published in the United Kingdom in 2022 by

Canelo
Unit 9, 5th Floor
Cargo Works, 1–2 Hatfields
London, SE1 9PG
United Kingdom

A CIP catalogue record for this book is available from the British Library.

Print ISBN 978 1 80032 886 0
Ebook ISBN 978 1 80032 885 3

Cover design by Head Design

Cover images © Shutterstock

Look for more great books at www.canelo.co

Printed and bound in Great Britain by Clays Ltd, Elcograf S.p.A.

1

To all Santas everywhere – for keeping the magic of Christmas alive

Chapter 1

'We've got a new inmate,' Seren Fletcher's aunt told her as soon as Seren walked into the care home's TV lounge.

Seren bent down and gave the old lady a kiss on the cheek. Despite her aunt being ninety-three, the old lady's wrinkled skin was soft and smelt of the powder she used on her face every single day, come rain or shine. She was also wearing bright red lipstick, Seren noticed, but most of it had bled into the creases around her mouth, giving her the appearance of a vampire with messy eating habits.

Great-Aunt Nelly patted the seat of the chair next to her, but Seren shook her head.

'Don't tell me you can't stay a while,' Nelly said, her face dropping with disappointment.

'I can stay for as long as you like,' Seren said, 'but the TV is so loud I can't hear myself think. Can we go somewhere quieter?'

'What did you say?' Nelly yelled, and Seren was just about to repeat herself when she caught the twinkle in her aunt's eyes.

'Oh, you,' she said, holding her arm out for Nelly to take.

Nelly shuffled slowly and stiffly forwards in her chair, then using her hands she pushed herself up until she was on her feet. Wobbling precariously, she grasped the proffered arm and caught her balance.

'Do you want your walker?' Seren asked, wincing at the old lady's rather firm grip. Nelly might look frail, but she had considerable strength in her fingers.

'I'd better had. It'll only get nicked if I leave it in here.'

'Surely not.' Seren was aghast; she'd not heard of there being a theft problem in the care home. She thought it was a good home, as far as these places went. It was bright and modern, had lovely gardens, and the staff to patient ratio was excellent. Not only that, the staff couldn't do enough for the residents and treated them with the care, compassion and dignity they deserved, so what Nelly was telling her was rather worrying, and she made a mental note to have a word with a member of staff before she left.

'This lot are a thieving bunch,' Nelly said, putting both hands on her walker and pushing it a fraction. Her steps were small and deliberate – one push of the walker, followed by one foot then the other, and the cycle was repeated.

Seren knew progress would be excruciatingly slow, but the old lady simply couldn't move any quicker; besides, Seren had nothing to rush off for. Dad wouldn't be home from work for ages yet, and this evening's tea was already prepared. Lamb stew with dumplings. Her favourite.

Slowly and carefully Aunt Nelly made her way down the carpeted corridor towards the day room. It was usually quieter in there, but not always – a lot depended on whether a game of cards was taking place, and on who was winning and who was cheating. Things had been known to get quite heated.

'Shall I fetch us a cup of tea?' Seren suggested when her aunt was finally settled in the thankfully deserted day

room. 'Then you can tell me all about this new inmate –
I mean, *resident*. Gosh, you've got me saying it now.'

'Yes, well, it feels like a prison, so you might as well
call the poor sods who are stuck in here inmates.'

'Aunty, it's not that bad!' Seren protested. 'I'll get the
teas.'

'Strong, mind you. I don't want any of that dishwater
stuff your father makes.'

Seren smiled. Her dad's tea-brewing was a non-event.
He was hopeless at it. He usually whipped the teabag
out of the mug before the water had a chance to change
colour. In their house it was Seren who made the tea, out
of respect for her tastebuds.

'There you go – strong as a builder's bucket,' Seren said,
putting the mug of tea on a side table, within easy reach of
arthritic hands. She cradled her own mug as she sipped at
the hot liquid and waited for her aunt to share her news.
There was always something going on in the care home
and Nelly usually had the lowdown. Despite the old lady
complaining about it being like a prison Nelly thoroughly
immersed herself in all the goings-on.

'A new bloke came for a visit today and he's moving in
at the end of the week,' Nelly said.

'What's he like?'

'He's young – eighty-five, I was told – and has a
daughter and a grandson, grown up, of course. He's got a
full head of hair and all his marbles, but then he should at
his age.'

Seren held her lips together in order not to smile.
Young, indeed! Aunt Nelly was only eight years older.

Nelly picked up her mug, took a loud slurp of her tea
and swallowed noisily. 'I've been told he's got Parkinson's,
and I can well believe it; he walks worse than I do, and

3

that's saying something. I've heard him speak though, and I don't think his speech is affected, thank the Lord. It's bad enough being stuck in here at all, without struggling to make yourself understood.' Nelly relayed this with a degree of satisfaction and Seren felt quite sorry for the man. No doubt her aunt would mine him for every scrap of personal information with as much doggedness as a miner pickaxing lumps of coal out of the rock face. She loved to know the ins and outs of everyone's business, and some would call her nosy but Seren knew she had a heart of gold and there was no malice in her.

'I thought about getting him a "welcome to the prison" present, just to be friendly, but...' Nelly shrugged, and glared stonily into her mug.

Oh dear, her aunt wasn't in the best of moods today. 'I can pick up something for you, if you like?' Seren offered.

Nelly shook her head. 'That's the thing, I don't know what he'd like, so I don't know what to get him.'

'Chocolates? Sweets? Beer?'

'Meh, the usual crap. That's what you buy people when you can't be arsed to think of anything.'

'Aunty! You can't use words like—' Seren lowered her voice even though there wasn't anyone else in the room and glanced over her shoulder before saying, '—*arsed*.'

'Why not?'

'It's not exactly ladylike, is it?'

'How old are you?'

'You know perfectly well how old I am,' Seren retorted.

'Seventy, is it? Maybe sixty-five? No one in their right mind would think you're only twenty-eight the way you talk. Ladylike? Pah! That kind of thing went out years ago, along with sitting with your legs crossed at the ankles.'

'It's a good idea if you're wearing a short skirt,' Seren pointed out.

Nelly narrowed her eyes. The creases around them deepened so much that her pupils were barely visible. 'Stop trying to change the subject.'

'What subject?'

'Present buying.'

'Oh, that.'

'Yes, that. Got any other suggestions? Ones where it seems like you actually care?'

'I do care but, like you, I've got no idea what this man does, or doesn't, like. What did you get the last new resident?'

'Funeral flowers. She died within a week.'

'Gosh. Oh, dear. I see. Um… that's awful.'

'Not for her, it wasn't. Heart attack in her sleep. She knew nothing about it. Lucky cow. That's the way I want to go. And the sooner the better if you ask me.'

'Yes, well, erm… how about a nice pair of slippers? I'm sure you can find out what size he takes.'

Seren didn't want to hear a repeat of how much her aunt didn't want to be here. And she wasn't referring to the care home, either. As far as Nelly was concerned, she was past her live-by date and should have been called home to heaven long before now. Not that the old lady believed in heaven, or hell for that matter – she just wanted an end to it because she was tired of being so old and frail, and she shared those thoughts frequently with anyone who'd listen. No doubt this new resident was in for an ear-bashing about it and Seren didn't envy him. 'What's his name?'

'Edwin something-or-other. I forget his surname. That's the problem when you get to my age – you lose your memory as well as your bladder control.'

'It'll be nice for you to have someone new to talk to,' Seren said, ignoring the waterworks comment and trying not to say anything that might set her aunt off. Nelly was clearly out of sorts today.

'I'm not giving him slippers. The rellies always make sure you have new slippers, a new dressing gown and new pyjamas when you come into a place like this. They must think it's like being in a sodding hospital and that you're in bed all day. Fat chance.'

'You'd hate lying in bed all day.'

'I hate daytime TV even more.'

'What have they got organised for this afternoon?' There was always at least one organised activity a day, usually more, and Seren knew her aunt sometimes took part.

'A quiz.'

'That's nice.'

'No, it's not.'

OK, then… Seren resisted the urge to roll her eyes at her aunt's unreasonableness.

Nelly scowled. 'I want something for Dorothy, too. It's her birthday next week.' Before Seren could say anything, she continued, 'And don't suggest chocolates, smellies or hankies. She'll get enough of that rubbish off her kids. No imagination, any of them. Grr.'

Did her aunt just growl? 'We can always look on the internet,' Seren suggested.

Nelly heaved in a deep breath and let it out in a whoosh. 'I want to see it for myself, not look at pictures – that's as bad as ordering out of a catalogue. It never looks the same when it arrives. And I want to touch things. You can't tell the quality of anything unless you give it a good feel.'

Right. There was only one thing for it... Seren gathered her courage. 'How about if I take you shopping?' she said, and she waited for the inevitable backlash.

'How's that going to work? Eh? Answer me that! The last time you took me shopping, your father had to come too because there was no way you'd have got me in or out of the car on your own. Even with his help, it took so long to get me into the wheelchair that it was almost time for the shops to close. And your father was so heavy-handed I had bruises on my behind that lasted a fortnight. Thanks, all the same, but I'd prefer to stay put and do without.'

That wasn't quite how Seren remembered the outing, but technically it was close enough. Despite how gentle Dad had been in helping Aunt Nelly into the car (which had been bad enough), and back out again (that had been even worse), she'd not been happy. And it had taken a while to manoeuvre the borrowed wheelchair up and down kerbs, and in and out of shops, with Nelly grumbling the whole time.

It couldn't have been easy for her aunt either; some of the racks and shelving units in the shops were pushed so tightly together that no one larger than a size 8 could slip between them, never mind a ninety-two-year-old in a wheelchair.

That had been over a year ago, and this was the first time since that Seren had plucked up enough courage to suggest another outing. Her relief when her aunt refused knew no bounds.

There was nothing else she could think of. Either Seren bought something and Nelly approved it (or not

– probably not, so she'd have to return it for a refund), or her aunt would have to pick a gift off the internet.

'How's work?' Nelly asked and Seren pulled a face.

'The same as usual.'

'You need to get out of that place.'

'Just because I work in a supermarket doesn't mean it's not a worthwhile job,' Seren protested.

'I didn't say it wasn't! But if you dislike it as much as I think you do, you need to find something else.'

Seren shrugged. 'I suppose. But I don't know what else I *can* do.'

Nelly snorted. 'You've got a brain in your head, so use it. Life is too short to waste it on a job you hate. Find something you like doing and go for it.'

Seren pulled a face again. Easier said than done. She wasn't sure what she wanted to do, or what she liked doing. Sad, really…

'You want to be careful,' Nelly told her. 'If the wind blows the wrong way your face will stay like that. Which would be a shame, because you've got such a pretty face, too.'

A sudden flurry – if Seren could call the shuffling and scuffing of assorted residents in the corridor a 'flurry' – made Nelly sit up and take notice. 'What day is it?' her aunt demanded.

'Wednesday.'

'Help me out of this chair. I don't want to be last,' Nelly instructed. 'All the good ones will be gone.'

What good ones, Seren mused as she helped Nelly to her feet and placed her walker in front of her.

'I can manage from here; you can get off home. Unless—' a speculative expression appeared on Nelly's face '— how do you fancy barging in front of this lot and holding them back until I get to the front?'

'Absolutely not.'

'I didn't think so. Spoil sport. You've got no gumption.'

Seren followed slowly behind as her aunt made her way towards the main entrance, musing on what gumption was and whether she was supposed to have it, and was surprised to discover the reason for the fuss was the arrival of a mobile library in the car park. Most of the residents would be unable to climb the steps leading into it, but the sides of the large vehicle lifted up to form a kind of awning, revealing shelf after shelf of books. Through the open door Seren could see more books inside. The librarian was handing boxes to one of the staff for them to take inside to those residents who were unable to come out, but many of them were milling around in the cold, eager to get their hands on the latest bestseller.

'Calm down, everyone,' the duty manager said. 'You don't have to go to the books, the books will come to you. So, if you'd all like to go back inside…?' He made jerking gestures with his head, which everyone ignored.

'Is it always this hectic when the mobile library shows up?' Seren asked her aunt, having watched the old lady push, shove and elbow her way to the front. She might be only four foot eight, frail and hunched over, and look as delicate as a baby bird, but she was a force to be reckoned with.

'It's the highlight of my week,' Nelly replied. 'I get to choose my own books – *if* I get the chance and other people don't grab the best ones.' She glared meaningfully at her fellow residents. 'Selfish lot,' she muttered under her breath, then added, 'We could do with something like this, but for gifts—' Nelly abruptly stopped talking. She stared at Seren.

Seren stared back, lightbulbs popping like crazy in her head. 'Are you thinking what I'm thinking?' Seren asked.

'I dunno what you're thinking, but I'm thinking there must be some enterprising person who will bring stuff to you without you having to go out for it. And I don't mean an Amazon delivery driver.' Nelly was so excited she was swaying on the spot, and Seren shot out a hand to steady her. 'Get on that internet of yours and tell them they've got to pay us a visit. It'll be worth their while.' She waggled her thin grey eyebrows and let go of her walker with one hand for long enough to rub her thumb against her fingers. 'Ker-ching!'

'I'll see what I can do,' Seren said. As her great-aunt had pointed out, there must be someone out there offering this very service, and once she'd found them she'd move mountains to make sure they paid her aunt and the other residents a much-needed visit.

–

There was nothing. Not. A. Darned. Thing. At least, not anything within reasonable travelling distance. Crossly, Seren slammed the top of the ancient laptop shut and slumped back in her chair.

'What's up, pumpkin?' Her dad was watching the news and shaking his head – Seren wasn't sure whether it was in disgust or despair. 'Look at that – some blighter has hung severed heads from the oak tree in the park.'

Seren sat up, horrified. 'Real ones?'

The camera zoomed in on the heads, and she was relieved to see they had once been part of dolls, not people. They looked awfully creepy, though.

'Don't be daft. Tinstone isn't London. It'll be for Halloween. Mark my words, as soon as that's out of the way and all the firework nonsense is over and done with, they'll be starting with the Christmas decorations. They've already got tubs of Roses and Quality Street in the supermarket.' Her dad shook his head.

'You *like* Christmas,' Seren pointed out.

'Not in flippin' October, I don't.'

Seren was about to say that October only had a couple more days left in it, but she let it go. She loved Christmas at any time of the year, and if she had her way she'd keep the decorations up permanently. Maybe not the inflatable Santa in the front garden, but certainly the tree and the twinkly lights on the outside of the house, and all those lovely baubles and garlands inside. She made the garlands herself every year, and the wreath for the front door and the centrepiece for the table, using fresh fir branches, strands of ivy, and bunches of holly and mistletoe.

When she had her own place, she'd—

'What's up with you? You've got a face like a slapped wotsit.' Her father pulled her out of her musings, chuckling loudly. Seren considered his laughter most inappropriate, considering he'd just asked her what was wrong.

'Aunt Nelly,' she said.

'What's she done now?' he asked, rolling his eyes and huffing.

'Nothing. It's just that she wants to buy some gifts and she can't get out and about to choose anything.'

Her father shot her a horrified look.

'Don't worry,' she added, hastily. 'She doesn't want to go *out* shopping. What she wants is for the shopping to come to *her*.'

'Thank goodness for that. I don't mind taking her out now and again, but when she said she needed the loo and that I'd have to go in with her to help her get out of her chair…' He shuddered.

Seren bit her lip, trying not to laugh. 'But you didn't take her; I did.'

'The thought was enough. She's a woman. I couldn't take her in the gents, and I certainly couldn't go in the ladies – I'd have been arrested!'

There had been a toilet for disabled use, but it had been locked and you had to fetch a key, and Nelly had said she couldn't hang on that long.

Nelly was her dad's aunt. His mum (Seren's grandma) was her sister. His mum was long gone and so were her other siblings, all seven of them. Nelly was the only one of that generation left, and Seren was thankful the old lady was still around. When she was gone, there'd only be Seren and her dad. There was her mother, of course, but she was living on the Isle of Man with her second husband and Seren only saw her a couple of times a year, so in a way she didn't count. To Seren, her mum hadn't counted for a long time, and since she was fourteen Seren and her dad had been a unit.

'Can't find anything suitable?' he asked sympathetically, looking at the laptop. 'How about smellies or slippers?'

'Ugh, don't go there. I suggested that and she shot me down in flames. She wants to have a look for herself.'

'The home has got a computer the residents can use – let her loose on that.'

'I mean, she wants to look at things in the flesh. And touch them. What she wants is a mobile library, but for gifts.'

'You're going to have to run that by me again.' Her dad looked thoroughly perplexed, so Seren explained.

'And there's no one on the internet who does that?' he confirmed when she'd finished telling him what she'd been searching for and how the mobile library had been responsible for her trawling the internet ever since she'd arrived home.

'There are one or two, but they're miles away, like in Scotland,' she said.

'That's no good, is it? You'll have to go back to the drawing board.'

'I'll have to go back and tell Aunt Nelly,' Seren moaned. 'She's not going to be happy.'

'You could always buy a few things and take them to her – you might strike lucky and there will be something she likes.'

'Yes, I suppose… If I keep the receipts, I can always take them back for a refund. The problem is, she doesn't know what she wants.'

'Do any of us?' her dad muttered, and turned the volume up on the telly, leaving Seren wishing she could do more to help her aunt.

'There's got to be someone local who has a mobile gift shop,' she sighed. 'There's bound to be a call for it, and not just for care home residents. There must be loads of people who are confined to the house or who find it hard to get out, and who'd love a gift shop that would come to them.'

She looked at her father for confirmation, but the only response she got was another shake of her dad's head.

Oh well, she'd done all she could – Aunt Nelly would have to make do with the internet or put up with Seren's choice of gifts.

Chapter 2

Daniel handed over the keys to his truck and gave Tobias a weak smile. Tobias was a whizz mechanic, and over the last couple of years he'd gone into business converting all kinds of vehicles into mobile homes and camper vans. He was doing Daniel a favour by taking a look at his truck's dodgy exhaust. He was doing him another favour by lending him a car for the duration, so at least Daniel had some wheels.

'Please don't tell me it's going to cost a fortune,' he begged.

'I'll do my best to keep the cost down,' his friend promised, slipping the keys into his pocket and turning his attention back to the camper he was updating.

'Thanks. I don't know what I'd do without you.' At least Daniel didn't need the truck urgently, because the end of autumn was the start of his quieter time. It was a pain, but people's thoughts tended to shy away from gardens and gardening in the run-up to Christmas, which meant, as a freelance gardener, he had considerably less work. It would pick up again in the new year (he already had two jobs booked in for January) but between now and then it was usually a lean time for him. He had a few bits and pieces that would take him into mid-November, but things were already starting to slacken off.

'I hope you don't find anything else wrong with it,' Daniel added, worriedly. He could barely afford to pay Tobias, even though he was only charging him mates rates.

Tobias sent him a sympathetic look. He knew all about Daniel's struggle to stay afloat financially during the winter months. 'Have you got any work lined up at all?' he asked.

'A bit. Not much. Although I have taken on some seasonal work this winter,' he said, then added without thinking, 'Nothing to do with gardens, though.'

'Doing what?'

'Santa Claus,' Daniel muttered, wishing he hadn't said anything. It was embarrassing enough doing the job, but now that Tobias knew about it, Daniel was going to get a right good ribbing.

True enough, Tobias chortled. 'You? Santa Claus? This I've got to see. Can I sit on your knee? Am I on your naughty or nice list?' He offered up a piece of insulation to the ceiling of the van he was currently working on and stared at it critically, a smirk playing about his mouth.

'Bugger off,' Daniel said mildly, wondering if he should offer to give Tobias a hand or whether he'd just be in the way. He loved working with his hands, but his tools of choice were spades and potting compost, not spanners and engine oil.

'Seriously, Dan, you'll be good at it. You get on well with kids.' Realising what he'd said, Tobias pulled a face. 'Sorry, mate. I wasn't thinking.'

'That's all right. It's not as though I'm Amelia's real dad.' Daniel didn't want to rake up his failed relationship with Amelia's mother again, so he was relieved when Tobias's phone rang.

'Hello, T&M Conversions,' Tobias said, jamming the phone into the crook of his neck as he tried to hold the length of thermal insulation in place with one hand. 'Hang on a sec, I'm putting you on speaker,' he said to the person on the other end.

Daniel made a "T" sign with his hands and Tobias nodded.

He'd have a cuppa, then get off; Tobias was busy and he didn't want to take up any more of his friend's time, as he was already putting himself out to fix the truck. Tobias was a good mate, even if he was a bit of a player when it came to women. He always had a new one on his arm and Daniel envied him his ability to attract the opposite sex without any apparent effort. He wished he was more like Tobias with his easy-come, easy-go manner, but Daniel couldn't help his own more serious attitude towards dating. He didn't take it half as lightly as Tobias did. Yeah, and look where that had got him, he thought: Gina.

As Daniel walked across the garage to the kettle, he had half an ear on Tobias's call and the other half on an Ed Sheeran song on the radio. It was about death and heaven, and was emotional enough to make him feel like crying.

'Do you do van conversions?' a man's voice asked over the phone's speakers, and Daniel glanced around in time to see Tobias let go of the insulation.

'We do,' Tobias said. 'What were you thinking of?'

'An ice cream van.'

'Er, you want to convert something like a transit into an ice cream van? Or you have an ice cream van you want to update?'

'I'm thinking of buying an ice cream van for my daughter. But not for ice cream.'

'As a motor home?' Tobias asked.

Daniel knew his friend had worked on stranger things, like a fire engine for instance. Any space in any vehicle could be transformed into campervan-style accommodation, as long as the client had the money. Tobias would supply the imagination and expertise to get it done – he was good like that.

'Er, not exactly,' the voice on the other end of the phone said.

'Then what, if you don't mind me asking?' Tobias pointed at a packet of biscuits lying next to the kettle and raised his eyebrows and nodded.

'As a gift shop,' the caller said.

'Right…' Tobias shot Daniel a look which said he thought the guy was pulling his leg.

'See, my daughter has an aunt – she's my aunt as well – who lives in a care home, and she had an idea when she saw a mobile library.'

'Your daughter or your aunt?'

'Me, actually. I'll start again, shall I? I am thinking about buying a used ice cream van and transforming it into a mobile shop. Can it be done?'

'It most certainly can.'

'OK, then. How much?'

Daniel carefully placed the packet of biscuits under his arm, picked up the mugs of tea and walked over to Tobias.

'Ta, mate,' Tobias mouthed at him, before turning back to his call. 'It depends on what you want doing.'

'Yes, of course, it does. But you can definitely do it?'

'Absolutely.'

'Rightio, all I've got to do now is buy it.'

'When you've got the vehicle, bring it in and we can have a chat and take it from there.'

'Okey-dokey. Thanks. See you soon.'

Tobias popped the phone in his pocket and turned his attention to Daniel. 'There's one thing I can say about my job – I'm never bored. A bit like you, really. No two jobs are the same and no two clients are the same.'

'I wonder if you'll ever get to meet this guy and the ice cream van he hasn't bought yet?' Daniel mused.

'No idea – but do you know who I'd like to meet?'

'Who?' Daniel took a slurp of tea.

'Father Christmas! Ho, ho, ho!'

Daniel sighed. He was never going to live this down, was he?

–

'Daniel, is that you?' Daniel's mum yelled down the phone, and he held it away from his ear with a grimace.

'Yes, Mum, it's me.' He was mildly concerned to think that a) she didn't recognise his voice and that b) she thought someone else would be answering his mobile.

'Good. I'm glad I caught you. I just wanted to tell you that Grandad is settled in. He's got that nice room I was telling you about, with the view of the garden. He's all unpacked and is looking forward to joining in with everything.'

'Great. I'll pop in to see him on my way home. Is there anything I can take him? Anything he needs or has forgotten?'

'Just yourself. He'll be thrilled to see you.'

'He saw me yesterday,' Daniel pointed out.

'I'm scared he'll think we'll forget him.'

'Mum, he's only been there a couple of hours. And it was his decision to go into a home.' Daniel still didn't understand why. His grandad's Parkinson's wasn't that bad, yet. But that was it, wasn't it – *yet*. It would get worse, and there was no telling how fast, or how severe the deterioration would be.

'I didn't want him to go,' Daniel's mum wailed, and he could tell she was close to tears.

'Neither did I. We'd have managed.' Somehow they would have done, although he had no clue as to how.

'Yes, we would have,' Linda said. 'I could have taken early retirement, and with home care and whatnot, we'd have coped.'

'I could have moved back home…' And that was where the whole argument for Edwin not going into a home had fallen apart. His grandad had been adamant that wasn't what he wanted for his grandson, and Daniel had recalled the heated conversations where Edwin had been furious that Daniel was happy to 'waste his youth' (Edwin's words, not Daniel's) on caring for an old man like him.

Never mind that Daniel was thirty-one and his youth was fast disappearing. Or that he'd have been more than happy to alter his lifestyle if it meant Grandad didn't have to go into a home. Anyway, he was hardly living the high life at the moment, was he, and he couldn't see the situation changing any time soon.

But Edwin, being of sound mind and fierce determin-ation, had insisted, and neither Daniel nor his mum had any say in the matter.

'Hello?' his mum called, and he realised he'd been silent for a while.

'I'm still here.'

'Fancy popping round for your tea? I've made a hotpot.'

'Lovely. I'll be there after I've visited Grandad.'

There was a pause, then his mum said, 'Don't get cross, but Gina phoned me. She said she can't get hold of you on your mobile.'

'That's because I've blocked her number.' A bolt of fear hit him in the chest. 'What did she want? Is Amelia OK?'

'Amelia is fine, as far as I know. But Gina was upset,' his mum said.

So, she was trying to get at him through his mum instead, was she? 'Low blow, Gina,' he muttered. 'Low blow.' He carried on in a voice his mum could hear, 'Yeah, upset she was caught. If I hadn't gone out that night, and had stayed in like I told her I was going to, I never would have caught her with her ex.'

'She claims nothing happened.'

'Tongues happened.'

'Yuck. I didn't need to hear that kind of detail,' his mother replied, then hesitated. 'It can't be easy for Amelia to have you in her life one minute, then out of it the next.'

'I know.' Daniel pressed his lips together. It wasn't easy for him, either. He missed the little girl like crazy, and he knew his mum was only trying to help, but... 'I can't say with Gina because of Amelia. If she was mine, it would be a different matter, but I've got no legal claim. I am just a guy who used to shack up with her mother.'

'There's no need to be crude. Two years is a long time in the life of a child.'

'Yes, it is, and I would never have become so involved with Gina if I'd realised what she was capable of.'

'The poor mite must be so confused. I bet she can't understand why you're not around any more.'

His mother had hit the nail on the head. Amelia didn't understand. But she wasn't his daughter, and even if she had been he wasn't sure whether he could commit to living with someone who had been unfaithful. He missed the little girl dreadfully – more than he missed her mother, if he was honest – but he couldn't take Gina back after what she'd done; and who was to say she wouldn't do it again?

Better to stop it right here, than have it limp along for another few months. Their relationship was over. Amelia had a father and Daniel wasn't it, although he'd wanted to be. That was the fella who Gina had been playing tonsil-tennis with – Amelia's real dad. It was extremely telling about the state of their relationship that when Daniel had seen Gina and Carl kissing passionately, his first thought was how pleased he was for Amelia to have her parents back together.

Daniel had been devastated for the little girl when he'd heard on the grapevine that Carl wasn't interested in taking up with Gina again, but at least it explained why Gina was hassling him now and wanting to get back with him.

Unfortunately for her, Daniel couldn't forgive or forget.

–

Daniel pressed the buzzer and waited to be admitted to the care home. Having never had any experience of places like this, he didn't know what to expect, and he was pleasantly surprised at the newness of the building and the landscaped grounds around it. Of course, he could only see the front of it from the car park, but his mother had assured him the residents had access to private gardens at the back of the home and they were equally as nice, if not nicer.

Once he'd stated his name and the reason for his visit over the intercom, the door opened and he stepped inside. Expecting to smell boiled cabbage and disinfectant, a waft of perfume drifted across his face from the vase of flowers on the main desk, followed by a hint of polish and the aroma of ground coffee.

The area he was standing in was light and airy, and appeared to be more like a hotel foyer than an old people's home, he thought, as he walked up to the desk to ask where his grandfather's room was.

'Edwin? You'll find him in either the games room or his bedroom,' the woman informed him, and pointed him in the right direction.

Apprehensively, Daniel set off along the corridor, taking note of the framed prints on the walls and the serviceable carpet underfoot. Yep, it still reminded him of a hotel – a low-to-mid-range one, but definitely not budget, and a far cry from the grim hospital-type environment he'd been expecting.

The sound of laughter and raised voices drew him on, and he glanced into open doorways as he headed towards the noise, passing a dining room, a kitchen and several bedrooms along the way.

As soon as Daniel reached the games room, he spotted Edwin. His grandfather was seated in a wing-backed chair, with a mug on a table next to him, watching two gents playing what looked like a complicated game involving cards and a wooden board. A pile of plastic counters sat in front of each man, and a crowd had gathered around them.

'He's cheating!' one very elderly lady shrieked, and others leapt in with various opinions, along with much raucous laughter and the occasional wave of a walking stick in the air.

Daniel took a moment to study his grandad, hoping the old man wasn't feeling lost or lonely, and was relieved to see him smiling and joining in. A gentleman to his right leant across and said something to him, and Edwin nodded.

As reluctant as Daniel was to interrupt what could be a budding friendship, he was nevertheless desperate to speak to his grandad and hear from his own lips that Edwin wasn't regretting the move. Mind you, it was early days and the novelty factor was still in evidence. Daniel would wait to see how Edwin felt about the home in a month or so.

As though he knew he was being observed, Edwin looked towards the door and when he saw Daniel standing there, his whole face lit up in a wrinkly grin and he beckoned him in.

Smiling, Daniel went over to him and gave him a kiss on his stubbly cheek. 'How are you, Grandad?'

'All the better for seeing you, my boy.' He scanned the room, saying, 'This is my grandson, Daniel, Linda's son. She was the one who was here earlier.'

A series of hellos and other assorted greetings came his way, along with waves and smiles, before everyone's attention returned to the game.

'It's the final,' Edwin said to Daniel. 'Another tournament starts next week. I've already put my name down, and for the Scrabble competition.'

'What are they playing?'

'Cribbage. Have you never played it?'

Daniel shook his head.

'Help me up and we'll go to the kitchen. I could do with a brew.'

Daniel held onto the old man's arms and hefted him gently to his feet, keeping a firm hold on him whilst he got the walker into position.

'Hey, that's mine!' a woman's voice cried. 'Get your own.'

'It *is* his own, you daft bat,' another lady said. 'Ignore her, Edwin. Nelly can't see for looking. Hers is behind her chair.'

'What's it doing there?' Nelly demanded swivelling awkwardly around in her seat. 'No wonder I didn't see it – I haven't got eyes in the back of my head.'

'Oh, shush.'

'Don't you shush me!' Nelly was trying to get to her feet, and Daniel wondered if he should help, but Edwin was already halfway to the door and Daniel decided to follow him.

'Don't mind that lot,' his grandad said. 'There's no harm in them. I've been told that Nelly is as cantankerous as they come, but she's got a heart of gold. She gave me a welcome-to-prison card. She'd made it herself, but it's the thought that counts. Shove a teabag in a mug, will you? I'm parched.'

Daniel looked around the kitchen and saw that it was equipped with a hot drinks dispenser, a fridge, a toaster and a microwave. 'Do you have to pay for this?' He pointed to the drinks machine, unable to see anywhere to put money in.

'Help yourself. It's part of the package.'

As Daniel set about making tea for them both, he asked, 'Is it really like a prison?' He kept his back to his

24

grandad, but he could see the old man's distorted reflection in the gleaming stainless steel.

'Good grief, no! It's great.' Edwin's expression was surprised. 'I know I didn't think your mum could cope with my health problems, but I'm not a masochist. If it was that bad, I wouldn't have moved in. It's pretty good so far. The food is decent, my room is nice, the staff are friendly, and the other residents seem a nice bunch. Did you know Nelly also gave me a pair of slippers as a welcome present, and when she gave them to me she apologised and said she *could* be arsed but it wasn't her fault because she didn't have many options. I have no idea what she was talking about. She's as batty as they come, but it was kind of her to give me a welcome present,' he added. 'Ta, son.' He took the mug with both hands, to steady it.

Daniel studied his grandad's trembling fingers to see if the shaking had grown any worse since the last time he'd seen him. He was forever checking for signs of the inevitable deterioration.

'She's got dementia, I expect,' Edwin continued. 'Poor lamb. It's an awful disease.' He peered at him over the rim of his mug. 'Old age is a bugger, which is why I don't want you getting to my age and not having lived your life the way you wanted to live it. Now that you and your mum are free of me, what have you been doing with yourself?'

'It's only been a couple of hours, Grandad,' Daniel chuckled. 'I've been trying to sort the truck out – I told you the exhaust was making a funny noise, didn't I? And I don't know what Mum's been up to since she settled you in this morning.'

'I told her to get her hair done or have a facial, but I bet she went home and cleaned my old room.'

'Yeah, she probably did,' Daniel agreed fondly, and he suspected she would have been sobbing as she did so, bless her. It was a good job he was popping in to see her after this, so she wouldn't be on her own. Even if she hadn't asked him for tea, he'd have called in anyway, just to check how she was coping. Grandad had lived with her for a good few years, so she was bound to be feeling strange now he wasn't there.

Daniel spent over an hour with his grandfather, chatting. He was quick to reassure his grandad that he hadn't forgotten the old man's birthday in a few days' time (no, Edwin didn't want a cake or balloons, or any other kind of fuss), but Edwin was more concerned with reassuring Daniel that his decision to move to the care home had been the right one. Although Edwin had only eaten two meals there so far, they'd both been lovely he told Daniel, and he proudly showed off his room, and the public areas such as the TV room and the gardens, and Edwin told him what he'd learnt of the other residents so far.

Daniel had to concede that his grandad appeared content with his lot.

As the old man had said so many times before, and he repeated again today, he felt he was able to come to terms with his illness much more now that he had round-the-clock care and didn't have to worry about how his increasing dependence was affecting Linda and Daniel's quality of life. No matter how vociferously Daniel protested, Edwin insisted that caring for an old man like him wasn't any life for a young man like Daniel. Or for his mum, for that matter.

'Linda can work for a bit longer if that's what she wants to do,' Edwin said. 'Or enjoy her retirement, now that she doesn't have to spend all her time looking after me. And you, young man, can see about finding yourself a proper girlfriend – one who treats you right and loves the bones of you – because that's what you deserve.'

'OK, Grandad,' Daniel said, smiling. But although his mouth was doing the right thing and he was making the right noises, his heart wasn't as keen on the idea. As far as Daniel was concerned, he'd had enough of women for a time, especially cheating ones with children who could get hurt.

Chapter 3

Halloween had come and gone and Seren was stacking boxes of Christmas crackers on the supermarket shelf when a voice cried, 'Mummy, Mummy, it's Seren!' and she turned around just as a small body launched itself at her.

'Oof!' Seren grunted as the head of a five-year-old child hit her full in the stomach and nearly knocked her off her feet.

'Freya!' Nicole rolled her eyes. 'Sorry – she got away from me.'

'I don't mind,' Seren said, kneeling down and hugging the little girl. 'She's got a hard head, though.' It would take her a minute to catch her breath properly after being headbutted in the belly button. 'Have you been a good girl?' she asked her goddaughter.

Freya nodded vigorously. 'I've been the goodest girl ever.'

Seren giggled. 'I'm glad to hear it. That deserves a kiss.' She gave the child a smacker on the cheek.

'Ew,' Freya protested, scrubbing at her face with her sleeve.

'She thinks she's too old for kisses, and too old to hold my hand when we cross the road,' Nicole explained.

'*I* like having kisses,' Seren said to the child. 'Especially since I don't get them very often.'

Freya stared at her curiously. 'Why not? Doesn't your mummy kiss you?'

'She does when I see her, but my mummy lives a long way away, so I don't see her very often.'

'I see mine all the time,' Freya sighed and shook her head, as if it was a chore to have her mum around.

Seren gave Nicole a sympathetic look. 'Is someone itching to spread their wings a bit?'

'Someone is trying to fly before they can hop.'

'I can hop – see?' Freya stood on one leg and hopped in a bouncy circle.

'And someone understands more than they should,' her mother added. 'We were passing, and she insisted we came in to see if you were working today. Sorry,' she repeated.

'That's OK. I love seeing her, and you too, of course.'

'If you love seeing her so much…?'

'You want me to babysit?' Seren deduced, smiling.

'Yay! Seren is going to look after me, Seren is going to look after me,' Freya chanted, at the top of her voice.

'Shhh,' Nicole said. 'Do you want everyone to hear you?'

Freya thought for a moment. 'Yes. I don't mind. It's not a secret.'

'You can't keep anything secret with this horror around.' Nicole ruffled her daughter's hair to show her she didn't mean it.

'Geddoff!!' Freya patted her curls back into place, and Seren stifled a giggle.

'When do you want me?' she asked.

'Tomorrow evening? I'm supposed to be going to a WI meeting with Marjorie, and Aaron was going to be looking after her, but he's been told he's got to work, so unless you offer…?'

'What do you mean *offer*? You asked.' Marjorie was Aaron's mum and Seren envied Nicole's easy relationship with her mother-in-law. She also envied her relationship with Aaron, because he and Nicole were madly in love. Seren would like to be madly in love and experience the bliss that Nicole felt. Oh, well, maybe one day…

'Offer, ask… it's the same thing,' Nicole said.

'Er, not really. What time do I need to be at yours?'

'Seven?'

'I'll be there,' Seren promised.

'Freya will be bathed and in bed – but she'll probably want you to read her a story.'

'Three stories,' Freya clarified, holding up four fingers and winking at Seren. 'And you can play with my dolls,' she said in a faux-whisper which was loud enough for her mother to hear.

Nicole pretended she hadn't, and Seren put a finger to her lips and said, 'Shhh,' which made the little girl giggle.

'We'd better let Seren get back to work before she gets told off,' Nicole said, taking hold of the child's hand. 'Say goodbye.'

'Bye.' Freya gave Seren a broad grin and a wave.

Seren waved back, smiling, and she continued to smile as Nicole led Freya away to the sound of Freya wanting to know if Seren would have to go sit on the naughty step and not have any sweets.

–

Seren preferred manning the tills because it gave her a chance to sit down. She also liked it because she could chat to customers whilst she scanned their purchases, without the manager assuming she was skiving off for a natter with a friend. Nicole hadn't been very far off the mark when she'd said to Freya that Seren would get told off, although the manager, Pamela, would couch the reprimand as a 'direction'; in other words, 'if you're free, please could you stock up the fruit aisle, round up the baskets, check the sell-by-dates' – anything which didn't involve taking time out to speak to someone. Thank goodness her shift was about to end. Maybe if it wasn't for Pamela she might like her job a little better, but as things stood now, she couldn't wait to go home.

As her mind turned to the evening ahead, she thought she might make a start on making some Christmas decorations. Seeing all the crackers, cards and wrapping paper today had got her in the mood to do something creative and she always loved making things for Christmas. Her speciality was garlands and wreaths to go on the door, using fresh greenery she would gather from the park. She often had compliments from the neighbours when they saw the Christmas wreath hanging from a hook above the knocker, and she occasionally made one for them, too. Her favourite bit, apart from seeing the finished result, was trying to come up with new designs, such as the heart-shaped wreath she'd made last year. Although, with the bright red holly berries scattered through it, it had possibly been more suitable for Valentine's Day than Christmas! All she would have needed to do was to swap the berries for roses, and she might have done if she'd had any reason to celebrate Valentine's Day. The lack of a love interest in her life was a bit of a drawback when it came to the fourteenth of February.

Seren was just catching her breath after a flurry of customers and was counting down the minutes to the end of her shift, when a man placed a bottle of whisky on the conveyor belt.

She glanced up at him automatically as she scanned the item, and he must have mistaken her casual look for something more critical because as he reached for his wallet he said, 'It's not for me, it's for my grandad's birthday. He likes a drop of whisky.'

'That's nice.' Seren's thoughts immediately jumped to Aunt Nelly's assessment of the gift of alcohol meaning the giver couldn't be arsed to think of anything else, and she stifled a grin.

'I've bought him a VR headset too. I hope he can work it.' The man frowned as he handed over the money.

'Wow, I wouldn't mind one of those myself.' It looked like the guy *could* be arsed, after all: unless he was buying it in the hope that his grandad couldn't operate it and would give it back to the guy. Who was seriously good-looking, Seren thought. Tall, broad-shouldered, flat-stomached and brown-haired. His hands, she noticed, had dirt ingrained in the creases, although the rest of him looked clean and tidy.

'He's eighty-six today, and has got Parkinson's. He's always wanted to visit the pyramids in Egypt but he never had the opportunity or the funds. I guess he never will, now.' He blinked and looked at a point over her shoulder, then his focus returned to her. 'I'd take him to see them but it's too late, so this is the next best thing. He had to move into a care home recently; only been there three weeks.' He laughed self-consciously. 'I don't know why I'm telling you this.'

'I have the sort of face that means people talk to me. I can be on an empty bus and if someone gets on, they always make a beeline to sit next to me,' she said with a smile to show him she didn't mind.

'You have a pretty face.' He stopped suddenly, looking horrified. 'Sorry.'

Seren laughed. 'I'm not! It's not often anyone tells me I'm pretty.'

'They should.' He was earnest, like he meant it, but he was embarrassed too, as the hint of blush on his cheeks testified.

Aw… Seren was touched. She was also impressed by his thoughtfulness in his gift choices for his grandad. But even as she thought it, she wondered if an eighty-six-year-old would actually know what a VR headset was, which was quickly followed by the thought that a mobile gift shop would be unlikely to carry such an object. She still did the occasional search of the net to see if a mobile shop close enough to go to the care home had miraculously popped into being since the last time she'd looked.

She handed the man his change, and as he took it she checked out his left hand.

No ring – but that didn't necessarily mean anything. She'd dated a gym-bunny once, who wore a signet ring that used to belong to his dad, but he always took it off when he was working out. She guessed this guy probably worked with his hands and he might well remove a wedding ring whilst he was at work.

'I hope your grandad likes his presents,' she said, as he returned his wallet to his pocket and picked up the bottle of whisky.

'So do I! It's hard buying gifts for people, even if they are your relatives and you know them well.'

'Definitely. I've already started thinking about what to buy people for Christmas.'

He shuddered. 'Oh, God, please don't mention Christmas.'

'Don't you like it?'

'I'm not a fan. It's far too commercialised. And expensive. And it starts too early. As soon as Bonfire Night is out of the way, all you'll see and hear is Christmas.'

'We've already started putting out Christmas stock,' she pointed out.

'Great! By the time Christmas comes, I'll be heartily sick of it.'

As he walked away, Seren couldn't resist humming 'I Wish It Could Be Christmas Every Day'. The guy shot her a sad look over his shoulder and shook his head. Then he grinned and winked at her, and she was glad she was sitting down, because if she'd been standing her legs would have turned to jelly.

The guy was seriously hot.

It was a pity she'd probably never see him again.

–

That was a lesson in how to make a fool of yourself, Daniel thought, as he strode out of the supermarket towards his car. What on earth had possessed him? He didn't normally chew the ear off total strangers and share personal information with them.

Mind you, the woman on the till did have cute ears, he'd noticed.

He'd noticed an awful lot more as well, such as the blonde hair piled on top of her head and the little wisps around her face. He'd also noticed her blue eyes, the smattering of freckles across her nose which he guessed might be a leftover from the summer, and her ready smile. He

hadn't been flattering her when he'd said she was pretty –
he'd been telling the truth. But it would have been better
if he had kept the thought to himself, and not announced
it to the whole shop. She must have thought he was a right
idiot. It was a good job he'd probably never see her again,
as the supermarket she worked in wasn't one he usually
frequented (he'd only popped in because it was so near to
the care home), so there was little chance of him bumping
into her unless he paid it a visit.

Putting thoughts of attractive checkout operatives out
of his head, he turned his mind towards his grandad and
what the old gent would make of the presents. The whisky
would be gratefully received he knew, but what about the
headset? Daniel hoped he'd like it. As he'd mentioned to
the woman on the till, buying gifts wasn't easy.

Edwin was in the games room again, but this time the
games that were being played were of the pass-the-parcel
variety. However, as Daniel soon discovered, the goal was
not to unwrap a layer of the parcel in the hope there'd be a
little gift inside as a prelude to the main one, but to try to
avoid unwrapping it. Therefore the parcel was doing the
rounds at an impressive speed for arthritic hands.

Each resident was wearing a party hat, along with
grimly determined expressions.

'This looks like fun,' Daniel said, after trying to kiss his
grandad on the cheek and being waved away: the parcel
was only four chairs away and as soon as it reached Edwin,
he grabbed it and almost flung it at the man sitting next
to him.

'It is,' Edwin said, bleakly.

'Why don't you want to unwrap a layer?'

'Because there's a forfeit inside some of them. Ooh, the
music has stopped. Open it, open it, open it.' Everyone,

apart from the woman in whose lap the parcel now resided, took up the chant.

Warily, she pulled the newspaper off it, revealing yet another layer underneath and a piece of A4 paper.

'What does it say?' someone shouted out.

'Hold your horses, I've got to put my glasses on.' Slowly and with tremulous fingers, the old lady took her glasses case out of her cardigan pocket, opened it, unfolded the arms, and slid them onto her face.

By this time, Daniel was invested – he simply had to know what was written on that piece of paper.

'Be spoon-fed trifle by the person sitting next to you,' she read out, and Daniel didn't think that was too bad, until she added, 'They have to be wearing a blindfold. I hope there aren't any pips in the trifle, because if there are, I'll have to take my teeth out.'

Daniel's eyes widened. 'Is this kind of thing normal?' he asked his grandfather quietly.

'Oh yes. It happens whenever anyone has a birthday. It's my birthday today, so we're celebrating.'

'I know, that's why I'm here. I've got you a present or two.'

Edwin's face lit up. 'Shall we go to my room as soon as this is over?' He frowned. 'On second thoughts, it might take a while. Let's go now.'

'How are you finding it, Grandad?' It had been two weeks – surely the novelty was wearing off and the old man would be beginning to realise what a mistake he'd made?

'I'm loving it.'

'Really?'

'Don't sound so surprised. I'm with people my own age – I can relate to them and identify with them.'

'Identify with them,' Daniel repeated woodenly.

'Is that so hard to believe?'

'Not at all.' He just hadn't thought his grandad would need to be around people his own age – it simply hadn't occurred to him that he and his mum weren't enough.

Edwin said, 'There was a programme on the telly about it. It said that being with like-minded people can boost your self-esteem and your self-confidence.'

'I see.'

'We have a good laugh. Mind you, some of them can get on your wick after a bit, but when that happens I bugger off back to my room and do my crossword.'

'Does that happen often?'

'Nah. As I said, we have a laugh.'

Daniel was forced to concede that his grandad did indeed appear to be happy. And he seemed to be a little more mobile lately, although the tremor in his left hand had become marginally worse over the past month or so. But then, that was only to be expected.

Edwin accepted the bottle of whisky graciously and placed it on the dressing table along with the cards he'd received – twenty-three in all, he announced happily, after showing him the one Daniel's mother had given him. Then his attention had turned to the neatly wrapped box in Daniel's hand, and he glanced at him excitedly.

'Go on,' Daniel urged, handing it to him. 'Open it.'

Edwin tore the paper off with all the eagerness of a child at Christmas, but he looked puzzled when he saw the contents. 'What is it?'

'It's Egypt,' Daniel said, causing his grandfather even greater confusion.

But when he explained what it was and showed Edwin how to use it, the old man was almost in tears.

'This is the best present, ever,' he kept repeating, and when it came time for Daniel to leave, he refused to take the headset off, he was so engrossed.

'Don't forget to go back to your party,' Daniel reminded him, as he prepared to go home.

'Meh, they'll all be watching Corrie by now,' he said. 'Or be asleep in the chair. This is wonderful. Just wonderful.'

'Take care, Grandad. I'll fetch you at half eleven on Sunday. Mum's doing a leg of lamb.'

Smiling when the only response he got was a vague wave of a hand, Daniel left his grandad to play with his new toy and stepped out of the room.

'Ow!' a woman squeaked, and he realised he'd just walked into someone.

'Sorry,' he cried, but as he shot out a hand to steady the poor soul that he'd almost knocked over, he saw it wasn't one of the residents, nor was it a member of staff. It was a visitor, and someone he recognised. 'Are you OK?'

The woman from the supermarket checkout stared up at him. 'Hello. How's your grandad? Did he like his presents?'

'He did, thanks. I take it you have a relative here?'

'My Great-Aunt Nelly; she's a bit of a character.'

Ah, the lady who gave Edwin the card and slippers as a welcome to the care home. 'Aren't they all,' he said dryly. 'I was in the games room earlier, and several of them were playing a forfeit version of pass-the-parcel.'

The woman laughed. 'Yes, they do that sometimes.'

'I left when it threatened to get messy.'

'The trifle stunt?'

'Yep.' He shuddered. 'I'm Daniel, by the way, and my grandad is Edwin.'

'Seren.'

She smiled at him, and his tummy somersaulted. Woah, what was all that about?

'No doubt I'll see you around,' she said, walking in the direction of the TV lounge.

Daniel hoped so. He really hoped so...

-

Daniel hadn't been living in his small, rented house for long, but it would do as a stop-gap until he found something he wanted to buy, in an area he wanted to live in, and at a price he could afford. He had stupidly given up his own little cottage with its wonderful garden to move in with Gina. Although it hadn't seemed a stupid move at the time. It had seemed logical and sensible. He'd been spending nearly every night at her house anyway, so the next step was for him to move in with her.

He'd sold his house for not a great deal more than he'd bought it for (the small profit he'd made was sitting in his bank account and he was being very careful not to touch it), thrilled to play happy families with Gina. And for a while, he had been happy.

Unfortunately for him, she hadn't.

She had been happy for him to pay the bills, put food on the table and buy nice things for her and Amelia, but that happiness hadn't extended to being monogamous.

In a way he didn't blame her. Carl was Amelia's father and it was only natural that Gina might want to resume her relationship with the man, even if it was more for Amelia's sake than her own. What Daniel *did* blame her for, was for not ending things with him first. It had seemed to him as though she'd been hedging her bets, and her attitude had been too cold and calculating for his liking.

Their split had not been pretty. He'd wished her well with Carl, and she'd alternately wept and pleaded, then hurled abuse at him when it was clear their relationship was over.

To his relief, he'd walked away with his heart more or less intact when it came to his love life. But when it came to Amelia, he'd been grief-stricken. He missed the little girl dreadfully, and he thought about her every single day.

It must be hard for Amelia not to have him there. He'd been such a large part of her life for nigh on two years, that she must be devastated. But, as he'd said to his mum, he couldn't stay with a woman he no longer loved for the sake of a child that wasn't his and one he had no legal claim to.

In some ways, he'd wished he had asked Gina to marry him and had formally adopted Amelia. At least then he could still be a father to her.

But he hadn't thought of it, and by the time he'd found his girlfriend in the arms of another man, it had been too late.

It didn't help that Gina, possibly sensing her daughter meant more to him than she did, had railed at him at the time that she'd make sure he never saw the little girl again.

Maybe it had been for the best. The last thing Daniel wanted was to upset Amelia. A clean break was better for her, especially if her mother took up with yet another man. Too many father figures in her life might only confuse her, and Gina's new fella might resent him anyway.

Not that Gina had a new man, that he knew of. But it was only a matter of time. Gina was the sort of woman who was never without a man for long, and it had been several months since things had ended between them.

After her initial denial, then anger (probably more because Carl hadn't been interested in getting back together with her, and she'd burnt her bridges with Daniel), Gina had changed tack and had thrown herself at Daniel, pleading that she'd made a mistake and begging him to take her back.

If he had loved her, he would have gone back to her in a heartbeat, but her infidelity had highlighted what had been missing in their relationship.

No, the pair of them were better off going their separate ways; she'd soon find someone else. As for Daniel…? Maybe it was time to think about dating again. Not all women were like Gina, and although his experience with her had made him wary of trusting again, he didn't want to be without love in his life forever.

An image of Seren, the woman from the supermarket, swam into his head and he smiled. He'd enjoyed their banter as he was buying the whisky, and maybe it was fate that their respective relatives were in the same care home. He wouldn't mind bumping into her again, and he knew where she worked so he could make sure that happened. He didn't want to come across as too keen, but if he began shopping there on a regular basis, he might get to know her better.

He was still smiling as he pulled up outside his house and got out of the truck: he'd got the impression that she had seemed to like him, too—

'Glad you're pleased to see me. I'm pleased to see you, too,' Gina said, and Daniel squawked in fright as he walked towards his front gate.

'Flippin' heck, Gina, you almost gave me a heart attack.' He put a hand to his chest, feeling the mad thumping beneath his T-shirt. 'What are you doing here?'

'I've come to see you, of course.' She stepped towards him.

Daniel stepped back.

A momentary flash of annoyance swept across her face, before she hastily rearranged her features into a more seductive expression. 'I've missed you.'

'Hmm.' He bet she had – she'd missed his contribution to her household expenses, more like. He knew he was being cynical, but he couldn't help thinking that way.

She simpered. 'Have you missed me? Now you've had a chance to calm down and think it over?'

Daniel hesitated. He'd not missed Gina, but he had missed being part of a couple. He'd missed someone being there when he got home from work, he'd missed a warm body to cuddle up to at night, he'd missed cooking a meal together, laughing at the TV together, sharing tales about their day...

'Amelia keeps asking after you,' Gina continued, and Daniel's heart clenched.

'That's not fair,' he protested.

'It's true – she does keep asking for you. Why don't you come round one evening? You can put her to bed and read her a story, then we could...'

He raised his eyebrows, daring her to complete the sentence.

'...have a meal and a chat. Talk things over. You never gave me the chance to put my side of the story.'

'There is no side: I know what I saw.'

'It was only a little kiss, for old times' sake. It didn't mean anything.'

Daniel looked up to the sky and took a deep breath, gathering his thoughts. 'I don't think me coming over is a good idea.'

'Why not? We were good together, weren't we? We had a laugh, and other things…'

'No.'

Gina stared at him, emotions flitting across her face, one after the other. The one which stuck was scorn. 'You'll regret it,' she said. 'You'll realise what you've thrown away and come running back to me. But it'll be too late – I'll have found someone else.'

'I hope you find what you're looking for,' he said, his heart heavy.

'Yeah, well, whoever it is will be better in bed. You were useless. No wonder I had to go looking elsewhere.'

Daniel had nothing further to say to her, and when she realised he wasn't going to be drawn into a slanging match, she gave him a final scowl, then flounced on her heel and marched off.

Glad to be rid of her, he hoped it was for good, but even though he was pleased to see the back of her, he still felt terribly sad and more than a little guilty when it came to Amelia, the poor little mite.

He vowed to be extremely careful in future about dating a woman with children; the last thing he wanted was for another child to get hurt.

Chapter 4

'Oh good, you're early. Don't take your coat off, we're going out,' Seren's father announced, as she walked into the house.

Seren blinked at him. 'I've only just come in. Can't it wait? I've had a hell of a shift. A delivery lorry got stuck in the loading bay, and I've been sworn at because we didn't have any bread. One of the tills decided to play up and managed to charge some poor soul nine hundred and forty pounds, instead of nine pounds forty, and we've got two people off sick. My feet are killing me.' She'd been on earlies today and had been dreading the manager asking if she could stay on for a bit since she'd been in at six a.m. Thankfully, Pamela hadn't mentioned it and Seren had been glad to escape. Now that she was home, she wanted nothing more than to have a cup of tea, put her feet up, and watch some late afternoon telly.

'I'll make you a coffee in your travel mug and you can drink it on the way – all you'll have to do is sit there. I'll do the driving.'

'Where are we going?'

'It's a surprise.'

Seren looked at him doubtfully; she'd been on the receiving end of a couple of his surprises before, and they weren't always good. Take that time he'd booked them both in for morris dancing lessons. Seren had nothing against morris dancers – she just didn't want to be one. Her father had thought it might be something they could both do together after she'd made the mistake of lamenting that she hadn't had ballet lessons when she was a child. He'd wanted to get a bit fitter and had thought morris dancing was an ideal way to go about it. He'd not factored in all the jumping and hopping around, which had come as a bit of a shock to his sixty-four-year-old knees.

'A *nice* surprise,' he added, seeing her expression.

'You always say that.'

'This time it's true.'

'Does it involve exercise, because I'm whacked. You'll be lucky if I can manage to walk to the car.'

'No exercise, I promise.'

'What time will we be back? I'm starving. What's for tea?'

'I thought we could pick up some fish and chips on the way home.'

'On the way home from *where*?'

'Oh, now, that would be telling.'

Seren threw up her hands in frustration and gave in to the inevitable. Her dad was behaving like a dog hearing the word 'walkies' – full of excited nervous energy and hopeful looks – so she went along with it. At least there was the promise of a fish and chip supper at the end of it, and her mouth watered and her taste buds tingled in anticipation.

She got in the car and settled back in the seat. 'Are we going far?' she asked, wondering if she had time for a snooze.

'Can't say.'

'For goodness' sake! You can at least tell me how long it will take. If it's more than ten minutes I can catch forty winks.'

'About thirty-five minutes, according to the satnav,' Patrick said, then shot her a worried look and put his hand over the screen.

Too late, she'd seen the postcode. Giggling, she picked up her phone and typed it in. Not sure what she was expecting to find, she was surprised to see the postcode was for a street in the middle of a housing estate.

She zoomed out, and saw there were a couple of shops and businesses highlighted, but nothing she would have thought her dad would be interested in.

Too intrigued to doze, Seren watched the world go by and wondered what he was up to. There was one thing to be said for living with her dad – he was unpredictable. But in a nice way. Sometimes she wondered who was the most mature out of the two of them, because he could, and did, act like a teenager at times.

Eventually Patrick indicated left, and the car turned off the main road and into the housing estate Seren had seen on the map, so she sat up straight and gazed around, although she wasn't sure what she was expecting to see. Nothing would surprise her when it came to her dad.

'We're here,' he declared, pulling into the side of the road in front of a house with an ice cream van on its drive.

'Where is *here* exactly?' Seren asked. It was starting to get dark, and all she wanted to do was to go home, have something to eat, and paint a bauble or two. She had lots of ideas and some new metallic paints she wanted to try out.

'We've come to collect that,' her father said proudly, pointing towards the house with the ice cream van sitting outside.

'What?' Seren looked but she couldn't see what he meant. It was just a house. And what did he mean by 'collect it'?

'I've bought it,' Patrick said.

'You've bought it? How? I mean, what with? Have you had a win on the lottery? And why buy a house here?'

Her dad wrinkled his forehead. 'I haven't bought a house. Whatever gave you that idea?'

'You just said you had.'

'I didn't.'

'You did!'

'I said I've bought *that*.' He pointed again, and Seren, who was about to continue arguing with him, paused.

Was he referring to the van?

Nah, he couldn't be. He didn't even particularly like ice cream.

'You don't mean the van… *do you*?'

'I do.' He looked as pleased as Punch and a coil of fear twisted in her stomach.

Please don't tell me he's going senile, she begged silently. 'What are you going to do with it? It's the wrong time of year to sell ice cream.'

'I'm not going to sell ice cream.'

'What, then? Hot chocolate? Candy canes? Ginger-bread men?' she scoffed. He was having her on; he *must* be.

'It's a thought – but what you sell is up to you.'

Seren put a hand to her brow. She had a headache coming on and she was beginning to feel nauseous. 'I don't understand.'

Patrick slung an arm around her shoulders and hugged her to him. 'It's obvious – you wanted a mobile gift shop, so this is it.'

She continued to stare at it. The van didn't look anything like the ones she'd seen on the internet. And didn't her dad say he'd bought it—

Seren rolled her eyes as the penny dropped. '*You want me to run a gift shop out of an ice cream van?*' she shrieked.

'That's the idea.'

'What on earth possessed you? Dad, I can't drive an ice cream van, and I certainly don't know anything about operating one.'

'But it won't be an ice cream van, will it? It will be a gift shop,' her father pointed out.

Seren nearly swore. 'No, it's so not a good idea. Let's get back in the car and go home. My tummy is crying out for that fish and chips you promised.'

'He gave her the keys to his car. I'll see you back at the house.' Her father looked so disappointed she could have cried.

'Aren't you coming with me?' she asked.

'I've got to drive the van back. I was hoping you would do that, but…'

'You really have bought it?'

He nodded.

'I thought you were exaggerating, or it was a turn of phrase.'

'I've bought it.'

'Oh, Dad. How much did it set you back?'

'I'm not saying. It was supposed to be a gift, so you could make your dreams come true.'

'My dream isn't to drive around in an ice cream van selling stuff. I was hoping someone else had that dream, and I could ask them to visit Aunt Nelly.' Seren was astounded, stunned, dumbfounded, and flummoxed that he should have gone to such lengths on the basis of her conversation with Aunt Nelly and a disappointing internet search.

Her father looked as though he was about to cry. 'Will you at least take a look at it? I can't leave it here – the chap I've bought it off wants it gone this evening.'

'If I must. I'll even drive it home, considering you've already paid for it.' She shook her head incredulously. 'But you can put it back up for sale tomorrow. Or use it yourself.'

Seren reluctantly followed her father as he made his way to the front door, rang the bell and waited for it to be answered.

She didn't say anything when the chap who was selling it handed over the various documents along with the keys, and showed them around the van.

The only time she made any comment was when the seller demonstrated the chimes, and the jaunty sound of a tinny '*O Sole Mio*' rang out, and even then she only muttered, 'Good grief,' and covered her ears as her dad started singing, 'Justa one Cornetto, geeve eet to meeee…'

'It's a lovely thought,' she said to her father once the man had gone back inside, leaving them alone with the ice cream van. 'I appreciate it, but when I said a mobile shop, I was imagining something more in the way of a large van, or even a bus; something people could climb aboard and browse.'

'You said yourself that it's a good idea, and that there is a market for it.'

'It's a good idea for *someone* – just not me. I can't see myself driving around the streets in this. Look at it. It's got a cone on the top, a couple of fridges inside, and an ice cream dispensing machine. It's got pictures of ice cream all over it and it's bubble-gum pink. *Pink*, I ask you!'

'It needs a bit of work,' her dad admitted.

'You think?'

'It won't take much to knock it into shape.'

She gave him a sceptical look.

'I know you were imagining something bigger, but think how manoeuvrable this is. You can take it almost anywhere.'

'The scrapyard?'

He ignored her comment. 'And you can play a tune to let people know you're on the street.'

'Imagine their faces when they pour out of their houses expecting to buy a 99, and what they get offered is a berry-scented candle. It plays *O Sole Mio*, Dad. It's an *ice cream tune*.'

'I expect it can be altered to something more festive for Christmas.'

Seren didn't know whether to laugh or cry. 'OK, say I agree to this madness… It needs a complete renovation, including a paint job.'

'On the plus side, it's got a brand new MOT, and the engine is in good nick and so's the underneath.' He kicked a tyre as if to prove his point.

Bless him, he was so excited and she hated to burst his bubble, especially since he'd already bought it. If money hadn't changed hands, she'd have dragged him away, but as things stood, she had no choice other than to drive the monstrosity home and hope she could persuade him to see sense.

Feeling a right idiot, she clambered up into the driver's seat and shoved the key into the ignition. She half expected nothing to happen even though it had started without a hitch when the seller showed them around, but the engine rumbled into life, and as she familiarised herself with the bite on the clutch and where the indicators were, she had a mischievous urge to sound the chimes again.

Seren knew her dad's heart was in the right place, but she couldn't help wondering what he'd been thinking. Aside from the expense of doing the van up, she already had a job, for goodness' sake – when was she supposed to fit in trawling the streets with her wares? Assuming she had any wares to trawl with. She had no idea what to stock, where to get the stock from, how much to charge, whether she needed a licence... There was simply too much to consider. And even if she was fully on board with the idea, it was already early November. The van would never be ready in time for Christmas.

She was about to pull off when there was a tap on the window.

Seren wound it down. 'What?' she asked, warily, fearful her father had something else up his sleeve.

'Just to let you know, I've arranged for you to take the van to a garage tomorrow. T&M Conversions in town; they'll give you a quote for... well... converting it. Then we'll know.'

Yes, we will know, Seren thought, although she didn't need to be officially told that converting the vehicle from an ice cream van to a travelling gift shop was going to cost a pretty penny. And she'd been trying to save all of hers for a deposit on a place of her own.

'It won't hurt to see what's what,' Patrick said. 'You might be pleasantly surprised.'

'And I might not,' she muttered under her breath.

She had a day off tomorrow, so she'd take it to the garage to show willing, and when they told her how much it was going to cost, her dad would realise that he had no choice but to sell it. All she hoped was that he wouldn't lose too much money. After all, who in their right mind wanted to buy an ice cream van at this time of year!

–

'Leave Aunty Seren alone,' Nicole told her daughter as Freya clambered onto Seren's lap.

Seren was sitting in Nicole's kitchen later that evening, feeling extremely bemused and more than a little shell-shocked. Nicole had taken one look at her face and had put the kettle on. Seren nuzzled the little girl's hair and inhaled deeply. She loved the smell of the child's fresh scent and her apple shampoo, and she cuddled her closer and gave her a kiss on the cheek.

'Did you bring me a present?' Freya asked.

Nicole gasped. 'Freya! No, she did not. Your birthday was ages ago and Christmas is weeks away.'

'It's fifty-two days,' Freya retorted, with a knowing look. Then she thought about it, and as she did so she became less sure of herself. 'Is fifty-two days a long time?'

'It's seven weeks, more or less. Six more Mondays in school.'

'I like school.' Freya scrambled down off Seren's lap.

'I know you do, but you always complain on a Monday morning when you have to get out of bed,' Nicole said.

The child wrinkled her nose. 'I wish school could come to me.'

'Well, it can't; so *you*, little Miss Bossy Boots, have to go to *it*.' Her mother punctuated each word with a kiss on her daughter's button nose.

Freya turned to Seren. 'Mummy… I mean, *Seren*… tell her I don't have to go to school.'

Nicole laughed. 'She called her teacher Mummy the other day. Most of the little ones slip up at some point.' She turned to Freya. 'Seren will tell you no such thing.'

'That's right,' Seren agreed. 'School is important.' She leant in to whisper in the little girl's ear. 'And it's much more fun than being stuck at home with boring old Mummy every day.'

'Go and play for five minutes before bed,' Freya's mum told her. 'Let the boring old mummies talk.'

'Seren isn't a mummy,' Freya said, with a frown.

'She doesn't have a little girl or boy of her own, but she is your godmother, so she's a kind of a mummy.'

'A god-mummy? OK.' Her frown cleared and Freya skipped off into the living room, leaving the adults alone to chat.

'What's up?' Nicole asked when they were finally able to speak freely.

'You're not going to believe what my dad's done,' Seren began with a huffed sigh.

'Don't tell me he's found himself a girlfriend?' Nicole's eyes widened.

'Fat chance! I wish he would, then maybe he'd stop dreaming up madcap ideas.'

Nicole placed a couple of mugs in front of them and slid into a seat. 'This sounds intriguing. Pray tell.' She put her elbows on the table, interlocked her fingers and rested her chin on them.

'He's only gone and bought an ice cream van, with a view to turning it into a travelling gift shop. And – this is where it gets even more bizarre – he intends for me to drive around the streets selling Christmassy stuff.'

'Wow, I didn't see that coming.'

'He's even gone and booked it into a place that will do it up for me. I'm supposed to take it there in the morning.'

'Crumbs. Was this a planned thing?'

Seren shook her head. 'I got home from work this afternoon, and he bundled me into the car, drove me to some guy's house, and told me he'd bought me an ice cream van.'

'Why would he do such a bizarre thing?' Nicole's eyes were wide with astonishment and became even wider when Seren told her the story behind it.

'I blame Aunt Nelly. If she wasn't so fussy and cantankerous, my dad would never have had such a ridiculous idea. Goodness knows what she's going to say about it. She'll probably think he's gone mad.' Seren bit her lip, not from concern about her aunt's reaction, but because of how she'd begun to feel about the idea as she'd driven the van home.

'Out with it,' Nicole said. 'You can't fool me – there's more.'

'I like it,' Seren confessed.

'The ice cream van?'

'No, the van is hideous!' She shuddered. 'But I do like the idea of a travelling shop. It's got potential, and there isn't anyone else with one for miles and miles. It's something to think about, and as my dad has actually bought it...'

Nicole was silent for a while. Seren had to admit it was a lot to take in. She didn't think she'd fully grasped it herself yet.

'Does that mean you're going to pack your job in?' Nicole finally asked.

'No such luck! I wish I could, but I don't yet know if I can afford to have it converted. At the moment it's this shocking pink colour – Freya would love it – has an ice cream cone in the middle of the roof like a weird vanny kind of unicorn, and it plays "*O Sole Mio*".' She sang the tune with gusto.

Nicole burst out laughing.

Seren observed her for a few moments with a disgruntled expression on her face, before her lips began to twitch, and soon she had tears rolling down her cheeks and a stitch in her side. It was quite comical when she thought about it.

'What will you do if it costs too much to renovate – if that's the right word when it comes to cars and vans,' Nicole wanted to know.

'Dad will have to sell it, and he'll probably get less than what he bought it for.'

'You could always sell ice cream,' Nicole cried, dissolving into hysterics once more.

'That's going to go down a storm in December in Tinstone. I'd be better off selling hot chocolate or mulled wine.' She caught a sudden flash of speculation in her friend's eyes. 'No, that's not going to happen,' Seren declared. 'There's bound to be a whole load of red tape around selling alcohol, mulled or otherwise. And even if I could afford to have the work done, time's ticking if I want to have it ready for the present-buying season – which is practically upon us already.'

'How much do you think it'll cost?'

Seren pulled a face. 'I've absolutely no idea, but however much this place charges I'll probably not be able to afford it. I don't know why I'm wasting my time.'

But she did know: excitement was quietly brewing deep inside her. *Could she do this?*

Perhaps she could...

Chapter 5

The ice cream van rumbled onto the forecourt of T&M Conversions and Seren cut the engine. A man with his head under the bonnet of a clapped-out old VW camper van straightened up and turned to look at her as she got out, and she noticed his eyes widen.

Yep, she bet he didn't get many ice cream vans rolling in... All she hoped was that he didn't want to buy a 99 with a flake and strawberry sauce, because he was going to be disappointed.

'What can I do for you?' he asked, wiping his hands on an old cloth and stepping towards the van. 'Is this yours?' He nodded towards the ice cream van, but his attention was on her. He had come-to-bed eyes and a sexy smile played on his lips. To say he was good-looking would be an understatement. It was a pity he seemed to be well aware of just how attractive he was.

'Apparently so,' she said, pulling herself together. He might be incredibly sexy in a 'man getting his hands dirty way', but he wasn't her type. Too cocky and self-assured for her taste. Mind you, if he asked her out, she probably wouldn't say no. Fair-haired and blue-eyed, with a stubbly chiselled chin, she felt a pull of attraction. Crumbs, it was like buses – no good-looking fellas for ages, then two came along at once, she thought, as an image of Daniel flitted across her mind.

'My father, bless him, bought it for me,' she said, dragging her thoughts away from the handsome hunk in front of her, and back to the reason why she was there in the first place.

'I remember… He said it's to be turned into a mobile gift shop.'

Seren rolled her eyes. 'It's a long story.'

'What's your vision for it?' he asked, and she blinked.

'The scrap heap?' she shot back.

'Seriously?'

Seren shrugged. 'It might be the best option for it. Look at it − not only is it ancient, it's also flamingo pink with a ruddy great big ice cream cone on the top.'

'I'm Tobias, by the way,' he said, smiling at her.

She felt herself smile in return. 'Seren Fletcher. Tell me how much it will cost to transform it into a kind of a travelling shop.'

'Nice name. Do you have anything particular in mind, Seren?'

'Not really. When I was looking at mobile gift shops, I was originally thinking of something bigger, like a bus, where people can get on and have a look around, but…' She grimaced. 'I was also envisaging it belonging to someone else.' The sneaking excitement of yesterday evening had given way to major doubts in the middle of the night, and she'd woken up this morning with the conviction that it would have to be sold as soon as possible. She was only bringing it to the garage today to humour her dad.

'Okaaay…' Tobias was studying her intently and she realised the impression she must be making.

'Sorry, I don't mean to be such a grouch, but my dad bought this behind my back based on a conversation we had about trying to find a gift shop that would come to the care home where my aunt lives – like the mobile library does. I searched on the internet and such things do exist, just not close enough.'

Tobias said, 'When I spoke to your father on the phone, he mentioned something about a care home and a mobile library, but I didn't know what he meant.'

'I wish I'd never told him about it,' Seren lamented. 'I'm not cut out for this.'

'Why not?' He tilted his head to the side as he looked at her.

'Because…' She blew out her cheeks and stared at him helplessly. 'Where do I start? I've not got the time or the experience. It's going to cost a fortune. I've already got a job. There's no way it would be ready this side of Christmas, which is kind of the whole point.' She checked off each item of concern on her fingers, then added, 'I'm sure I can think of plenty more reasons, but those are enough to be going on with.'

'When you say mobile gift shop, what's the reasoning behind it? Is there a need for such a thing when you can order anything and everything online and it'll be delivered straight to your door with just the click of a button?'

'I blame my Aunt Nelly. She can be a right pain in the backside. It all started when an old gent moved into the home, and she wanted to buy him a "welcome to the prison" present.'

Tobias's eyes widened. 'It's not that bad, is it?'

Seren giggled. 'No, it most definitely isn't. It's a good home and the staff are brilliant. She just hates being there, but that's no reflection on the home – she'd hate being anywhere. As far as she's concerned, she should have died years ago. She says she's lived too long and she's nothing but a burden.' Seren snorted. 'As if! We love her to bits and wouldn't want to be without her.'

'The van?' Tobias reminded her.

'Oh, yes, how could I forget!' She shot the ice cream van a sour look. 'As I was saying, Nelly wanted to buy this man a present, but she poo-pooed everything I suggested and refused to let me show her anything online. She said she wants to see things for herself before she decides to buy. Then when the mobile library pulled into the car park at the home, we had the same idea about trying to get a mobile shop to pay the home a visit.' She gave a deep sigh. 'I looked online but there is nothing within travelling distance, and when I mentioned this to my dad, he must have got it into his mind that it would be something I'd want to do.'

'Don't you?'

She gave him a withering look. 'Hardly!' Hadn't this guy listened to a word she'd said?

'How hard can it be to sell things?'

'You'd be surprised.' Seren squinted at him. 'Whose side are you on?'

'No one's. And before you get your knickers in a twist about me touting for work, I've got more than enough to be going on with. You're probably right about it not being ready before Christmas. It would be a squeeze to fit you in.'

'Good. That's another nail in the coffin. Not only will it cost an absolute fortune, but it won't be ready in time, which was the whole point. My dad will have to put it back on the market.' Mild disappointment stirred in her tummy but she ignored it. Her running a travelling Christmas gift shop was a ridiculous idea.

'Do you want to know how much it'll cost?' Tobias asked.

'Go on then. Hit me with it.'

'I don't know.'

'What do you mean, *you don't know*? Surely you must have some idea?'

'It depends on what you want.'

'I don't *know* what I want. Apart from wanting it out of my life. Can't you give me a ballpark figure? I'll have to tell my father something,' she added.

He sighed. 'Just for you to know, I think your idea is a brilliant one. There must be loads of people, and not just in care homes either, who can't get to the shops easily and who don't like, or can't use, the internet.'

'Hmm… If you say so.'

'Anyway, it doesn't matter what I think. If you don't fancy doing it, or you feel it's too risky, then that's up to you.' He sighed. 'Leave the van here and I'll do a proper quote for you.'

'Thank you so much.' Once her dad saw how much it would cost, she'd have no trouble persuading him to sell it.

Just then a car rolled onto the forecourt and came to a stop, and when the driver alighted, Seren's eyes widened. It was Daniel, the guy whose grandfather had just moved into Tinstone Care Home.

'Are you converting this into a camper?' he asked Tobias, his attention on the ice cream van. He didn't seem to have noticed her.

'A travelling gift shop,' Tobias supplied. 'Or we would be if Seren, here, wanted it to be. She's not keen on the idea.'

Seren's attention was on Daniel while Tobias was speaking, and she saw him start at the mention of her name.

When his gaze shot to her, she smiled widely at him.

'Hi,' Daniel said, smiling back. 'A travelling gift shop, eh? Neat.'

'Seren's not convinced,' Tobias said.

'Do you really think it's a good idea?' she asked, addressing her question to Daniel. She didn't trust Tobias to give her an unbiased answer since he'd be benefitting by way of being paid to convert it.

'Yes, I do,' he replied. 'My grandad mentioned that your Aunt Nelly was complaining about how few options some people had when it came to present buying. I, for one, think there's a market for it.'

Seren was torn. It *was* a good idea, but... 'It's just, I don't know where to start.' Her eyes narrowed and she stared critically at the van. 'That cone would have to go.'

'You could put a present up there instead,' Daniel suggested.

'It plays "*O Sole Mio*"!'

Daniel burst into laughter. 'The "just one Cornetto" song? Nice.'

'It really isn't,' she giggled, then sobered as she thought about what her dad had said. Could this be the start of a new career? Did she have the courage? 'I can't properly consider it until I know how much it's going to cost me.'

Tobias sucked his teeth. 'Let's have a chat about what's feasible and what isn't, then I'll have a better idea. Dan, I expect you've got things to do. The keys are in the truck. It was only a spark plug, this time.'

'Cheers. Thank God for that. When it started misfiring, I had visions of it being something serious.

What with that and the exhaust the other week…' He trailed off.

'You can settle up with me next time I see you,' Tobias said, jerking his head towards a truck with the words Daniel Oakland Gardening Services emblazoned on the side.

Seren saw Daniel raise his eyebrows at Tobias and give him a knowing look. Then she watched him walk over to the truck and get in. As he drove off, she wondered if she'd see him again any time soon, and she hoped she would: out of the two men, Daniel was more her type.

Tobias cleared his throat, bringing Seren out of her reverie.

'It needs a paint job,' she said without hesitation, forcing her attention back to the matter at hand. 'I refuse to drive around with cartoon pictures of ice cream cones plastered all over it.'

'OK. What else? How do you envisage the selling part working?'

She moved to the side of the van and stroked the sliding window. 'I'd like to keep this.'

'I think you should. You'd have difficulty fitting any customers inside, so you're probably going to have to do the selling via the hatch, so you'll need shelves that are clearly visible from the outside.'

She still wasn't convinced of the van's feasibility as a travelling shop, but she'd hold fire for now. It wouldn't hurt to get a quote and maybe it wouldn't be too hideous. So she spent the next half an hour batting ideas around, listening to what was, and what wasn't, doable, until finally, a clear picture emerged of what it was that she wanted.

It was surprisingly simple – clean lines, neutral interior, cream bodywork. Classy, almost, but with a hint of quirkiness. She liked it, and the spark of excitement fanned back into a flame as she imagined how good the old van would look once it was done.

Maybe her dad was on to something after all.

–

What on earth was she doing? Where did she intend to go with this? How much was it going to cost? Who'd buy her goods? Was she being a fool? What did she know about selling anyway?

Seren straightened up and arched her back. She'd been poring over the laptop for hours and she didn't think she was much further forward than she'd been at the start.

She'd arrived home from dropping the van off at T&M Conversions with her head swirling with questions, and after spending ages on the internet, she still didn't have the answers to many of them. To be fair, some were unanswerable, although she had discovered that she would need a licence if she wanted to be a mobile trader. When she'd phoned the council, she had been informed that it would take a couple of weeks but she could do it online. She also found out that she could purchase a temporary one, which covered her for up to twenty-eight days, which was considerably cheaper than buying a permanent one.

She checked the calendar and calculated that for her to make full use of a twenty-eight-day trading licence, the van would have to be ready to go by the last week in November, which didn't give Tobias from T&M Conversions much time.

Gah, what was she doing?

She must have asked herself the same question at least ten times in the previous hour, and she still didn't have any idea.

'Are you all right, love?' Her dad was standing in the doorway of her bedroom, a look of concern on his face.

'Not really.'

'I've caused you a bit of a headache, haven't I? I'm sorry.'

'It's fine. At least it's given me something to do on my day off, other than clear out the cupboard under the stairs, or fill my face with chocolate while watching *Countdown*.'

'It's going to be hard work, isn't it? I should never have bought it. I'm sorry, I wasn't thinking.'

'It's done now, so I should at least give it some serious consideration. Tobias is getting back to me with a quote for the conversion, plus I know what needs doing when it comes to all the rules and regulations surrounding street traders. And I've done some research into care and residential homes within a thirty-mile radius. I've even phoned a couple of them to gauge their reaction, and they've all been positive.'

'I should have thought about doing market research before going off half-cocked and bidding for the van on eBay.'

Seren agreed with him but saying so would only make him feel bad. 'We guessed there would be a demand for it,' she said, instead. 'My main problem, though, is what to sell and where to get it from.'

'How about the garlands and wreaths you make? I'm sure they'll go down a storm.'

Seren wrinkled her nose. 'I only make them for us.' She always made a new wreath for the front door every Christmas, using fresh holly, ivy and mistletoe, and she made garlands, too – one to twine around the stairs and another to drape around the mantelpiece. She was always pleased with them and they were often admired, but she wasn't certain how she felt about selling them. She honestly didn't think they were good enough.

'What about the craft fair at the town hall on Saturday?' Patrick suggested. 'There are bound to be some local sellers. You could ask them if they'd be interested in supplying you with stuff to sell. You could either buy it outright at a reduced rate, or – and this is the better option for you – ask them if they'd be willing to display their stock in your van for free. They name the price they want to receive for their goods, and you charge a percentage on top of that when you sell it, which you get to keep. That way, everyone wins.'

Seren was stunned. What a brilliant idea!

If it worked.

She'd be a total stranger to these people – why would they trust her with their stock? But the more she thought about it, the more feasible it sounded. There was no harm in asking. If all of them said no, she'd have to go back to the drawing board.

Seren felt her father's reassuring hand on her shoulder, and she tilted her head to rest it against his forearm.

'This could be the start of something special,' he said. 'I know you can make this work; I have every faith in you.'

Seren wished she had even a fraction of his faith. But there was one consolation – she didn't have to give up her job to give this a go. She'd be able to fit it in around her shifts in the shop for the time being. And if it didn't work out, all she would have lost was her time (and her savings, but she didn't want to think about that), and at least she'd have given it her best shot.

Chapter 6

'*Hi, it's Tobias from T&M Conversions. I've got that quote for you. Are you able to call in, because there are a couple of things I want to go over with you.*'

Seren listened to the message on her phone, thinking how rumbly and deep Tobias's voice was, but not too deep – not like the voice on the film trailers for thrillers and such like. His voice was as sexy as he was, and rather uncharitably she wondered if it was natural or whether he practised the smooth, rich tones.

Her shift had been nine to five today, and he'd left the message on her phone earlier but she'd been unable to take the call. She wondered if it was too late to pay him a visit, then decided it wouldn't be any bother to take a detour and walk home via his garage. It was only a little out of her way. Half an hour was nothing in the scheme of things, and the exercise would do her good. Never mind that she'd been on her feet all day: standing around filling shelves or checking the dates on fresh food couldn't be compared to a brisk walk on a chilly November evening. It would do her good and blow away the cobwebs.

Wrapping up warmly in her padded coat, and winding a scarf around her neck, she took her hair out of its bun and ran her fingers through it, rubbing at her scalp and letting out a groan of relief. Letting her hair down (literally, not figuratively) was the best part about leaving work and, scalp massage finished, she shook her hair out, letting it fall around her ears to keep them warm.

Once outside the shop, she wished she'd thought about putting some lipstick on, but it was too late now; besides, she was going to a greasy, grimy garage, not a nightclub. Tobias would have to take her as he found her. And why she was even thinking about her appearance, she honestly didn't know.

The roller doors were still up and the lights were on when she turned into the street where the garage was located, she could see Tobias – he had his back to her and his head under the bonnet of a boxy truck.

Not wanting to make him jump and risk him banging his head, she stomped across the forecourt, her flat shoes clomping on the tarmac and she also coughed loudly.

It did the trick.

'Hi,' Tobias said, straightening up and turning around. 'How are you today?'

'Good thanks. You?'

'Busy.' He picked up a soiled rag and wiped his hands on it, which only served to smear the grime around rather than remove it. 'Let me wash up first. Would you like to wait in the office?'

'OK.' With a quick glance at the ice cream van (which didn't look any less ice creamy or any more appealing than the last time she'd set eyes on it) Seren walked into the office and sat down. It was as tidy as she remembered it being from her previous visit, and it was remarkably clean for a garage.

'Sorry about that,' Tobias said, appearing in the doorway and making her jump. His hands were cleaner, although he had a smudge of dirt on his cheek.

Seren got a tissue out of her bag and offered it to him. 'You've got an… um…' She pointed to her left cheek.

His hand went to his right one.

'Other side. Oil or dirt. Not sure.'

'Could be either. Or both,' he said, rubbing at his face with his fingers. 'Gone?'

'Yeah.' More or less. She was beginning to wish she hadn't mentioned it in case he thought she was flirting with him. He was rather sexy and she enjoyed looking at him, but there was no way she was going to let him know she thought that.

From the smirk on his face, she didn't think she'd been very successful at hiding it.

Instead of sitting on the other side of the desk, Tobias sat in the seat next to her, so close she could smell his aftershave and an underlying aroma of engine oil.

'Before I show you the quote, I've done a couple of drawings to give you an idea of what it will look like when it's done,' he said, pulling a buff folder towards him and opening the flap. 'What do you think?' He took out several sheets of paper and fanned them out across the table.

Take a card, any card, she thought inanely as she scanned them, then she began to focus as she saw what he'd drawn. 'Is that my van?'

'It could be, if you're happy with my suggestions. Feel free to tell me if there are any aspects you don't like – or if you hate the whole concept.'

'Hate it…?' she repeated, dazed. The drawings were wonderful and the finished van looked far better than she ever could have imagined. 'I like all of it,' she said, her voice coming out all squeaky.

'Good.'

'I love the colour scheme,' she added.

He simply nodded as though he'd been expecting her to. If these drawings were any indication, he was very good at what he did, and she hoped the finished article would look the same as the drawings.

'What about making it look Christmassy?' she asked, because wasn't that the whole point of the van in the first place?

'The easiest thing to do would be to buy some festive decals. They are so easy to put on and take off, and you could swap them around to suit what you wanted to push.'

That seemed a reasonable solution. 'What about the tune?'

'I've not had a good look at it, but I shouldn't think it would be a problem to change it to something more festive.'

That was another hurdle out of the way. It seemed the universe was intent on her doing this. But there was one other thing...

'Hit me with the quote,' she said.

Tobias slid another piece of paper towards her.

Seren turned it over and nearly cried. *How much?* That was most of her savings, gone. Just like that! But she'd known it wasn't going to be cheap, so perhaps she should be more surprised that the quote wasn't higher.

Was she serious about this? Or had she been wasting everyone's time?

She had to make a decision now, she realised. If she dithered, even for a week or two, she'd lose too much time and it would be pointless going ahead with the conversion at all.

'OK, let's do it,' she declared. 'But only if you can have it ready in two weeks. We're at the beginning of

November and if it takes any longer than that I'm not going to get the most out of it.'

'It's a deal.' Tobias held his hand out.

She took it, intending to shake firmly, but he held her hand a little longer than was necessary, so she hastily snatched it back. It wasn't that she minded him holding her hand, but she wasn't used to men like Tobias paying her attention. And, of course, there was always the issue that she might be imagining it and she was in danger of making a fool of herself.

'I'd better be off,' she said, getting to her feet. 'No doubt you want to close up, and I've got to get home and start contacting people who might be willing to give me their stock to sell on nothing but a promise. There's a craft fair in the town hall on Saturday, and my dad suggested I ask some of the sellers if they'd consider supplying me with their wares on a sale or return basis. Wish me luck.'

'I'm sure you don't need it.'

She pouted. 'I'm pretty sure I do. I'm going to wait until just before closing time, when hopefully it's quiet, and I'll sock it to them then. Can I hang on to the drawings, so I can show people? Hopefully that will be more impressive than me trying to describe it.'

'Yes, of course. I'll be in touch when it's nearing completion, or if I hit a snag.'

'Please don't say something like that,' she pleaded.

'I'm sure it'll be fine. I've had a good look at the van, and it should be straightforward enough.'

Seren smiled shakily. She'd never spent so much money in her life before and she felt a little light-headed. 'Do you want a payment upfront?'

He shook his head. 'Not at all.' He paused. 'How about going out for a drink on Saturday?'

Ooh, so she hadn't been imagining things – Tobias *was* asking her out.

'I'd love to,' she said, but it was only after she was walking home after agreeing when to meet and where, that she wondered if she really did want to go on a date with him.

Oh, well, she'd said she would, and at least it would get her out of the house for a few hours. Besides, a date with a man as good-looking as Tobias wasn't to be sneezed at, even if she didn't fancy him as much as she thought she should.

Chapter 7

Daniel stood in his bedroom mirror on Saturday morning, took the Santa suit out of the bag and slipped the jacket on. He was due to play Father Christmas in a department store in town in a couple of hours, but he thought he'd better check his outfit first. He'd tried it on when he'd bought it, but he'd been so eager to leave the shop that he hadn't noticed anything apart from that it fitted OK – if he ignored the looseness around the stomach area, that is.

A cushion should sort that out. Perhaps he could borrow one from his mum? Or maybe a pillow would do the trick? He didn't want to play Santa, but he was committed now so he didn't intend to go into it half-heartedly. He wanted to make a good job of it and if shoving a pillow inside the voluminous jacket added to the illusion that he was Father Christmas, then that's what he would do.

The pillow worked a treat, although he did have to cinch the belt tightly to ensure it didn't slip, and when he popped the trousers and the hat on, he began to look the part. The fake beard came next, along with a surprisingly silky long white wig, and stick-on eyebrows. There was even a little pair of round glasses to complete the look, and when he stood in front of the mirror he was relatively pleased with the result.

At least no one would recognise him in this get-up. He barely recognised himself. The only recognisable part of him was his eyes and he didn't think anyone he knew would get close enough to him to notice. Apart from his mum – she'd jokingly threatened to pay him a visit and sit on his knee, and she might even bring Mrs Williams from next door with her to cause him double the embarrassment.

Yeah, thanks, Mum…

Finally he couldn't put it off any longer; he had to leave now, else he'd be late.

He quickly removed the Father Christmas suit, folded it neatly and put it back in the bag, then he grabbed the keys to his truck and took a deep breath. He could do this. He liked children and they seemed to like him, for the most part. Although he wasn't a people person (which was one of the reasons he liked being his own boss and working alone) he could socialise if he needed to. And today, he needed to.

When Daniel pulled into the car park he still felt relatively calm. Even when he passed his favourite florist who had a wonderful display of Poinsettias and winter greenery in the window and was tempted to go in and have a look around, he hurried past. He knew that if he did pop in, it was a safe bet that he'd either buy a plant, or some bulbs, or a ceramic pot… or all three; which would defeat the object. If he spent his earnings today on things for the garden, he might well be forced to eat toast for dinner for the rest of the winter.

Daniel wrinkled his nose. He might be exaggerating somewhat right now, but nearer to Christmas when gardening work had dried up almost completely and he was living on what he'd managed to save earlier in the year, he wouldn't be pleased. So, he clutched the bag containing his Santa suit more tightly, and instead scuttled off towards the department store.

He wasn't due to start work until eleven a.m., so he headed directly to one of the tills, and told the young man standing behind the counter why he was there.

'Cool,' the guy said. 'I used to love going to see Santa.'

Most kids did, Daniel mused as he followed the lad across the shop floor to find the manager. He used to enjoy it himself, but he'd never for one minute thought he'd be the person wearing the red suit.

After he was shown the staff room and where he could change, the chatty manager led him back out onto the shop floor to inspect the grotto.

'Thanks so much for filling in for us,' the woman gushed. 'Having a Santa's Grotto is one of the reasons the public come into the store, and we'd hate to disappoint anyone. Our regular Santa has a wedding to go to, one he couldn't miss.' She gave him an apologetic look. 'Sorry it's only this one time, but if we ever have need of another Santa, can we give you a call?'

'No problem,' he said, unable to envisage being a regular Santa; he wanted to get this job under his belt first. 'Um, I've never been a Santa before,' he confessed. 'This is my first time.'

'Aw, bless. You'll be fine. You'll love it!'

Daniel wasn't so sure and his answering smile felt a bit strained.

'Tanya will be your helper today. People buy their tickets to see Santa from one of the tills and take them to Tanya who then brings them through to you, so all you have to do is speak to the children and give them their gift. Here's the grotto – what do you think?'

The grotto was situated at the far end of the store's Christmas section. People had to walk through various shelves of assorted gifts such as scented candles, soaps and plush toys, and then past an impressive range of decorations, all of which were colour coordinated. There were also ceramic houses that lit up, a Santa's train set on its own track, and an array of mechanical Father Christmases, polar bears, and reindeer, all of them displayed on dressers and tables, and arranged in a way that would entice people to buy. Heck, Daniel was sorely tempted to purchase a few items himself, and he didn't even like Christmas that much. The whole display was so inviting it made him feel quite festive.

But the *pièce de résistance* was a large, dark, walk-through tunnel which showcased the many lights the shop had for sale. On either side were Christmas trees, lots of them, in different sizes and colours, and all were brightly lit and twinkled in the dimness. Snowmen and other figures were dotted between, glowing and sparkling, and everything was coated in a fine dusting of fake snow. Christmas songs were playing and the scent of oranges, spice and berries wafted through the air.

The grotto was at the far end of this tunnel, and Daniel had to admire the store's sales technique. Faced with all this Christmas stuff, especially whilst they were queuing, people had plenty of time to contemplate the Christmas decor they had at home and to consider upgrading. It was certainly a sight to behold.

Daniel walked up to the grotto and studied it. It was built out of plywood and painted to look like a gingerbread house. Children entered at the one side, then walked across to where he would be sitting at the other end, next to a fake fireplace with streamers and lights to give the impression of flames. Daniel noticed a tag saying how much the fireplace was and where it could be found – the department store wasn't going to miss any opportunity to make a sale. His chair was a rather uncomfortable-looking wooden throne, with holly-shaped lights draped around it, and several large boxes filled with presents next to it. He guessed that all the decorations in the grotto, including the Christmas tree in the corner, were from the shop's own stock.

He had to admit – despite the obvious sales pitch – that it was cheerful and festive, and would undoubtedly appeal to children, and probably the grown-ups accompanying them.

Feeling dreadfully apprehensive, he went back to the staff area to get changed and have a nervous wee, and by the time he arrived back at the grotto, several families were already milling about, waiting to see him.

Oh, God… He just hoped he didn't let the side down.

–

Daniel felt as though he had spent the last eight hours felling a tree. With a pocketknife. In the dark.

He was absolutely shattered. His throat was sore, his mouth was dry, he was losing his voice from talking so much, and his face ached from all the smiling he'd felt obliged to do. Then there was also the sore backside he had from sitting so long, an aching back – for the same reason – and more tension in his neck than he'd ever had in his life. Add all this to the headache he'd been brewing due to the aforementioned tension and the lack of fresh air, and he was a physical wreck. Who could have known that sitting in a chair and talking to small children was so exhausting?

He was emotionally drained too, mostly from being so nice for so long, but also from trying to cajole awestruck or reluctant children to speak to him. The adults with them (he'd been advised never to call them parents, but to refer to them as the child's 'grown-up') were usually keen for their children to get the most out of the experience, and many of them were also pretty desperate to hear what their charges wanted Santa to bring them, but some children just didn't want to talk to him and he didn't blame them. If he was a kid, he wouldn't have wanted to talk to himself either.

Shattered, aching and hungry, Daniel was delighted and relieved when it was time to remove his Santa suit and go home.

He intended to shower, change into slouchy clothes, and stuff his face with pizza, in that order. Watching some mindless programme on the telly was also on the agenda, preferably something he didn't have to think about too much. He might even treat himself to a beer; there were three in the fridge that had been there since Wednesday and they should be lovely and cold by now.

It wasn't his preferred way to spend a Saturday night, but even if he'd had plans to go out, Daniel wasn't convinced he'd have been able to force himself to leave the house once he'd stepped over the threshold.

He must be getting old…

Taking deep lungfuls of cold air, Daniel hurried away from the cloying, artificially perfumed warmth of the department store, and walked tiredly towards his truck, holding the bag with the Santa suit in his hand. If he was honest, he'd be happy if he never saw the darned thing again, but he had jobs lined up for several weekends between now and Christmas Eve, and some days during the week, too.

He was thinking about the next place he was due to work at – a Christmas fayre in a nearby town – when he spotted a familiar figure standing outside The Thorn and Thistle fiddling with his phone. Daniel debated whether to turn on his heel and slink off in the opposite direction, but as he dithered Tobias glanced up and saw him.

'Wotcha, mate,' Tobias said. 'Where are you going?'

'I'm on my way home,' Daniel said, hoping Tobias wouldn't ask him where he'd been or what he'd been doing, because he didn't want to lie but neither did he want to share what he'd been up to today. 'What about you?'

'I would ask if you fancied going for a pint, but I've got a date.'

'Why am I not surprised!' Daniel joked. The man had more dates than a wholefood shop at Christmas. Which reminded him, he should get some for his grandad, because Edwin adored the sticky, sweet fruit.

'Remember the woman with the ice cream van? Seren? I'm meeting her for a drink,' Tobias said.

Daniel remembered, all right. He hadn't been able to forget her. Every time he visited his grandad, he'd hoped to catch sight of her. It had crossed his mind to call into the shop where she worked but he hadn't, worried that it might look too obvious.

He wished he had, because Tobias had asked her out before he'd found the courage to, and now it was too late – she wouldn't look at him twice after going on a date with Tobias. Women fell for Tobias faster than trees for a logger's saw. And they usually stayed felled. Daniel had lost count of the number of broken hearts Tobias had left in his wake.

Tobias will love her and leave her, the same as he'd done with all his other girlfriends, Daniel lamented silently, and he was about to say he hoped Tobias would have a good time (even though he didn't strictly mean it) and hurry off home, when Seren came hurtling around the corner and almost skidded to a halt.

'I'm not late, am I?' she asked, breathlessly. 'Oh, hi, Daniel.'

'Hello.' Daniel's heart lurched at the sight of her and a pulse began to throb in his temple. Goodness, she looked amazing. Her cheeks glowed, her hair shone in the street-lights, and she looked elegant in a long woollen coat and high-heeled boots. She was wearing lipstick, and his gaze was drawn to her full mouth and her ready smile.

He gave her a half-smile in return, wishing he was the one who she had been hurrying to meet and not his friend.

'You're not late. I've only just got here myself,' Tobias said.

There was an awkward moment when Daniel wondered if the two of them were going to go for a hug, so he hastily made his excuses and left. He didn't want to witness any embracing – or worse – and neither did he want to hang around like a spare part.

Feeling rather sorry for himself and wishing he was more like Tobias and less like himself, Daniel made his way home.

Finding out that Tobias was Seren's type was a depressing end to what had been a most unsatisfactory day.

When Seren had tottered around the corner on her too-high heels and saw Tobias lounging against the wall of the wine bar talking to Daniel, her heart had sunk.

For some inexplicable reason she was reluctant for him to know she was going on a date with Tobias. It was rather silly, considering Daniel hadn't shown any interest in her and she didn't even know whether he was in a relationship. The absence of a ring meant nothing. Most of the people she knew from school were living with someone and hadn't formalised their union with a marriage certificate.

He'd looked shocked to see her, and he'd quickly made his excuses and left. She was sorry to see him go, which concerned her – that she was even thinking about Daniel made her wonder if she should be here with Tobias. He might be hot, but he wasn't her type and she suspected she'd only agreed to go out for drinks with him because she was flattered that such a good-looking guy would be interested in her.

She'd never been one of the popular girls in school, and boys hadn't been queuing up to ask her out. The few dates she'd been on had been with those boys who most girls didn't look at twice – the nerdy ones, the swotty ones, the ones who were shy and introverted.

As she'd grown older, she'd been asked out more, but she hadn't been under any illusion she was a catch. Neither had she fallen for any of them. The relationships she'd had in the past had been brief and unsatisfactory, and she was reluctant to jump into another one.

But it stroked her ego to be asked out by someone as good-looking and as smooth as Tobias, even though she was under no illusion that it would be anything more than a quick fling for him. If she let it get that far, which she wouldn't.

Still, there was no harm in giving him the benefit of the doubt. Underneath his confident and self-assured manner, a shy guy might be lurking, and she hadn't been out for ages with a member of the opposite sex, so this was quite a treat.

Seren became aware of Tobias staring at her as she watched Daniel dash off, and she gave him a wide smile. 'Shall we go inside? I'm freezing.'

Gallantly, Tobias opened the door and gestured for her to go ahead of him, and she gave him another smile as she stepped inside. So far, so good, she thought.

When he asked her what she wanted to drink, she chose a small white wine and was pleased to see he had a soft drink after he'd told her he was driving. She'd arranged to meet him in town, but if the evening went OK and he offered to drive her home, she'd probably accept rather than take a taxi. She liked to keep her options open when it came to how she was getting home; a couple of disastrous dates had made her rather wary of being dependent on anyone else for transport.

They took their drinks to one of the high tables with equally high stools, and Seren was thankful she was wearing trousers. As it was, she had to enlist Tobias's help to clamber onto the seat, but as he held her arm and helped her up, his hand warm on the sleeve of her silky blouse, she discovered she didn't have the kind of reaction she would have expected to have had in response to his nearness: no fluttering in her tummy, no catching of her breath, no hint of desire. She'd had as much reaction to him as she would have done if she was having a drink with Aunt Nelly.

Interesting… And slightly disappointing. Although she didn't for one moment consider Tobias as relationship material, it was disheartening to think he didn't do anything for her when it came to romance.

Ah, well, at least she knew where she stood, so she decided to simply enjoy the evening for what it was and be relieved not to have the internal debate about whether they would kiss at the end of the evening, or whether he would ask her out again. It was going to be no to both of those things.

'How is the van coming along?' she asked as soon as they were settled. Seren felt a bit precarious on her perch, but at least the atmosphere in the wine bar was lively and upbeat. The place was trendy, with lots of steel and glass, and done out in shades of white and grey. The drinks menu, which was above the long shiny bar, was lit up and advertised cocktails she'd never heard of. What was a Pornstar Martini anyway?

'I thought you might ask, so I've taken a couple of photos,' he said, getting his phone out and showing them to her.

'Gosh…' Seren swallowed nervously. The inside of the vehicle was totally empty; the van had been gutted. The outside, though, had been resprayed. 'What colour do you call that?' she asked.

'Vanilla.'

'Seriously?' Tobias nodded, and her lips began to twitch. 'How appropriate.'

'That's what I thought. But at least this way you can change things up a bit if you wanted.'

When he'd given her the quote (she still felt cold and clammy when she thought how much this was costing her) and she'd agreed for him to do the conversion, Tobias had suggested she go for a neutral paint job, with the addition of decals, if she wanted, for decorations. It was a sound idea. If (when?) she decided to sell it on, all she'd have to do was remove the decals and all person-alisation would disappear, which might make the van a more attractive prospect for the next buyer. It also made having a respray far cheaper, which had been music to her ears.

'I'm so glad you've got rid of the ice cream cone,' she said.

'I've got rid of "*O Sole Mio*", too,' he told her. 'The sound system you've got isn't as old as the van. Although it's not the most up-to-date model, it does allow you to put a pre-loaded USB stick in it. I hope you don't mind, but I took the liberty of uploading some Christmas carols onto it.'

'You did?' Seren beamed at him. 'That's wonderful! I had visions of having to buy a new sound system. I looked them up online, and they're not cheap.'

'I've still got the shelves and the storage to construct, and the interior lighting to rig up, but the hardest part is done.'

'When do you think it'll be ready?' Seren's palms felt damp – this was starting to become very real all of a sudden.

'In a couple of days, slightly ahead of schedule.'

She gazed at a spot over his right shoulder as she thought frantically. 'That's fine. I've booked in for a couple of Christmas fayres and markets, but the first one isn't until a week Saturday. Hopefully it'll be well attended. There's a whole load of things going on as well as the market – they've got street performers, a candle-lit procession in the evening, and a Santa's grotto.' She swallowed nervously. 'The extra few days will give me enough time to familiarise myself with the van and sort out the stock.'

Her dad's idea of speaking to local crafts people had been a good one, as she'd found out when she went to the fair and spoke to some of them. A few people hadn't wanted to know but others had been enthusiastic, and they'd agreed that as soon as the van was ready she'd get in touch with them and arrange to collect some of their stock.

'I still can't believe I'm doing this,' she said. 'I keep cringing when I think of the amount of money I'm spending, but at least I don't have to shell out a fortune to fill the damned thing.' She explained the arrangement she'd come to, adding, 'I think I'll be selling half Christmas things and half gifty stuff. I've also been making Christmas wreaths and garlands, so I'm not totally reliant on other people. I've managed to get hold of some nice ivy from the park, and the holly tree down the lane near where I live has got some lovely berries on it.'

She was about to show him some photos (she was particularly pleased with her wreaths, having experimented with a couple of new designs) when she realised Tobias wasn't interested. He had a kind of glazed expression in his eye, so she picked up her wine and took a sip of that instead.

'You might bump into Daniel,' Tobias said.

'Might I?'

'He's a Father Christmas.'

'Pardon?'

'Santa's grotto? He might be the Santa at some of these places. I tried to get him to tell me where and when, but he went all shy on me.' Tobias chortled. 'I was going to ask if I could sit on his lap!'

'What a magical and lovely thing to do.'

'You think?'

'Don't you? Someone has to be Santa, to keep the myth going, and I think it's wonderful that Daniel is doing it.'

'All those screaming kids and grumpy parents? Better him than me.'

Indeed, Seren thought. Tobias didn't seem the child-friendly type.

'I think it's a very nice thing to do,' she insisted.

'You do realise he's getting paid for it? He's not doing it out of the goodness of his heart. It's just a job to tide him over until his gardening work starts up again in the spring.'

She replied, mildly, 'Why shouldn't he be paid? I should imagine the organisers aren't letting children visit Santa for nothing.' And it wasn't as though he could be Father Christmas all year round, was it? She suspected that many people who held down seasonal jobs like that, would have other things lined up for the rest of the year.

Tobias shrugged and stood up, nodding at her empty glass. 'Same again?'

Seren was on the brink of refusing and saying she had to leave, but it wasn't fair on him to let her love for all things Christmas ruin the evening. Some people, like her, adored the festive season, others not so much. She understood some of Tobias's cynicism – it was terribly commercialised and most things were barely veiled attempts to persuade people to part with their cash. But wasn't she about to do the very same thing?

She might kid herself that she was providing a service, but at the end of the day she had to make it viable if she didn't want to be out of pocket.

'Go on then, but let me get these,' she said, slipping inelegantly off her stool and reaching for her purse.

'If you insist.' Tobias handed her his empty glass and she made her way to the bar, feeling a little disheartened. This date wasn't going as well as she'd hoped.

There was no spark on her part, and he seemed a little patronising when it came to Daniel's job and dismissive of it too, as though it was beneath him. Tobias might be easy on the eye, but there was no connection there, so when he offered to take her home later that evening, she refused.

'It's OK, I'll grab a taxi,' she said.

'Are you sure? It's no bother.'

'I'm sure. I don't want to put you out.'

'You won't be,' he said. 'But if that's what you want...?'

'It is.'

'I'll wait with you until your ride shows up.'

'You don't have to,' she said, feeling awkward. He was being so nice about it; maybe she'd misjudged him?

'It was fun,' he said as they stood outside the wine bar, Seren scanning the road anxiously for any vehicle that looked remotely like a cab. 'We must do this again.'

'That would be nice,' she replied vaguely, then realised her taxi had arrived and she sighed in relief.

Ever the gentleman, Tobias opened the door for her, but just as she was about to get inside, he pulled her into an embrace and went in for a kiss.

At the last moment, Seren turned her head so his lips landed on her cheek, and she gave him a swift squeeze and drew away.

His smile was rueful as he watched her clamber into the car. 'I'll let you know when you can pick the van up or if there are any niggles. I'm not anticipating any,' he added hastily as Seren's eyes widened in worry. 'Good night, Seren.' He shut the door.

''Night.'

The taxi pulled away and she glanced back at him, hoping she hadn't hurt his feelings. She was just in time to see him smiling at two young women who had emerged from the wine bar, and as she watched, she saw one of them peel away from the other and saunter over to him, hips swinging.

Nope, Seren hadn't hurt his feelings in the slightest.

If it wasn't for the fact he was working on her van, she had a suspicion that he'd have forgotten she existed the moment he closed the door on her.

Seren sank back into her seat and let out a slow breath: at least she'd got out from under her dad's feet for a couple of hours even if she hadn't found true love this evening.

It was strange though, but at that very moment Daniel's easy smile and crinkly eyes floated across her mind, and instead of thinking about the date she'd just been on, she found herself thinking about the date that was never going to happen.

Chapter 8

Traditionally mid-November was, for Daniel, time for the annual mulch. In his eyes, the apparently dormant winter months should be almost as busy as the rest of the year. Just because most things looked as though they were dead or dying, it didn't mean to say they were (although even the autumn-flowering annuals were now past their flower-by date) and he believed every garden could benefit from some TLC at this time of year to prepare it for next spring and summer.

Earlier that morning Daniel had visited the woods not far from his mum's house. It was one of those bright winter mornings where the air was crisp and clear, and there was still a hint of warmth in the sun's weak rays. It hadn't rained for a while and fallen leaves crunched underfoot, although some of their fellows still clung stubbornly to the branches overhead and glowed ochre, gold and burnt umber. It was cold enough to see the breath clouding in front of his face and he inhaled deeply, relishing being outdoors. No matter what the time of year or how poor the weather, if he had a choice, he'd be outside.

After a brisk walk to stretch his legs and to try to banish the horrors of yesterday spent in Santa's grotto, Daniel gathered all the fallen leaves he could and stuffed them into a couple of large hessian sacks. When he got them home, he used a shredder to chop them up, and then spread them over his flower beds to provide a natural barrier to the elements plus a decent bit of compost as the leaves broke down. He did the same to Mrs Williams's garden next door.

She loved her garden but was too old and doddery to do much more than deadhead the odd rose or two. Gradually, over the years, he'd started to help her more and more, until he now took care of her garden as well as his mum's. In turn, Mrs Williams would sing his praises to anyone who'd listen. It was an arrangement that suited them both, as she was occasionally able to throw some work his way. That wasn't the reason he did her garden for her, of course – he would have done it regardless – but it was a bonus, because although she lived in a modest stone-quarried, slate-roofed, semi-detached house like his mum, she had friends who owned far more substantial properties which often had far larger gardens.

He was just tipping the wheelbarrow up and jiggling it about a bit to persuade the last of the mulch to go where he wanted it to, when Mrs Williams tapped on her kitchen window and beckoned him inside.

Bless her, she always had a cup of tea for him and a biscuit or two to go with it, so he quickly finished what he was doing and stowed the spade and his gloves in the barrow, ready to wheel back home later.

He knocked on the back door and walked in, heading straight for the utility room to wash his grubby hands, and when he was done he found the old lady in the kitchen, pouring tea into mismatched china cups out of an ancient brown teapot. He knew from experience that the liquid would be strong enough to clear a drain, so he took one of the Garibaldi biscuits she'd laid out on a plate and bit into it, hoping the residual sweetness would take the edge off the tea.

'Mulching, is it?' she asked, placing a delicate cup on the table in front of him, before sitting down, her own drink clasped in her hands. It always amazed him that she didn't burn herself, but he'd long ago come to the conclusion that she had asbestos hands. She relished the heat and hated the cold, and Daniel often had to shed layers of clothing when he was in her house after he'd been outside, because he was in danger of overheating.

'Mulch, I said,' Mrs Williams repeated when he failed to answer her, poking him in the arm with a bony finger.

'Sorry? I was miles away. Yes, mulching. I'll also spread some manure on your roses when I can get some.'

'How was the thingy?'

'The what now?'

'The...' She tapped her hand crossly on the table. 'You know, the... I hate it when that happens. I can't find the word, but I can visualise what I mean... Father Christmas!' she yelled, making him jump.

Daniel winced. He wished his mother hadn't told Mrs Williams, but the elderly lady had a way of winkling information out of people, and she knew things she had no right knowing just by the sheer force of her personality. He'd heard her called nosy and interfering, but he preferred to think of her as being genuinely interested in people. Despite the age difference, Mrs Williams had been a good friend to his mum, and she was like an honorary grandmother to Daniel. Many a time Mrs Williams had looked after him for a couple of hours in the school holidays, or had taken him off his mum's hands for a while so she could have a break when things became too much for her.

'So, how was it?' Mrs Williams repeated impatiently.

'OK, I suppose.' He hoped he would get used to it. At least it was a job – one he'd have preferred not to have to take – and it beat working in a shop, which was the other option for seasonal work at this time of year. And it certainly beat the risk of going under. He was hanging on by his fingernails as it was; having so little work from November to January would have seen him having to pack in his gardening business if it wasn't for his Santa gigs. Maybe next year he'd start applying for jobs at the beginning of autumn when there was more choice. He'd considered being a delivery driver, but by the time he'd bitten the bullet and decided to apply for some jobs, there hadn't been many vacancies around.

'Daniel!'

'What?'

'You haven't listened to a word I've been saying. *I said*, I know of a job going if you want it.'

'As Father Christmas?'

'No, you silly boy. A gardening job. Minty Carruthers owns Fernlea Manor, and ivy is causing her problems. She wants someone to remove it. She needs some renovations done but the ivy has to go first. It's a listed building, you know. Anyway, I told her you'll do it. She can't pay much because she's desperately trying to raise funds to carry out the renovations. You know the type – sitting on a fortune in property but not a bean to her name. I told her you were desperate for work.'

Cheers, thanks a bunch, he felt like saying. Still, paid work was paid work and it wasn't as though he had anything else lined up – apart from playing Santa again on the weekend.

'I said you'd give her a call,' Mrs Williams told him, passing him a piece of paper with a telephone number on it, written in an ornate, curling hand.

'I will, thanks.' Anything was better than having to be Santa again. He stood up and drank the last of his tea. 'I'd better be off: Grandad is coming for lunch.'

But before he picked Edwin up, he intended to phone Minty Carruthers.

—

Edwin was dressed in his Sunday best when Daniel arrived to fetch him later.

'We're only having lunch at Mum's,' Daniel said, hoping his grandad didn't think they were going to a pub or a restaurant for a meal.

'I know, but I do have standards. Unlike some people.' He gave Daniel's jeans and sweatshirt a meaningful look.

'It's comfortable,' Daniel protested.

'You might want to think about wearing nicer clothes if you want to find yourself a girl. Speaking of which, how is Gina? Your mother told me she'd phoned.'

'She turned up at my place the other day, wanting us to try again.'

'Don't be tempted, my boy.'

'I'm not. I just feel sad about Amelia.'

'I expect you do, but the girl is her mother's responsibility, not yours. It wouldn't be fair on you or her if you got back together with Gina because of the child.'

'I know.'

'You need to get out there and find yourself a girlfriend who doesn't think of you as a meal ticket,' Edwin added.

Daniel was about to stick up for Gina, then had second thoughts because that was precisely how Gina did view

93

him – as someone to help pay the bills, do the DIY and the garden (obviously) and look after Amelia. She was selfish through and through, and he was well rid of her. His grandad often spoke a great deal of sense, and Daniel wished he'd spoken up sooner. Then again, would he have listened? He'd loved Gina in the beginning, and he doubted if he'd have had a word said against her back then.

'The garden is looking nice,' Edwin said, as Daniel parked on the road next to his mum's house.

'It always looks nice,' Daniel said. 'I make sure of that.'

'You're a good boy, but you can't be forever doing things for everyone else, and never doing anything for yourself. You've got your own life to lead, so lead it.'

'Hmm, I haven't had much luck with that lately.'

'If you mean Gina, don't let one rotten apple stop you from making cider.'

Daniel blinked. His grandad came out with some things. The old man was right, Daniel knew, but it was only two months since he and Gina had split up, and he hadn't met anyone yet who sparked his interest. He ignored the voice in his head that said 'oh yes, you have' because the voice was referring to Seren, and Tobias had already staked his claim.

He tried not to think about how their date went last night. It was none of his business and would only make him more disgruntled. Besides, Tobias would no doubt fill him in with the details the next time he saw him, no matter how little Daniel wanted to hear them.

It was like old times having Grandad at the dinner table, and Daniel was pleased to see him there. He'd joined his mum for a meal most evenings and every Sunday since Edwin had moved into the care home, thinking she might be lonely on her own after looking after his grandad for so long. Daniel might as well move in with her for the amount of time he spent at her house, but he was determined to retain some independence. Besides, he didn't want to confess to any new girlfriend that he lived with his mum: he didn't want to come across as any more pathetic than he already felt.

Not that he was likely to have a new girlfriend any time soon.

Which brought his train of thought neatly back to Seren…

'Tobias is converting an old ice cream van into a travelling shop of some kind,' he said, around a mouthful of crispy roast potato. His mum made the best roasties ever.

Edwin shoved a forkful of green beans into his mouth, chewed and swallowed. 'A travelling shop, eh? What will it be selling?'

'Gifts, I believe,' Daniel said. 'Maybe if there was one in the area, your friend in the care home wouldn't have given you slippers.' He chuckled and a pea went down the wrong way, making him cough.

'I like my slippers.'

'I bought you a new pair when you moved in,' Linda said.

Edwin reached across the table and patted his daughter on the hand. 'So you did, love, but you can never have too many pairs of slippers.' He paused. 'To tell you the truth, I've never seen Nelly wearing any. Maybe I ought to buy her a pair in return?'

'Do you think it's a good idea?' Daniel asked.

'Probably not. If she wanted to wear slippers, I suspect she'd have bought some for herself,' Edwin replied.

'Not the slippers; the travelling gift shop.'

'I dunno. I suppose.' Edwin frowned. 'Will you still take me Christmas shopping this year?'

'Of course I will,' Daniel promised.

His grandfather was quiet for a moment, the only sounds in the dining room being the clink of cutlery on plates and chewing. 'I can't get your present, not while you're with me. I had to ask your mother to buy something for you last year.'

'What's wrong with that?' Linda said, reaching for the gravy boat and pouring a generous dollop onto her plate. 'I have excellent taste.'

If Daniel's memory was correct, his grandad had bought him a gnome. It had been naked, apart from a mankini. Where on earth was he supposed to put it, he'd wondered at the time, and had ended up hiding it in the middle of his mother's hydrangea. Therefore, Daniel seriously doubted his mother's self-proclaimed good taste.

'So maybe there is a call for a travelling gift shop,' his grandad said thoughtfully, as their eyes met. He was clearly remembering the gnome, too. 'I prefer picking out something myself, rather than relying on your mother.' Edwin and Daniel shared another meaningful glance, and Daniel bit back a smile. He thought he'd shown a great deal of enthusiasm and appreciation for the gnome, but he obviously hadn't been able to pull the wool over his grandfather's eyes.

'Daniel has been working in the garden this morning,' Linda said. 'Mulching. You miss having your own garden, don't you, love?'

'It's lucky I can work in yours,' Daniel said to her with a smile.

'Talking of work, how is it going?'

Daniel grimaced. 'I've just phoned someone Mrs Williams put me in touch with, who wants me to remove some ivy from the walls of her house. She doesn't want me to start until the week after next though, so I've not got a lot on between now and Christmas.'

'You've got your Santa thing, though,' Edwin pointed out. 'Surely that'll tide you over?'

Daniel rolled his eyes and sighed. 'Mum, have you told everyone?'

'Your grandfather isn't everyone,' Linda retorted.

'You told Mrs Williams.' Daniel wished she hadn't done that.

'She's not everyone, either. She's like family. There's no need to be embarrassed. We've all done jobs we didn't like to make ends meet. There's no shame in it.'

'I'm not ashamed,' Daniel objected. 'It's just not my thing. The kids are cute – mostly – but I feel such a fraud.'

Edwin chortled, 'So you should! The real Santa is still at the North Pole this time of year.'

'Ha, ha, very funny. Seriously, it's a responsibility I could do without. What if I let something slip? I don't want to be known as the man who told a kid that Santa isn't real, or that it's the grown-ups who bring the presents.'

His mother leant across the table and chucked his cheek. 'You're a good boy,' she said as he twisted away in embarrassment. He was too old for cheek-pinching. 'You'll make a good father.'

But that was the problem, he realised, as a memory of Amelia opening her presents last year swam into his mind – he'd thought he already had.

Chapter 9

Seren had her heart in her mouth when she walked into the garage a few days after her damp squib of a date with Tobias on Friday, but it wasn't because she'd be seeing him again – it was because this was the day she was going to pick up her ice cream van that was now a gift shop.

As she stepped inside and saw it parked in the corner, tears gathered in her eyes.

It was beautiful.

Gone was the unicorn horn of an ice cream cone on the roof. Gone was the depiction of various kinds of ice cream along its side. The previous owner's name had also been obliterated.

Instead, she was staring at a van with the same outline as before, but the colour was the muted creamy one that Tobias had shown her in the photos the other night, with the addition of a spray of holly above the side window, along with ivy, mistletoe, and candy canes. It seemed that Tobias had been listening to her after all when she'd wittered on about making wreaths and garlands.

'Do you like it?' Tobias asked, appearing at her side.

'It's wonderful,' she whispered, awestruck at just how perfect it looked. 'Are those—?' She pointed to the pictures, hoping they weren't permanent.

'Stick on? Yes. As we discussed.' He shrugged. 'You can change them if you want.'

'I'm not changing anything,' she replied, adamantly. 'Can I take a closer look?'

Tobias laughed. 'You can do what you like with it – it's yours.'

Seren stepped forward tentatively, scared it wouldn't look as good in close-up, but to her relief it looked even better, as she could now see inside.

'I've given you as much storage as I could, without hindering your movements,' Tobias said, as she stood on tiptoe and peered into its depths.

The wall opposite the sliding window contained several shelves, each of them angled downwards slightly, and for a second she wondered why that was until she realised that the angle would showcase her stock better to her customers. To prevent everything from falling off, Tobias had placed a clear Perspex barrier along the edge of each one.

Opening the driver's door, she climbed in and went into the back. It looked equally as wonderful from this perspective, and she could see the cupboards underneath the counter and the craftsmanship that had gone into everything. There were boards either side of the window with holes in them and hooks hanging from them, and when she went to slide the window across, she realised that instead of the one pane of glass sliding across the other leaving an opening half the size of the window, Tobias had altered it so that both sides slid back, meaning the opening was twice as large. He'd even constructed a tiered display to sit on the exposed counter.

Blimey, he'd thought of everything.

Leaning through the hatch, her eyes glistening with tears and her heart full of gratitude, she flung her arms around him and gave him a massive hug. 'Thank you, thank you, thank you!'

Laughing, he hugged her before gently extricating himself, and pushing her back inside so she didn't fall out through the window. 'You're welcome. Even if I say so myself, she does look good, doesn't she?' He waited for Seren to join him on the ground before he asked, 'What are you going to call her?'

'Um… I hadn't thought about it,' Seren admitted.

'You have to have a name for your business,' Tobias insisted.

'I've been so busy concentrating on getting it up and running, I haven't thought about a name for it.'

'How about The Christmas Gift-mobile? Or Wheelie Great Gifts?' he chuckled.

Seren groaned. 'That's awful. I'll have to have a think.'

'When you've decided on a name, give these people a call.' Tobias handed her a piece of paper. 'They make decals. They're not too expensive and can do a fast turn-around. That's who I used.'

'I don't know how I can ever thank you,' she said, still feeling emotional, although she wasn't sure which emotion was taking pride of place – delight, excitement, fear, apprehension…

She caught the look he gave her and wrinkled her nose. 'Let's don't go there,' she warned playfully. 'I think we both know dating each other isn't going to work out for us.'

'Pity,' he said, sounding sincere. 'You're a beautiful woman.'

'Aww…' She could feel her cheeks reddening. 'Flatterer.'

'I know, I practise.' He grinned and she simply had to grin back. He was irrepressible and she liked him, but not in that way. He definitely wasn't boyfriend material.

'There's a couple of things I want to show you before you take the van away,' he said, opening the cab door and indicating she should sit inside.

Seren climbed into the driver's seat and Tobias stood on the step, leaned across her and pressed a button. The van lit up like a Christmas tree inside and out, and Seren gasped.

'Oh, my, that's gorgeous.' She gazed around the van with delight. Tobias had used tiny gold fairy lights to highlight the inside, and strings of them were entwined everywhere. It looked like a fairy grotto and her imagination ran wild as she envisioned it filled with baubles and stars, Santas and elves, all twinkling and glowing in the pretty lights.

'That's not all,' he said. 'Knowing the British weather and how fickle it can be at this time of year, I installed this.'

He pressed another button and Seren heard a rumbling sound. She squished around in the seat to find where it was coming from and was astounded to see an awning in the same colour as the van slowly emerge from above the window.

'You have thought of everything,' she said, then a thought occurred to her. 'How much are you charging for this?' She hadn't agreed to this, and neither had he phoned to tell her he was planning on doing it. They'd agreed on an amount, which she was only just able to pay as it would use almost all her savings, and she hadn't budgeted for anything extra.

Tobias stepped down. 'It's included in the quote I gave you.'

'It is? I don't remember seeing anything about an awning.'

'I took it off another vehicle I'm in the middle of upgrading and it would only have gone to waste as the owner wants something bigger. So I thought I'd put it on yours.'

'It looks brand new,' she said.

'Yeah, it does. They hardly used it. I gave it a scrub, tested the electrics, and there you have it. But that wasn't all I wanted to show you. See that box there, with the knobs? Turn one of them.'

Seren sent him a curious look but did as he asked, wondering what new surprise he had in store for her.

The uplifting tune of 'Joy to the World' rang out, filling the garage with tinkling music.

'Wow…' By now Seren was speechless.

'I've pre-programmed it with six tunes altogether,' he told her, and Seren spent a delightful minute or so, turning knobs and listening to the brief snatches of music. Her favourite, and the one she thought she might use if she ever found the courage to patrol the streets in her Christmas van was 'Jingle Bells'. It simply had to be.

As Seren drove off, having said goodbye to Tobias and thanked him yet again, she was so overcome with Christmas spirit that tears trickled down her face.

She was doing this – she really was!

–

Aunt Nelly was bundled up in a long-sleeved jumper, a woolly cardigan, a heavy-duty mac, a scarf and a pair of lime green leather gloves. She was also beaming fit to burst as she regarded the transformed ice cream van which was sitting in the care home's car park.

'Are you pleased with it?' she demanded and Seren nodded.

'I think it's lovely, and it'll look even better when it's fully stocked.' That was where she was off to next – to collect stock from those crafts people who had agreed to let her sell their items on a sale or return basis. Before that though, she couldn't resist stopping off at the care home to show her Great-Aunt Nelly. After all, she'd been instrumental in Seren having the idea in the first place.

'You must bring it back when you've got something to sell,' Nelly instructed. 'Now, take me back inside before I freeze to death, and you can make me a cup of tea while you're at it.'

'Yes, ma'am.' Seren saluted her, then supervised as the old lady shuffled her walker around so it faced the right direction and made her slow, careful way indoors.

'When are you planning on going out in it?' Nelly asked, when she was settled in the day room with a cup of tea and a mince pie on the side table next to her.

'I'm going to a Christmas market on Saturday to break myself in gently, plus I've got a couple of others booked in. If they go OK, I might risk going to a care home or two, and maybe a trawl around the streets.'

'You need to be more proactive than that,' Nelly said, slurping her tea. 'You've got to make the most of the run-up to Christmas.'

'Don't forget, I already have a job, and it's not going to be easy fitting it all in. They'll probably want me to work extra shifts the nearer we get to Christmas.'

Nelly made a snorting noise. 'You're wasted in that supermarket. They work you to the bone and they don't appreciate you.'

It wasn't as bad as her aunt was making out. The work could sometimes be hard, and she certainly wasn't appreciated, but didn't every employer expect their staff to give a hundred per cent? It was just a shame Pamela was such a dragon. Seren had quite enjoyed working there until Pamela became manager.

'Tell her to stuff her job,' Nelly was saying and Seren tried not to roll her eyes. Her aunt hadn't worked for over thirty years and things had changed. If Seren did what Nelly suggested, then Seren would be frantically trying to find employment without a reference. If she did intend to change direction and leave her current job, she fully planned on having another one to go to. Simply walking out wasn't an option.

'You've got your van, now,' Nelly said.

'But I don't even know if I'll make a profit,' Seren objected.

'Nonsense. Of course you will. I have every faith in you.'

Seren was glad someone did, because she didn't have much faith in herself. 'I think I've rushed into this with my eyes closed,' she said. 'I've used all my savings on it – or I will have done when Tobias sends me his invoice. And I don't even have a name for it. He suggested calling it *Wheelie Good Gifts*.'

Nelly bared her false teeth. 'That's awful.'

'I know, but I don't have anything better.'

'I do. *Serendipity*.'

Seren's mouth dropped open. Why hadn't she thought of that? The name was perfect!

–

It was dark by the time Seren headed back home with her van loaded with boxes from those people who had enough faith in her to trust her with their valuable stock.

She was shattered. It had been a long day, starting with doing an early shift at work (seven a.m. start), picking the van up as soon as she'd finished, followed by a quick visit to her Aunt Nelly, then a great deal of driving around to make sure she had enough things to sell at the very first market in three days' time. It was rare to have a Saturday off, but she'd traded shifts with a member of staff who had a day trip to London booked during the week, and she also had the following Saturday off so she'd booked into a Christmas Fayre in the grounds of a posh manor house. She should head off home and start labelling the stock up and arranging it in the van, but she wasn't due to go into work until the afternoon tomorrow, which meant she had all morning to do that, so she decided to drop in to see Nicole and show off Serendipity (or Dippy, for short, as she decided to call it). She knew Freya would love it, and she couldn't wait to see the little girl's reaction.

The child's squeal of excitement made Seren's ears hurt, and even Nicole was impressed.

'It's gorgeous,' her friend said when Freya had calmed down enough so they could hear themselves think.

'Fancy a quick ride in it?' Seren asked the little girl. 'If that's OK with your mum?'

'Please, Mummy, can I?' Freya hung off Nicole's arm, a pleading look on her face.

'Only if you're quick,' Nicole said. 'It's your bedtime in ten minutes and you've got school tomorrow.'

'We'll just go around the block,' Seren said, and as soon as Freya was safely strapped in Seren drove slowly to the end of the road, turned left, then turned left again. It was only a short trip, but Freya was ecstatic, and she nearly squealed herself out of her pretty pink trainers when Seren let her play one of the tunes.

'Can I do it again?' Freya asked, as the final notes of 'Ding-Dong Merrily on High' ended.

'Sorry, sweetie, I'm only allowed to play it once and then I have to go somewhere else if I want to play another one.' The regulations on playing the sort of tunes ice cream vans played were surprisingly strict.

'Can we go somewhere else?'

'Another time. Mummy said it's your bedtime and I'm really tired too, so as soon as I've dropped you off, I'm going to go home to bed.'

'My mummy doesn't go to bed when I do,' Freya said, suspiciously.

'Your mummy has to stay up to make sure your uniform is ready for school tomorrow,' Seren said, improvising wildly.

Freya seemed happy enough with Seren's explanation and when Seren parked Dippy outside Freya's house, the little girl shot inside to tell her mum all about her adventure.

Nicole came outside to speak to Seren before she left. 'I've told her to put her PJs on,' Nicole said, 'but I bet she won't. Procrastination is her middle name: she'll do anything to delay going to bed. Whereas I, on the other hand, can't wait to lay my head down on the pillow.'

'Me, too. I'm exhausted, and I've still got so much to do before Saturday.'

'I was thinking about popping along to offer some support and to help out for a couple of hours if you want me to, considering it's your first one. Freya will be with her nan for the day because—' Nicole glanced over her shoulder, then whispered '—I need to do some shopping for presents for you-know-who.'

'That would be fantastic. I'm dreading it.'

'You'll be fine,' Nicole said. 'What could possibly go wrong?'

'Don't get me started. How about the van breaks down? Or I don't sell anything? Or everyone hates the idea. Or—'

'Or an alien might come down and steal all your baubles,' Nicole finished. 'This is the start of what could be a great opportunity. The hard bit is done: you've got a fantastic travelling shop and you've got lots of stuff to sell.'

Seren wailed, 'I keep getting cold feet.' She couldn't believe how quickly her emotions swung like a pendulum from happy and confident, to anxious and scared, and back again, with a couple of stops at panic-town along the way.

Nicole rubbed her arm. 'I expect you do, and it's going to be hard juggling your job and your van, but once you are established you can jack your job in and concentrate on this new chapter in your life.'

'I suppose by doing it this way it might take longer to get the business off the ground but at least I've got some income coming in,' Seren mused. 'I'm not shelling out for stock to sell at the moment, either. It might mean I don't make much of a profit on each item, but over time it should all add up. I do make a decent profit on my wreaths and garlands though, so I need to get off home and make a couple more. It's quite therapeutic.'

'I'll take your word for it,' Nicole said, hugging her goodbye. 'Now, chin up. It'll be fine.'

It's got to be, Seren thought as she got in the van. Her life savings were sunk into this and she didn't know what she'd do if it all went horribly wrong.

Chapter 10

Seren manoeuvred Dippy through the old town's narrow streets, a frown of intense concentration on her face. It didn't help that it was so early in the morning that it was still dark, she didn't know where she was going, and she was so tired she didn't know what to do with herself.

If it wasn't for Nicole sitting in the passenger seat and giving her loads of encouragement, she might have considered turning around and going home.

Fortunately there was nowhere to turn easily so it was impossible to act on the temptation to turn tail and run. She knew that once the van was parked, and they were all set up and she had a coffee inside her, the Christmas spirit would start making its presence felt and she'd hopefully get some lovely festive vibes, made all the more intense by the atmosphere of the Christmas market.

An official in a neon yellow vest over a heavily padded jacket flagged her down, and Seren came to a stop and wound down her window. The woman was clasping a clipboard in one gloved hand and a pen in the other, and her breath steamed around her head. Seren handed over the relevant paperwork, and once she'd been checked off the list the woman gave her a printed map of the market and pointed out their pitch on it. Seren thanked her and handed the map to Nicole.

'We're next to the medieval market house,' Nicole chortled as she checked the map, and she slapped the dashboard. 'Yes!'

'That's good?'

'Of course it is! It's right in the middle of the main street. It says here that the whole street will be cordoned off and it'll be pedestrian access only, and we've got a spot right in the middle of it. Woohoo!' She jabbed a finger at the map. 'Plus, there's a Santa's grotto almost directly opposite us. Every kiddie under the age of ten will be nagging to see Santa, so we should get loads of passing trade.'

Seren hoped so. This fledgeling business of hers depended on the success of sales at this event and the others she'd arranged to attend in the run-up to Christmas.

It took her a bit of to-ing and fro-ing to position the van but as soon as it was in its correct place the pair of them leapt into action, and because of Tobias's well thought out interior design, it didn't take long before they were ready to start serving.

The market didn't officially open until ten o'clock and it was only just gone eight, so Seren said, 'There's a stall over there selling coffee. I'll go grab us some. Will you be all right on your own until I get back?'

Nicole nodded and rolled her eyes. 'I'll be fine.'

Seren knew she would be, especially since she was only going to be a few metres away, but this was her baby, her responsibility, and Nicole was only here out of the kindness of her heart and because she was a darned good friend. Nicole knew how nervous she was and had given up a precious Saturday when she didn't have to look after Freya, to look after Seren instead. Poor Nicole should be having a lie-in, followed by a leisurely breakfast, topped off by an unhindered shopping session and perhaps treat herself to lunch out. Instead, she was helping man a mobile shop in the middle of a draughty high street. The least Seren could do was to keep her friend fed and watered.

It was starting to get light and the street was choc-a-bloc with traders and stallholders setting up their stalls, but a few people were already browsing and Seren guessed it was going to get busy very soon and very quickly. So to go with the coffees she bought a couple of bacon rolls. With a hot drink and some food inside her, she'd be ready for anything.

Hopefully…

–

'I'm starting to feel rather Christmassy,' Seren declared an hour and a half later. She was standing inside Dippy and gazing around it happily, Nicole by her side. It looked brilliant and she was immensely proud of it, even though it had been Tobias who had done all the hard work, and nearly all the stock had been made by other people's hands.

'You always feel Christmassy,' Nicole said, draping an arm around her shoulders.

'It looks good, though, doesn't it?'

'It sure does. And I love the name – it's so you.'

Seren beamed. Aunt Nelly's suggestion to call it Serendipity had been inspired, and the van now had the name emblazoned on it in red, gold and green. Tobias's recommendation for the decal producer had been spot on, and as soon as she'd agreed a font and a colour scheme, the company had done her a massive favour and had shipped the decals to her by express delivery. That was one of the reasons she was so tired this morning – she'd been up half the night sticking them on: not an easy task by torchlight, balancing on a step ladder and in the bitter cold.

It was a relief to see that she hadn't made too bad a job of it now that she was able to see it in the daylight. Maybe one of the decals could do with being a bit more to the left…? She sighed; it was too late to do anything about it today, and to tell the truth she was frightened to take it off and try to reposition it in case she couldn't get it to stick on again, and it hadn't been cheap so she couldn't afford to pay for a new one. Which reminded her, Tobias hadn't sent her his invoice yet and she wanted to pay him so she knew where she stood financially. She must remember to give him a ring on Monday and ask him about it.

'It'll be fine,' Nicole said, giving her a squeeze. 'You'll see. Anyway, you've done the best you can – I don't see how you could possibly make the van look any more inviting.'

Seren continued to stare at it. It looked amazing, even on a dull morning in late November in what was normally a sleepy little market town in the Cotswolds. Already there was the noise and bustle of eager shoppers, and the smell of mulled wine, hotdogs and roasting chestnuts filled the air. Soon the streets would ring to the sounds of assorted carols, chatter and laughter, which all added to the festive atmosphere.

The angled shelves lining the trailer's back wall were perfect for baskets of baubles and stars, angels and robins, and other decorations which caught the light and shone invitingly, and the displays of garlands, wreaths, woven stockings, plush elves, cuddly robins, and edible candy canes were cheerful and enticing. Seren defied anyone not to be tempted. Out of everything, Seren's favourites were the snow globes, and she was immensely grateful to the kind lady who'd taken a chance on her and had given her an impressive range of them to sell on her behalf.

Nicole's weakness was candles, especially scented ones, and she had busily sniffed her way through most of them, and with them all laid out in a pretty display, the van was enveloped in the wonderful fragrance of orange, berries, vanilla, chocolate, nutmeg and cloves.

Seren's tummy rumbled loudly and her thoughts turned to a second breakfast. The first one had barely touched the sides, and the smell of the candles made her long for a hot chocolate drink with marshmallows on the top and lots of whipped cream, and maybe a cookie to go with it.

'Are you hungry?' she asked, and Nicole laughed.

'You clearly are. Do you want me to break out the sandwiches?'

Seren sniffed, her nose filled with the delicious smell of crepes from a stall further up the road and she tried to resist. She'd made cheese and pickle sandwiches the night before with the express intention of not spending her hard-earned profits on eating out. But… Seren sniffed again, her mouth watering.

Nicole gave her a pointed look.

'How about if we compromise?' Seren suggested. 'We'll eat the sandwiches later and I'll treat us to a hot chocolate now.'

Nicole appeared to be mulling it over, but Seren could tell she'd already succumbed to temptation. 'Go on then. We might as well grab a drink before it gets any busier. And if you don't mind, I'd like to have a look around the market to see if anything takes my eye – I've still got loads of presents to buy.'

'Of course I don't mind! You're doing me a massive favour just by being here. I don't expect you to have your nose to the grindstone all day. We'll have our hot chocolates, then you go exploring.'

There were already loads of people around and Seren could see a queue starting to form outside Santa's grotto. The wooden hut was currently locked and shuttered, but fairy lights gleamed from the rafters and at some point during the past half an hour three rather realistic reindeer had come to mechanical life and were gently moving their heads to the sound of 'Jingle Bells'. Fake snow lay around their hooves and behind them sat Santa's sleigh, with a toy elf standing on top of a stack of brightly covered presents, waving his arm, and another climbing down a little ladder, then climbing back up again. As a grown-up Seren was enchanted, so she could only imagine how a small child would feel on seeing this delightful scene for the first time.

Hugging herself with excitement, the joy of the festive season swirling through her and making her feel quite giddy, Seren headed towards the grotto. There was a stall selling hot drinks, cakes and cookies situated next to it, and it was already doing a brisk trade. Several people strolling past were holding cups of hot chocolate (one even had a candy cane in it!) and they looked delicious. She hurried over to the stall, anticipating the feel of silky-smooth chocolate on her lips, and sweetness bursting on her tongue—

She didn't notice the man cutting across her until she'd barged into him, her shoulder catching him in the chest.

'Oomph!' The impact sent her staggering back, and she thought she was going to fall but his hand shot out and grabbed her forcibly by the arm. 'Ouch,' she cried again.

'Sorry,' the man released her so abruptly, that she almost lost her balance once more.

His head was lowered and she followed his gaze, realising he'd dropped a Santa hat. Hastily, she stooped to retrieve it, feeling guilty, but as she did so he reached for it at the same time, and his forehead collided with hers with an audible crack.

Abruptly, Seren's legs went from under her, and she sat down heavily on the freezing tarmac, her teeth clacking together. 'Ow,' she moaned, clutching her head.

'Are you all right? Oh, it's you. Um, hi...' a familiar voice said, and Seren looked up to see Daniel's face inches from hers as he crouched down to check on her.

Stars hovered around his head and for an awful second Seren thought she might be suffering from concussion, until she realised it was the fairy lights of the grotto twinkling behind him.

Crossly she was about to retort 'do I look all right', but as she gazed at him her irritation melted away. She blamed her inability to hold onto her annoyance on the hazel eyes gazing down at her in worry. She also blamed it on his aquiline nose, sculpted cheekbones and the brown hair that curled around his ears and flopped over his forehead. A hint of stubble and a chiselled jaw didn't help, either. Daniel was a handsome-looking man.

Abruptly, he held out a hand.

Seren took it and he hauled her to her feet.

She staggered again, almost falling into him, but caught herself in time, putting out a hand and feeling soft fluffiness under her palm. When she looked down, she saw he was holding a Father Christmas outfit in his arms.

'Sorry,' she said. It had been her fault, not his, so she had no right to be annoyed with him. And even if she did, any hint of crotchetiness had well and truly disappeared. She should have been concentrating on where she was going, and not on images of hot chocolate.

'It's OK,' he replied, but he didn't look happy and she hoped he hadn't hurt his head too badly; hers was sore and she'd probably have an impressive lump and a headache later on, but maybe he'd come off worse than she had.

'Are you all right?' she asked.

'Fine. No harm done.'

'Good, well… I'd better leave you to it. I've got to get back to the van.' She glanced over at it and he followed her gaze. 'Nice to meet you again, and sorry for the…' She pointed to his head and rubbed her own ruefully, giving him a small smile.

He nodded, then bent to retrieve the Santa hat and plonked it on top of the pile of clothing he was holding.

'Good luck for today,' he said, looking at the van. 'Not that you'll need it.' He continued to stare at it, not meeting her eye. 'Tobias has done a good job.'

'Yes, he has,' she agreed enthusiastically, and beamed at him when he glanced back at her.

To her surprise, he hastily looked away again. 'I'd better go.'

'Of course.' She had to stop lingering too, but she couldn't help asking, 'Is that for you?' She nodded at the Santa suit he was holding. 'I'm only asking because Tobias said you were playing Father Christmas.'

The frown he gave her made her wish she hadn't mentioned it. 'Thanks, Tobias,' he muttered, then said a little louder. 'Yes, it's mine.'

'How lovely. What a wonderful way to get into the Christmas spirit, all those eager children and their little faces.' It was a pity Nicole hadn't been able to bring Freya to see Father Christmas, but it would have been too long a day for the little girl. She was better off spending it with her granny. Maybe another time…

Daniel grimaced. 'If you say so,' he said. 'Look, I've got to go. It's been nice talking to you.' And with that, he walked away.

Seren watched him go, bemused and rather cross once more. OK, the collision had totally been her fault, but there was no need for him to be so cranky about it. She hadn't walked into him on purpose, and from the feel of things she'd come off far worse than he had. And why was he so miserable about dressing up as Santa Claus anyway?

She rubbed her head again, her eyes tracking him.

She hoped for the sake of all those children who were waiting to see Father Christmas that he cheered up and found some festive spirit, otherwise there were going to be a lot of disappointed kids and aggrieved parents in a bit.

But as she waited in line for the drinks, she couldn't help wondering why Daniel was so bad tempered. Was it only because he was being forced to dress up as Santa to supplement his gardening business, or was there some other reason?

Oh, well, it was unlikely she'd ever get to find out, so she pushed him from her mind. She had more important things to think about than a grumpy Father Christmas.

–

'That'll be seven pounds fifty, please,' Seren said, popping the little train tree decoration into a paper bag, and thanking the customer.

The stall was doing well; she'd sold a fair amount of stock already, and there were still a few hours to go, culminating in a candle-lit procession through the town once it got dark.

'Do you mind if I pop to the loo?' she asked Nicole, who'd only just returned from a visit to the ladies herself. Thank goodness Nicole was here otherwise Seren would have to have kept her legs crossed all day! She'd need to have a serious re-think about the remainder of the fayres and markets she had lined up, and how she was going to cope on her own. Still, it was easy enough to close the window on the van and lock it up, even if she did have to leave the wreaths and garlands outside.

'I'll be as quick as I can,' she promised.

She was forced to dodge around the ever-present queue to see Santa and, as she slipped between the waiting people, she glanced at the grotto and realised she was at just the right angle to see inside.

The little hut was so pretty with its fake snow, red and green striped bunting, and the twinkling lights woven into the ivy and holly draped along its eaves. There were shutters on the window, which were currently open to reveal a charming scene of elves hard at work making toys through the glass, for the waiting children to look at as they moved closer to the door, and Seren saw many little ones standing on tiptoe and peering in. It made her heart melt to see the shining faces as they turned in awe to their parents. This was what Christmas was all about – magic and wonder.

Seren hesitated, torn between knowing she shouldn't leave Nicole on her own for too long, and wanting to indulge in a little Christmas magic herself. She clearly remembered the intense excitement she used to feel when she'd visited Santa when she was a small girl, and her unwavering belief that he was real. She'd been so eager to assure him she'd been good, and she'd tried so hard to not be on the naughty list, so please could she have a doll's house.

Looking back, her parents hadn't had a great deal of money to spare on extravagant gifts like doll's houses, but they'd managed to get her one and it was only much, much later when she was all grown up that her mum had let her into the secret that she'd bought it from a charity shop. It had been in pretty poor condition, but her mother had spent many evenings after Seren had gone to bed painting it and making tiny curtains and blankets.

'Excuse me, are you waiting to see Father Christmas?' a little voice said, and Seren looked down to see a small boy gazing at her with a worried expression on his face. 'Because if you are, you're a bit old,' he added.

'Callum! Don't be so rude. Sorry…' His mother looked mortified, but Seren found it hilarious.

'I'm not going to see Santa, although I would like to.' She glanced inside the grotto, but from this angle all she could see was a pair of legs, the feet encased in chunky black boots. She wondered if Daniel was any happier than he'd been earlier, but as she'd not noticed any unhappy faces leaving the grotto, she assumed he must have cheered up.

'Santa doesn't bring presents for grown-ups,' the little boy informed her. 'Only for kids, like me.'

'Only if you've been good,' Seren replied. 'Have you been good?'

He nodded vigorously, and his mum smiled indulgently. 'He has his moments,' the woman said, ruffling his hair.

Seren stood to the side, not wanting anyone else to think she was in the queue, and craned her neck, hoping she'd be able to see more of Daniel.

That was better, she could see all of Santa now, and not just his feet. He was talking to two small girls, possibly no older than three or four, both of them identical. Their eyes were wide, and one of them had a thumb in her mouth. Seren saw them nod, and she noticed Santa's eyes crinkling with merriment, and she heard him cry 'Merry Christmas!' as he handed them each an identically wrapped present.

Aw, that was so sweet.

She was about to make a move when Daniel glanced through the open door and saw her looking.

He cocked his head as their gaze met, and his eyes locked onto hers. For a second he looked incredibly solemn, then he smiled at her: not a jolly Father Christmas smile, but a small sad smile, barely visible through his fake beard. A smile that made her want to rush over and wrap her arms around him. It also made her stomach do a backward flip – goodness, he was incredibly sexy. Or at least his eyes were, because that was all she could see of his face.

The moment fled as swiftly as it had arrived; one of Santa's helpers stepped forward to usher the next child into the grotto and Seren's view of him was obscured by a pair of red and white stripey tights, and a green and red elf costume.

Blinking and wondering what all that was about, Seren hurried away. She'd lingered long enough; Nicole must be wondering where she'd got to!

–

Seren reversed the van into a space outside her house, taking several goes until she was happy that she'd reversed the darned thing properly and it wasn't sticking out into the road too much, then she switched the engine off, slumped back into her seat and stared into space, over-whelmed with exhaustion.

A knock on the window made her jump and she turned to see her dad peering in at her. 'Are you coming in?' he yelled. 'Or are you going to stay there all night?'

Wearily she unclipped her seat belt, opened the door and almost fell out onto the pavement.

Her dad's arm shot out to steady her. 'Are you all right?'

She pulled a face. It was supposed to have been an attempt at a smile, but she had the feeling she was gurning. 'I'm cold, exhausted and starving.'

'Did it go OK?' He looked worried and she hastened to reassure him as she locked Dippy.

'It went well, and I sold loads.' She tried not to pull another face at the thought of all the reconciliation and paperwork she had to do to ensure her suppliers were correctly paid. She'd kept meticulous records throughout the day, but there was always room for error. 'It was good fun,' she added, 'But it didn't half take it out of me, and I've got to go into work tomorrow.' She dreaded the thought.

Yawning hugely, Seren hoisted the bag with the day's takings in it and followed her dad inside.

A wall of welcome warmth hit her, and once she'd divested herself of her coat, fleece, scarf, gloves, boots and one of the two pairs of socks she'd been wearing, she dropped down into the squashy sofa with a groan.

'Can I make you a cuppa?' her dad asked, and she nodded gratefully, then glared at his retreating back when he pressed the button on her cuddly Father Christmas as he walked past, sparking the toy into jerking life as his mouth moved mechanically to the tinny sounds of 'Jingle Bells'.

As if on cue, the moment the Father Christmas had ground to a halt, the Christmas clock above the fireplace briefly played 'We Three Kings Of Orient Are', announcing it was nine o'clock.

No wonder Seren was tired. She and Nicole had been on the go since six-thirty this morning, and not only was she tired, she ached like the devil, her face hurt from smiling so much, and she was starting to lose her voice from all the talking she'd done. She also hadn't had anything to eat since twelve-thirty when Nicole had bought them a slice of game pie from the deli stall opposite, to go with their sandwiches.

After drinking her tea and telling her dad all about the market (she may have mentioned Daniel once or twice), Seren had a hot bath to warm up, then wrapped herself in a soft throw – a special Christmas one with a happy snowman on it – and kissed her dad goodnight. She made herself a mug of hot chocolate (although it was nowhere near as yummy as the one she'd drunk earlier today) and settled down to do some sums.

An hour later she was finding it hard to keep her eyes open. She'd counted the money, prepared a float for the next fayre, written out the takings, less her commission, for every supplier, and had made a note of what had sold well, what stock was left and what she needed more of.

She was now bone-grindingly weary and was falling asleep in the chair.

Oddly, though, when she retired to bed and nestled into her pillow, she found she was unable to sleep. Daniel's face kept intruding into her mind, and she couldn't help hoping she'd bump into him again soon – preferably not literally next time, as she still had a sore spot on her head from today's encounter.

Crossly, and in desperate need of rest, she told herself that even if she did see him again, he wasn't interested in her; he'd made that abundantly clear. So why was she unable to get him out of her mind…?

Chapter 11

Daniel loved old manor houses because they usually had wonderfully old and well-established gardens to accompany them. This one was an exception. What had once probably been magnificent lawns to the front of the house had been mostly tarmacked over, and what was left of the lawn now had a giant marquee plonked on it.

Miss Carruthers (she'd been quite acerbic on the phone when he'd accidentally called her *Mrs*) was waiting to greet him as his truck crunched up the potholed drive the following Wednesday afternoon. It was a dim and dismal day with lowering clouds, and it was starting to get dark already.

'I need it done urgently,' she informed him brusquely. 'The manor has an event on at the weekend, and I'd like it completed by then.'

That explained the huge white tent. But it didn't explain why she'd made him wait until this week to remove the offending ivy, when he could easily have done it last week and saved rushing the job.

Daniel studied the front of the house, and from where he was standing the encroaching ivy didn't appear to be too much of a problem.

'Not here,' she told him. 'Around the back.'

She moved out from under the rather grand porch entrance and shooed him away. He stood to one side as she marched past, a thin, slight woman possibly in her late sixties or early seventies, with a hairstyle reminiscent of Princess Anne's and an expression of exasperation on her face. The drive swept around the side of the house, and he guessed that was where they were heading, as he followed behind and gazed up at the house.

It had seen better days, but it still bore a hint of its former grandeur in the columned porch, the enormously tall windows on the ground floor, and the smooth butter-yellow stone that the building was constructed from. Daniel couldn't even hazard a guess at the number of rooms within its walls, but he knew he'd love to see inside at some point.

'Ah, I see what you mean,' he said, when the rear of the grand old property came into view. Hardly a window could be seen for foliage.

'It's evergreen,' Miss Carruthers added, unnecessarily.

'It's going to be messy,' he warned. There was no simple way of stripping the clinging strands of vines from the walls without making a mess on the ground below.

'Yes, well, do the best you can,' she instructed. Her mouth was a thin straight line and her eyes were narrowed in dislike as she glared at the offending climber. 'As I said, I need it done urgently. The builders will be here on Monday.'

It was going to be tight. Ivy was a nuisance to get rid of, as its tendrils burrowed into the stonework and refused to let go without a fight. Even then they left marks on the bricks, as a ghostly reminder.

He moved closer to the wall and gave one of the tendrils a tentative tug. It came away with a small protest, and he snapped it off.

'I can't do much today,' he advised; the light was fading fast. 'I'll make a start in the morning, if that's all right with you?'

'It'll have to be,' she retorted sourly.

He got the feeling she'd be more than happy for him to work throughout the night, but he didn't intend to go up a ladder in the dark. However, there was something he could do right now which wouldn't take very long, and that was to saw through the trunks of the ivy. He'd cut them as close to the ground as possible. Ideally this should have been done months ago to allow the plants to die back and make their removal easier.

When he mentioned it, all Miss Carruthers said was, 'Get on with it, then.'

'Don't you want me to give you a quote first? It'll take me a good two days to remove this lot.'

She pinned him with a steely gaze. 'Phoebe – Mrs Williams to you – assures me that you won't charge more than the job is worth. Please don't disappoint me.'

'But you don't know how much—'

'Be here bright and early tomorrow. You can collect your payment on Sunday – I'll have the money for you by then. Will cash do?' Her tone indicated that cash would have to do, whether he liked it or not.

Irritated, Daniel began to walk back to his truck to fetch the necessary equipment. He could make a start, at least.

'And please park your vehicle around the back in future,' she instructed as a parting shot, leaving him with the definite impression that hired help such as himself, should be neither seen nor heard.

As he set to sawing and cutting, Daniel felt like he was taking part in an episode of *Downton Abbey* and he wondered if he should have doffed his bobble hat to her.

He didn't care, though; he was doing what he loved and getting paid for it. And anything was better than dressing up as Father sodding Christmas. He still had nightmares about last Saturday – although it had more to do with Seren. Of all the people to bump into him, it had to be her. Fate must have been having a good old chuckle at his expense.

He had been tempted to ask himself 'what were the chances?', but that would be silly. He'd known she was planning on using the former ice cream van as a travelling gift shop, so he should have anticipated that he might see her at one of the events he was also booked into. He might have got away with not being recognised if he'd been dressed in his suit, with the wig, the beard, the eyebrows and the little round glasses. He might even have got away with it if he'd bumped into her without the darned suit in his hands, as he could have told her he was there to do some Christmas shopping. But he had to meet her as he was carrying his suit to the grotto, when it was pretty evident why he was at the market.

Not only that, Tobias had obviously filled her in on what he was doing and the reason he was doing it, and Daniel felt like a total failure. He might have his own business, but it wasn't a thriving one like Tobias's was. Seren must think he was a total loser, despite her saying she thought him playing the part of Santa Claus was wonderful. She probably hadn't meant it and was just being nice.

He also hadn't failed to notice how her face lit up when she'd said Tobias's name. It looked like his friend had made yet another conquest.

As he sawed through the surprisingly sturdy trunks of the vines, Daniel again thought how pretty she was. Cute, even. In his mind's eye he could see her long blonde hair, wide mouth, and blue almond-shaped eyes. Cornflower blue, that was the colour. Or maybe grape hyacinth? Or was bluebell closer? And she'd felt so light, as though she'd hardly weighed anything when he'd yanked her to her feet.

Stop it, he told himself. Thinking about her only served to make him crotchety and he was irritable enough already. For once, not even his beloved gardening was helping to lift the grumpy funk he'd been in since Saturday.

At least he had two days at the manor, doing what he loved, and he was mercifully free of Santa appearances until the following weekend, so that was something to be thankful for.

But no matter how hard he sawed, or how much he tried, he still couldn't shift Seren's face from his mind.

Chapter 12

'Pinch, punch first of the month,' Seren said, and added, 'White rabbits,' for good measure.

'I thought you were supposed to say white rabbits before you say anything else when you get up in the morning,' her dad pointed out. 'You've been singing since we set off.'

'Singing doesn't count.'

'Saying "good morning, only twenty-four days to Christmas" as soon as you got out of bed, does,' Patrick argued.

'I'd forgotten that.'

'And you're supposed to pinch and punch,' he added, putting his hand up to ward her off and shrinking back in the passenger seat in case Seren took his advice.

'Stop being so bah humbug,' Seren said. 'Oh, wow, look at that lofty pile.'

They'd just driven through a pair of impressive, if rusty, wrought iron gates to see Fernlea Manor sitting at the far end of a wide, unkempt drive.

'It's gorgeous, but I'm not sure I'd want to live there. Imagine the heating bills! And it looks like it could do with some TLC.' Trust her dad to think of the practicalities when Seren was bowled over by the romance of the place. 'It's falling down,' he added. 'Bet that's going to take a pretty penny to do up. I wonder if that's the reason they're holding a Christmas Fayre in the grounds?'

'I was listening to something on the radio about that,' Seren said, wondering where they were to park the van. 'Some lord was being interviewed and he said it costs an arm and a leg to keep these old estates going. Which is why so many owners either hand them over to the National Trust or open their doors to paying visitors. That's what the owner of this place might be doing. Maybe the profits for today will pay for a new gargoyle or something?'

A man stood halfway down the drive and as they approached, he put up a hand. 'Set up there,' he said, pointing to the circular area in front of the house. 'There are facilities around the back, where that van is going.'

Seren saw a large white truck inching around the corner and even from here she could see its suspension bouncing wildly on the rutted drive.

'Traders aren't allowed in the house under any circumstances,' the man added.

'What if we need the loo?' she asked, and as was always the way, as soon as she thought about it she needed to go.

'As I said, the facilities are around the back.' The man tutted and shook his head. Seren heard him mutter something under his breath as he walked off to see to the vehicle behind her, but she couldn't catch what it was.

Suitably chastised, she pointed Dippy to where she'd been told to park.

Several traders had already arrived, and as they drove slowly past the entrance to the marquee, Seren could see stalls being erected and people bustling to and fro with boxes and crates, trestle tables and signs. She was so glad her van needed the minimum of fuss to get it ready. Open the window, roll out the awning, then lift the assorted pretty baskets out from underneath, and Serendipity was ready to go. The only other thing to be done was to hang the garlands and wreaths (which were turning out to be best sellers and incredibly profitable, considering Seren made them herself) and grab a coffee before 'The Christmas Fayre at the Manor' opened to the public.

It sounded grand, and Seren hoped it would attract lots of customers. She couldn't wait to have a look around either, especially in the marquee where the food stalls were. Images of handmade chocolates, speciality cheeses, and artisan gins and liqueurs floated through her mind, whilst outside the space was starting to fill up with catering vans selling mouth-watering items such as hot chocolate with Baileys, pulled pork sandwiches, and roast chestnuts.

Her tummy clenched in excitement – God she *loved* Christmas!

Seren pulled Dippy into its allotted place and got to work, her dad helping. She was so grateful he was here because she didn't think she could manage by herself, although she was feeling considerably better about today now that she'd got one market under her belt. Fingers crossed, she hoped this one would be as profitable.

She'd find 'the facilities' (hoping they weren't as grim as they sounded) and then she'd treat them to a coffee. Or a hot chocolate, since it was Christmas. Leaving her dad alone for a few minutes, she headed off around the side of the manor house and into a large courtyard surrounded on one side by the house itself, a tall stone wall with bushes and trees poking over the top on another, and outbuildings on a third side.

It was busy here too, with people coming and going, and vehicles looking for parking spaces, and she stopped for a moment to get her bearings and try to work out where the loos were.

Ah, there they were, she saw, as she read a handwritten sign on a piece of cardboard. They were at the far end of the outbuildings, and she made her way towards them, hoping they would be clean.

Thankfully they were, although functional was the word that came to mind as she washed her hands in the tiny, chipped, enamel sink, and was forced to dry them on the hem of her scarf. If this was what visitors had to use, no wonder the manor house was so run down – it certainly didn't encourage repeat visits.

As she exited the facilities, she noticed a tall ladder propped against the rear wall of the house and a man balancing at the top of it. He was removing the ivy growing around one of the upstairs windows, and from the marks on the brickwork and the scattering of leaves, small branches, and twiglets on the ground beneath, Seren assumed he'd worked his way across the whole lot. She didn't envy him – she hated heights, and he must be freezing.

She had just begun to walk across the courtyard and back to her dad and Dippy, when a bang and a crunch made her jump. The noise was caused by a transit colliding with the side of a silver Twingo, and it looked as though both vehicles had aimed for the same parking slot.

Worried, her eyes shot to the man on the ladder, fully expecting him to have lost his balance and fallen, and she breathed a sigh of relief to see him still perched there. It was short-lived, though, when she noticed the man wobble precariously, and her heart was in her mouth until he steadied himself.

Seren sagged with relief, feeling a little shaky, and she wondered if anyone else had noticed a man in danger of plunging to his death, but everyone's attention was on the occupants of the pranged vehicles.

Seren glanced back at the man again to check he really was OK and that he wasn't about to fall off, and froze.

He had twisted around and was gazing down at the scene of the minor accident, but almost as though he could feel someone watching him, he looked her way and their eyes met.

It was Daniel. 'Of all the gin joints in all the towns in all the world…' she thought, her heart leaping at the sight of him. She'd been half-expecting to see him, but not up a ladder. She'd hoped he might be playing Santa, considering a grotto was advertised as part of the attraction, but the last place she would have thought to look for him was fifteen metres above the ground.

Hastily, she broke eye contact as she remembered the accident, and turned her attention to that instead. The driver of the transit had got out and was talking to the driver of the Twingo, who was still in his car. Neither bloke looked happy, and the elderly gentleman who was behind the wheel of the Twingo was grimacing and rubbing the back of his neck.

For a second she debated whether to offer to help, but there were enough people around already and she suspected she'd only get in the way. Besides, she didn't have first aid training and neither had she witnessed the accident, so she would be of little use.

Glancing back at Daniel she saw he was still staring at her, so she gave him a small wave of acknowledgement, then wished she hadn't as she imagined him letting go to wave back.

He gave her a single nod in return.

Seren smiled at him, then walked back to Dippy, but all the time she felt he might still be staring at her, so when she was about to turn the corner, she risked a quick look over her shoulder.

To her disappointment, he'd gone back to removing the ivy and was taking no notice of her whatsoever. It reinforced her view that he wasn't interested in her.

'What took you so long?' her dad asked, when Seren finally arrived back at the van with two mugs of hot chocolate.

'Sorry, there was a prang in the car park. An old guy in a Twingo and a transit van. Guess who I just saw?' She put them on the counter and straightened one of the woven baskets. This one contained angels in every colour imaginable.

'Who?' Her dad sipped his drink and licked his lips. 'Mmm, this is good.'

'Santa Claus.'

'Really.' Her dad gave her a 'so what' look.

'Not the *real* Father Christmas—' she began.

'I didn't think so, because he's still at the North Pole,' Patrick interrupted with a chuckle.

'—the guy who was Father Christmas at the market last weekend,' Seren finished.

'The fella who's got a relative in Aunt Nelly's care home? There's a Santa's grotto. I expect that's why he's here.'

'He was up a ladder, clearing ivy off the back of the house.'

'Interesting.'

'Ivy?'

'No, my little star... that you felt you needed to share that bit of information.' Her father's gaze sharpened and he focused on Seren.

Seren squirmed under his stare. 'What?' She wished he wouldn't call her his 'little star' – it made her feel as though she was a celebrity of some kind, when in reality Seren meant 'star' in Welsh. She blamed her parents' choice of name for her on a weekend in Llandudno shortly before she was born, although she supposed it was better than some of the names they might have come up with after their stay in the seaside resort.

Her father poked her in the ribs. 'You know what. Why such an interest? You must have mentioned him at least six times. More times than that Tobias guy you went out with.'

'I've hardly mentioned him at all.'

'Hmm.' He raised his eyebrows. 'You can't fool me – you like him.'

Seren almost dropped a delicate pair of glass skates and yelped as she caught them just in time. 'Don't you think you'd be better off concentrating on customers rather than on my love life?'

'You haven't got a love life. Anyway, there aren't any customers yet; the fayre isn't due to open until ten.' Abruptly Patrick stopped talking, and Seren turned to see what had caught her dad's attention.

An ambulance was rumbling slowly down the drive, and Seren watched as it made for the back of the house and disappeared out of sight.

Oh, no...

'Where are you going?' he cried as she shoved the glass skates she was still holding into her dad's hands and climbed out of the trailer. 'Rubbernecker!' he called after her when she failed to answer, but Seren took no notice.

She didn't want to rubberneck – she wanted to check that Daniel hadn't fallen off his ladder.

Dashing around the corner of the house, she came to a halt. The ambulance was alongside the Twingo and a paramedic was already speaking to the driver. Crumbs, Seren wouldn't have thought that a little bump like that would have resulted in the need for medical intervention.

'I hope he's OK,' she said to the person standing next to her.

The woman snorted. 'Wimp. He says he's got whiplash. I ask you!' The elderly woman pursed her lips and narrowed her eyes. 'This is not good for business.'

'I don't think the fayre is open to the public yet,' Seren said, trying to reassure her. Here was someone who could do with a dose of Christmas spirit. The woman looked sour enough to have been chewing lemons, and her voice was cut-glass sharp.

'I know it's definitely not open. I haven't given Mason the word yet,' the woman said.

Who was Mason and what word was this woman going to give him, Seren wondered as she scanned the crowd who'd gathered to see what was going on.

There was no sign of Daniel.

The woman tutted loudly. 'I wish they'd get a move on. There's nothing wrong with the chap. Anyone can see that. He's probably hoping for compensation. Well, he won't get any off me!'

Had the woman also been involved in the accident? Seren didn't think so, but then again, she hadn't been looking. She'd been too intent on checking that Daniel was OK.

'Oh, for goodness' sake!' the woman exclaimed when the paramedic who'd been treating the driver of the Twingo, helped the elderly gentleman out of the car and into the back of the ambulance. The van driver got into the Twingo, started it up and moved it out of the way, before handing the keys to the paramedic, who returned them to their rightful owner. Then the medic got in the back of the ambulance, closed the door and the ambulance slowly drove away.

'Is he coming back?' the woman standing next to her demanded, and Seren wasn't sure whether the question was aimed at her or not.

'Um, I don't know.'

'Marvellous. That man was my Father Christmas.' The woman tutted again, then clapped her hands and shouted. 'Is there anyone here who can play Father Christmas?' She glared at the onlookers, who were beginning to drift away. 'Anyone? There must be *someone*. The fayre has been advertised as having a Father Christmas,' she added as though that made any difference. 'Surely *one* of you can pretend to be a jolly fat man in a red suit?' She lowered her voice and said to Seren, 'Oh dear, he was supposed to bring his own suit, too. Now what am I going to do? Mason? Mason! Where is the dratted man when you need him? He was here a minute ago.' She scanned the parking area, her eyes narrowed, until her attention came to rest on the ladder which was now empty.

'And where is the damned gardener? He'd better not be shirking.'

'He was up that ladder the last time I saw him,' Seren said, helpfully.

'Where is he now?' the woman wanted to know, looking at her for the first time.

'I don't know,' Seren began, but the woman barged past her as she spotted someone.

'There you are, Mason. I've been looking for you. We have a problem – we have no Father Christmas. Do you happen to have a suit you can wear?' The woman smiled, and Seren shuddered. It was like watching a shark grin.

She felt rather sorry for Mason, the chap who had spoken to them when they'd first arrived – no wonder he'd been so irritable when he'd told her about 'the facilities'. She'd feel the same if she had to put up with a boss like this. Oh, hang on a minute, she did have a manager who was just as obnoxious.

Mason said, 'Nope. No suit, and I don't do Father Christmas. You'll have to find some other poor sod. I've got to open the gates.' He stomped off, leaving the woman glowering after him.

'I honestly don't know what I pay him for,' she said. 'Right. Plan B.'

'What's plan B?' Seren couldn't help asking.

'*I* will have to be Father Christmas.'

Seren spluttered. 'You?'

'Yes, me. There's nothing else for it.'

'I've, erm, got a Santa hat you could borrow, but as for the beard and the rest of it…' Seren trailed off, trying to suppress a giggle as she imagined this sour woman with her dad's Father Christmas hat jammed on her head. Then she froze, as a thought occurred to her. 'The man up the ladder, Daniel, he could play Santa,' she said slowly. 'He's done it before.'

'Why didn't you say so? Daniel? Daniel! Where are you, man?' the woman turned to Seren. 'I'm Miss Carruthers and I own this place. If you see Daniel please send him to me. I'll be in the house making a pot of tea.'

'Not for me, thanks, I've got to get back. My dad will be wondering where I am.'

'The tea isn't for you, silly girl, it's for *me*. I need a cup of Earl Grey to steady my nerves. Please find Daniel for me, and when you do, tell him I wish to speak with him.'

'Yes, ma'am.' Seren almost curtsied.

'Don't be flippant. This is serious.' With that, Miss Carruthers stalked off, leaving Seren staring incredulously after her.

Chapter 13

Daniel headed towards one of the catering vans, anticipating a hot coffee and a cookie, thinking it might be a good idea to make himself scarce until the drama at the rear of the house died down. He didn't want to risk being up a ladder with so many people milling about, and it wouldn't do to drop foliage on their heads, either. He'd finish the job off when all the fuss had died down.

He had hoped to have completed it by now, but the ivy had proved to be incredibly stubborn and he'd been forced to wrestle every single strand from the wall. It was certainly putting up a fight and he had to admire it for that, even as he cursed and cussed, and nearly fell off.

Two days had morphed into three, but there was only a small amount left to do, so he was hoping to finish by midday.

'Daniel?'

He'd know Seren's voice anywhere and he looked to see where it was coming from.

'Hi,' he said, trying to ignore the sudden leap of his pulse. At least she'd seen him when he'd been up a ladder and doing some vaguely gardening-related stuff this time, instead of wearing a silly red suit. 'Are you here for the fayre?' He was gratified to discover that he sounded calm and cool, especially since it had been a shock to see her staring up at him like that.

After the accident between the transit and the Twingo, he'd spotted her van as soon as he'd walked around the front of the manor house, and he wondered if his decision to take a break hadn't had more to do with seeing her. If he was honest, he'd gone looking for her, despite his best intentions.

'I was hoping to find you,' she said, and his pulse leapt again. 'Miss Carruthers wants to speak to you.'

Oh, that was why Seren was looking for him. Because Miss Carruthers wanted him. He might have guessed, he thought, wondering why the elderly lady had sent Seren to find him. Did they know each other? Was Seren some kind of relation?

'What does she want?' he asked.

'She needs a Santa Claus and she thought you might be able to help.'

'Come again?'

Seren smiled and his heart skipped a beat. 'She wants you to dress up as Father Christmas,' she explained.

Daniel was taken aback. That was the last thing he'd expected – clear the guttering whilst he was on the ladder, maybe repair the downpipe which he'd noticed was leaking… but not that.

'Uh, uh.' He shook his head. 'No way.'

Back in the early autumn when he'd been applying for Santa jobs, he'd been disappointed not to have had anything lined up for this weekend. But after the first couple of Santa sessions, he'd been relieved, despite the lack of income. Then this ivy-clearing job had come along, and it didn't matter that he wasn't Santa until next Saturday because he was doing what he loved and was getting paid to do it.

Yet, now here he was, being asked to do the very thing he didn't want to do.

'No. Categorically not,' he said, in case she hadn't understood.

'She's desperate,' Seren said.

So was he – desperate not to do it. Besides, he had a job to finish.

'At least go and talk to her.' Seren smiled winningly up at him, and his heart faltered again.

Crossly he shook his head once more. 'There's no point in speaking to her if I'm not going to do it.'

But even as he refused, he knew he *would* speak to her; he owed the elderly lady the courtesy of hearing her out. He couldn't simply ignore her. He'd have to see her tomorrow anyway when he came back for his wages.

He didn't like being rude, and neither did he wish to upset a client, especially one he was hoping might put more work his way; the garden was in desperate need of some attention and he was itching to get his hands on it.

'OK, I'll speak to her. But I'm still not going to play Santa,' he insisted.

'That's up to you, but one of the people involved in the accident earlier was supposed to be Father Christmas and he's been taken to hospital.'

Daniel frowned. 'I didn't think it was that bad. It was only a fender-bender, wasn't it?'

'I thought so too, but apparently one of the drivers has got whiplash. He was rather elderly, so they've taken him to hospital and no one knows when he'll be back. Certainly not in time to dandle hordes of excited children on his knee.'

Daniel shook his head. 'I don't dandle. No sitting on Santa's lap.'

'That's a shame. I used to love doing that when I was little. It was my favourite part about seeing Santa.'

'Not the present?'

'Funnily enough, no; although I was always pleased to be given one. It was the joy of seeing Santa that was more important to me, telling him what I wanted and thinking of him being back at the North Pole instructing his elves. Then I'd imagine him loading sacks of presents on his sleigh, one or two of them mine, and flying all over the world on one magical night to deliver them. It's up to you, of course,' she added, beginning to move away. 'But just consider all those children who think they'll be seeing Santa today, and who'll be incredibly disappointed.'

Seren's expression was one of disappointment, too.

God, he so didn't want to do this, but she was making him feel guilty, making him feel it was his fault if children were upset. 'I'm not really Santa. My real job is a gardener.'

'I know, but it's not as though you haven't played Father Christmas before. Would it hurt you to be Santa today? Think of the children. Do it for their sakes.'

Daniel gave her a pained look. That was below the belt.

As though sensing he was wavering, she added, 'They deserve to think of Christmas as a magical time – don't let them down.'

He wanted to be annoyed with her, but the pleading, hopeful expression on her face undid him. 'OK, I'll do it. On one condition.'

'What is it?'

'Don't tell Tobias. I know I'm asking a lot, but I can't take the teasing.'

'You're not asking a lot at all. I'm hoping I'll not see him again any time soon – because if I do, it means something has gone wrong with the van. Actually, you'll probably see him before me, so if you do, could you remind him that he still hasn't sent me the bill for the conversion. I've left a couple of messages, but he hasn't got back to me.'

Daniel felt for her. Damned Tobias and his philandering ways. Seren was too nice to be messed about. 'I'm sorry,' he said. 'I hope you're not too upset.'

'Why should I be upset?'

'Because of the way he's treating you. I can tell you like him.'

Seren's eyes widened. 'You mean...? *Ha!* Yes, I like him, but not like *that*.'

'You went on a date with him.'

'So I did, but it was just the one. I haven't been out with him since, and I don't want to go out with him again. He's not my type.'

Daniel swallowed, his heart in his mouth. 'But I thought...' He took a deep breath. It was now or never, and he wasn't averse to throwing in a spot of blackmail if it meant she'd say yes.

'In that case, I change my terms. I'll play Santa today if you'll have dinner with me.' There, the ball was in her court. If she refused, she'd be the one responsible for making hordes of kids cry.

But when her face lit up and she said, 'I'd be delighted to,' he felt a grin spread across his own lips. Maybe playing Santa wouldn't be so bad after all...

–

Daniel was in a quandary and had been for most of the day. The source of his dilemma was Seren. Had asking her to dinner been a good idea, considering he'd almost blackmailed her into it? She'd agreed readily enough, but that was probably because she didn't want to upset small children. Unlike him, who'd have been quite happy to have ignored their distress and carry on with the job he was there to do – which was clearing ivy from the wall.

That wasn't strictly true. He would have *wanted* to carry on with it, but his conscience had already started to prick at him and he would have agreed to play Santa without Seren feeling obliged to have dinner with him. But when she'd told him she wasn't dating Tobias, his heart had begun to sing and he hadn't been able to resist asking her out.

But why, oh why, hadn't he asked her straight and not made it a condition of him playing Santa? What a wally.

He wouldn't blame her if she changed her mind or was having second thoughts. She probably thought he was some kind of weirdo and was even now plotting how to get out of the deal.

Should he go and find her when the fayre was over and ask her properly? Or should he let her off the hook and tell her he wasn't going to insist on dinner?

Embarrassment coursed through him as he guessed what she must think of him, and he'd felt this way ever since he'd gone to find Miss Carruthers to tell her he'd be Santa and realised how he must have come across to Seren.

Thankfully, there were only two more children to see before the fayre ended, although he was still no nearer to making a decision about what he should do.

He was currently sitting in a rather grand chair in the corner of a very grand sitting room, waiting for the next child to be shown in, and mulling things over yet again. Although it wasn't a particularly large room (Miss

Carruthers had called it the snug), it had high ceilings, a polished wooden floor with an ornate rug covering most of it, a grand fireplace with flames crackling and roaring, and a stocking hanging from the mantelpiece. On the other side of the chimney breast was an impressive tree wrapped in tinsel and decorated with what appeared to be antique baubles. Daniel hoped to goodness that none of them got broken.

Miss Carruthers stood at the door, taking 'donations' as she called them, but what it actually amounted to was a five pound entry fee for children to tell Santa what they wanted.

To Daniel, the scene could have been one from a Christmas card. It was certainly evocative of a Victorian Christmas, complete with a side table holding a glass of sherry (which he was more and more tempted to drink as the day wore on), and a couple of ginger thins. She'd even gone to the trouble of placing a fountain pen and a scroll of yellowed paper, half-unfurled, next to it. His very own naughty or nice list.

Helpfully, in the absence of an elf, Miss Carruthers was writing each child's name on a label and plastering it onto their chests as they came through the door, so he could at least pretend he knew who the kids were. It had been his suggestion when he was hastily donning the Santa suit that he'd thankfully left in a bag on the passenger seat of his truck. If he was going to do this Father Christmas thing, he at least wanted to do it properly, and he realised that knowing the children's names added to the magic of the experience for them.

Finally there was only one child waiting to see him and he smiled when the small girl broke free of her mum's hand and came charging towards him. She nearly tripped over the edge of the rug, windmilled her arms, then continued with her headlong rush.

Daniel braced himself for impact, but she came to a jerky halt a hair's breadth away from his knees and stood there, her eyes wide and a solemn expression on her heart-shaped face.

She clasped her hands together and looked at him warily.

'Ah, yes, Charlotte,' he boomed, surreptitiously reading her label. 'Have you been a good girl? Or a naughty girl?'

'Good girl,' she whispered, blinking owlishly.

'No coal for you, then,' he chuckled. 'What would you like for Christmas?'

'A kitten.'

Daniel pulled a sad face and said, 'Kittens don't like it at the North Pole.' He risked a glance at the mum's face. She was shaking her head and biting her lip, so he carried on, 'It's far too cold for them, even in a room with a nice warm fire. And imagine how cold they'd get on my sleigh?'

'You could wrap them up warm,' the little girl said.

'That's a good idea, but there's no seat for them on the sleigh. They'd have to go in the back with the presents, and they might get squashed or fall out, and then they'd be lost and frightened.'

He shot another glance at the child's mother and winked at her when he saw the relieved expression on her face. She smiled at him gratefully, as did the girl's father. He was carrying a tiny baby in a sling across his chest and Daniel guessed that the parents had their hands full with this new arrival without any more additions to the family in the form of a feline, however cute.

'Is there anything else you'd like Santa to bring you?' Daniel asked.

'Yeth, pleathe,' she lisped. 'A tractor.'

The little girl's mother nodded furtively.

'I think I can manage that.' Daniel picked up the scroll, unfurled it a little, then reached for the pen and pretended to write. 'Charlotte,' he said slowly, moving the pen across the page a millimetre above the paper's surface, angling it so the child couldn't see that he wasn't actually writing anything. 'Tractor.' He looked up at Charlotte. 'Any particular colour?'

'Red,' she said, without hesitation.

'I'll have to see what colour paint the elves have got in the cupboard,' he told her, not wanting to make promises her mother might not be able to keep. 'There, I've written it down. Now, remember, you've still got to be good between now and Christmas morning, because I'll be watching. Do you promise?'

Charlotte nodded.

Daniel reached into a sack behind his chair and pulled out a gift-wrapped present. He had no idea what was in it because Miss Carruthers said she'd taken care of the present buying and wrapping; he just hoped it was age-appropriate. On the other two occasions that he'd dressed up as Santa, an elf had handed him a present out of one of the sacks. There had been several and their contents had been based on age and gender.

He sat back in his chair and breathed deeply, letting the tension flow from his shoulders. It was hard work being so jolly all the time, but he did, however, feel a sense of achievement. It wasn't comparable to that which he felt when he'd cleared an overgrown flower bed of weeds or when he'd pruned an unsightly, straggly shrub into a more compact shape, but it was there nevertheless.

Miss Carruthers stepped into the room and closed the door behind her. Daniel couldn't be certain, but he thought she was smiling. It was difficult to tell because although her mouth was curling up ever so slightly at the corners, she still had a flinty look in her eye.

'All done,' she announced, briskly. 'Thank you for stepping up to the mark.'

'You're welcome.' The experience hadn't been as bad as he'd anticipated, and he decided he must be getting used to it.

'I expect you to return tomorrow to finish removing the ivy,' she said. 'You can't leave a job half done.'

'I didn't intend to.' Daniel blinked; it hadn't been his idea to down tools. It had been hers, and he'd been doing her a favour by playing Santa. Anyone would think he'd been skiving off.

'Good, because you won't receive a penny from me until it's completed to my satisfaction. I'll also pay you for today in the morning. Cash.'

She'd mentioned being paid in cash previously and it suddenly occurred to him that she might have been relying on the profit from the Christmas Fayre to pay him. And possibly to go some way towards the other renovations she'd mentioned.

'I'll be back first thing in the morning,' he assured her, taking off the Santa jacket and peeling off the fake facial hair.

'Make sure you are,' was her parting shot as she left him to get changed.

Suitably attired in his own clothes once more, he gathered his courage and went to find Seren.

She was handing the last of the wreaths to a man standing inside the former ice cream van, but when she saw him, she said, 'Can you finish up, Dad? I just want to have a quick word with Daniel.'

'So that's Daniel, is it?' The man peered down at him, and Daniel squirmed, wondering what Seren might have said about him and hoping it wasn't too bad.

'Look, I'm sorry if you felt obliged to go out with me just so I'd play Santa today,' he began, moving away from the van so her dad couldn't hear.

'I don't feel obliged,' she retorted. 'I'd have gone to dinner with you regardless, if you'd asked.'

'You would?'

She beamed at him. 'I would.'

'You don't feel browbeaten into it?' He had to make sure.

'Absolutely not.'

'Phew!' He pretended to mop his brow. 'That's a relief. So, Friday…?'

'Friday it is. We'd better swap phone numbers, just in case.'

'Good idea.' He told her his mobile number and watched her key it into her phone. A second later his phone rang and he saved her number. 'I'll give you a call when I've booked somewhere,' he said. 'Any preference? Or are there any foods you don't eat, such as meat?'

'I'll eat most things,' she said. 'Although, I don't like sprouts.'

'I'll try not to book us a table in a sprout restaurant,' he joked, then said, 'I'll let you get off home. See you Friday, but I'll be in touch before then.'

'Great. See you— Oh, before you go, have you got any idea what'll happen to all that ivy?'

'Um, I expect it will either be composted or burnt.'

'Do you think they can spare any? I could do with some to make more garlands and wreaths.'

'I'm coming back tomorrow to finish up, so I'll ask if you can have some if you like?'

'Would you? That would be fantastic.' And with that, she stood on tiptoe and gave him a quick peck on the cheek, then hurried back to her van, but not before she threw a smile over her shoulder at him.

Daniel, his pulse pounding, put his fingers to the spot where her lips had connected with his skin and felt like cheering. The thought of going on a proper date with her was sending his heart rate into overdrive, and he had the most wonderful feeling that she might like him.

He hoped so, because he liked her more than he'd liked any woman for a very long time – and that included Gina!

Chapter 14

Seren awoke on Sunday on cloud nine. Yesterday had been brilliant, both in terms of the Christmas fayre and being asked out on a date by a fit, hunky fella, and she was still fizzing with excitement, a warm glow enveloping her. She felt she was on the cusp of a whole new life.

Even being told to check the sell-by dates on the chilled meals section didn't dampen her spirits, and neither did she let Pamela's whingeing about how she should have been in yesterday and not swapped her shift, get to her. Staff swapped shifts all the time, but for some reason the store manager had got a bee in her bonnet about it.

Bah humbug, Seren thought. Some people were just born miserable and some people worked hard at it – she wasn't sure which category Pamela fitted into, but she sure as hell wasn't going to let the woman's sour mood bring her down.

Not having another Saturday off between now and Christmas was going to be a problem though, because most of the Christmas markets and fayres Seren fancied attending were on weekends, but she fully intended to make use of her day off on Thursday. She wasn't expecting miracles, but she had been in touch with her aunt's care home to ask if she could visit, and another old people's residential complex on the other side of town had been happy for her to take her van along. It was a start, if nothing else.

She also planned on taking Dippy out for a drive to see if she could drum up any trade. The thought of trawling the streets with assorted Christmas tunes blaring out like a festive version of Mr Whippy (with handmade luxury chocolates instead of a 99) was daunting, but after all, that was what she and Aunt Nelly had envisioned when they'd got the idea of a travelling gift shop. To be truly mobile she had to go to the customers and not expect them to come to her. If she only concentrated all her efforts on events such as markets, she would be no different to those outlets on the high street.

With happiness flooding through her, Seren got on with what she was paid to do and tried not to think about her burgeoning business, or her date with Daniel on Friday. Because she'd found that if she wasn't thinking about one of them, then she was thinking about the other, with Daniel occupying the lion's share.

It was while she was daydreaming about his hazel eyes and strong-looking hands that her phone vibrated in her pocket, making her jump. Furtively, she hurried to the back of the shop and through a door marked 'Private'. Only then did she take her mobile out to check to see who the caller was.

Her heart did a flippy-flip when she saw it was Daniel.

'Just a sec,' she hissed into it, and darted out to the loading bay. At this time of day it was usually empty and the store had had a delivery earlier, so she wasn't surprised to see she had the area all to herself.

After wedging the door open with a piece of wood for that express purpose, and making sure she was standing just outside the reach of the CCTV camera which was trained on the loading bay, she turned her attention to her phone and the man on the other end of it – the man who made her have butterflies in her tummy whenever she thought of him, the man whose face she couldn't get out of her mind.

'Hi,' she whispered. 'Sorry about that. I'm at work, so I've got to be quick.' She glanced through the crack in the open door but didn't see anyone.

'I've spoken to Miss Carruthers and she says you can have all the ivy you want, but you've got to take it away asap, otherwise it will be burnt.'

'I see. Um…' Seren dithered, wondering how much greenery she could feasibly get in the van now that it was full of stock. She could always borrow her dad's car, but it was only a small hatchback and he was ever so fussy about it. All the leaves, twigs and other assorted flora which would inevitably need cleaning up would drive him to distraction; no matter how thoroughly she vacuumed up the mess, he would spot a bit she missed.

Daniel solved the problem for her. 'I'm here now with my truck,' he said, 'so how about I load some on and drop it round to yours this evening? You can pick out the best bits and I'll get rid of anything you don't want.'

'That's kind of you. I'll be home by five, so any time after that.' She gave him her address and was about to say she was looking forward to seeing him, when she heard a noise beyond the door. 'I've got to go,' she whispered, and swiftly ended the call and slipped the phone back into her pocket.

'There you are! I've been looking everywhere for you. What are you doing out here?' Pamela glared suspiciously at her.

'I... erm... just needed some fresh air,' Seren said, hoping her face didn't show her guilt at telling a porky.

'Have you had enough?' her manager asked, sarcastically. 'Or would you like some more?'

'I'll come back in now,' she said, feeling rather cross. Perhaps she shouldn't be out here when officially she should be on the shop floor, but there was no need for Pamela to be so shitty about it. The woman was quick enough to reprimand her for the smallest infringement, but there was never any mention of the times Seren had gone above and beyond, staying after her shift ended to sort out a problem or skipping her break because they were short-staffed. It wasn't as though Seren made a habit of popping outside for a cigarette, unlike others she could mention (she didn't smoke), and she rarely took phone calls at work. But she'd been praying Daniel would keep his word and give her a ring.

She was so pleased she'd taken the call – even if it had landed her in hot water with Pamela – because with Daniel dropping off some ivy for her, she'd get to see him again a whole lot sooner than Friday. Yay!

–

'I think your fella is here,' Patrick said, sticking his head around the shed door and letting all the warmth out. 'A van has pulled up outside. Do you want me to show him in?'

And risk her dad saying something Seren wished he hadn't? No thank you! 'It's OK, I'll do it. I'll ask him to bring the van around the back, rather than traipse half of Sherwood Forest through the house.'

Seren had been trying to keep herself occupied by sorting out her garland and wreath-making materials in the shed (the only place her dad would allow her to make them), and her tummy turned over as she hurried through the house to the front.

Daniel was just getting out of his truck when Seren shot outside, shutting the door firmly behind her and dashing onto the pavement.

'Hi,' she said, suddenly coming over all shy. She peeped into the open bed of the truck and saw a mass of green foliage. 'Is that for me? Gosh, it's a lot.'

'I knew I had the right address when I saw your van,' he said, then he made a face. 'Did I go overboard?'

Just a bit, she thought. She'd never use all that. 'A little, but at least that means I get to pick out the best bits. I need to find somewhere else to park the van,' she added. 'It's a bit big to leave outside the house on the road. The neighbours will start to complain. But I don't want to park it too far away because I want to be able to keep an eye on it.'

Daniel looked towards the house and Seren followed the direction of his gaze. One of the drawn curtains twitched and she knew her dad was watching.

Quickly she said, 'Can you drive your truck around the back, then I can put the ivy straight in the shed. It'll save tracking it through the house.'

'Good idea. It'll make one hell of a mess otherwise. Get in and you can direct me.'

Her house was in the middle of a terraced street, with generous gardens to the back and a lane beyond that. The lane was only narrow, but the refuse lorry was able to get down there, so hopefully Daniel's truck would be able to do the same.

Seren clambered into the cab and clicked the seatbelt in, conscious of how near she was to him, and how his fresh outdoorsy scent filled her nose making her feel light-headed.

He drove slowly and carefully, but her fears regarding the width of the lane were unfounded and she breathed a sigh of relief when he brought the vehicle to a halt where she indicated. Jumping to the ground, she hurried to open the gate.

Daniel dropped the tailgate on the truck and followed her into the garden, where he stopped and blinked. 'This is a nice size,' he said.

'It's a pain to mow,' she said over her shoulder, as she scuttled up the path towards the brick shed next to the house.

'You could put a hard standing or even a garage here, if you wanted,' he said, following at a slower pace and looking around, although she wasn't sure how much he could see of it in the dark. 'For your travelling shop, I mean.'

Seren opened the shed door and ushered him inside, shying away as he stepped through the door in case she made a fool of herself; she felt an urge to kiss him, and she stamped down on it ruthlessly. Now was not the best time to jump him – it was dark and cold, they had a tonne of greenery to unload, and no doubt he wanted to get off home.

'Wow!' he cried halting just inside the doorway. 'You certainly like Christmas, don't you?'

'I do,' she replied. 'But a lot of this isn't mine. It's the stuff I'm selling on a sale or return basis. The wreaths, garlands and centrepieces are mine, though.' And that was because they were incredibly cheap to make. If she had to buy all the things she'd been provided with by her suppliers, she would either be in debt or Dippy would look terribly sparse.

'They're lovely,' Daniel said. 'I didn't get a chance to have a good look at them yesterday. I'll bring the greenery in, and you can sort through it. Whatever you don't want, I can put back on the truck.'

By the time she'd selected the strands of ivy she wanted to keep, Seren was frozen to the bone. She'd switched the paraffin heater off earlier because the door was constantly being opened and closed and it seemed wasteful to keep it on, but as soon as the last length of foliage was neatly hung on a hook originally meant for a garden fork, and all the discarded and excess bits had been put back on the truck, she closed the door and turned the heater up to full.

'Would you like a coffee to warm up?' Seren asked, gesturing to a battered table with a small coffee machine and two mugs sitting on it.

'Great idea. I'll make it, you warm yourself. You look like you're freezing.'

'I am.' She smiled at him gratefully, holding her hands out and groaning as welcome warmth seeped into them. 'Aren't you cold?'

'I'm kind of used to it,' he said, putting a pod into the machine. 'I spend most of my time outdoors, although I'd be lying if I said I liked the winter. I tolerate it.'

'Tobias said you don't get much gardening work at this time of year.'

'I don't. Which is why I'm doing the Santa thing.'

'You don't seem to like it much.'

'It's OK, I suppose. Each time I do it, it gets easier. It's not talking to the kids that bothers me, it's the commercialism.'

Seren was pleased that his reluctance had nothing to do with children, and she could sort of empathise with the commercialism thing – which was ironic considering what she was doing. But somehow it felt totally different to the items the supermarket sold. There it was all about bulk sales and moving so many units of stock, and with no opportunity to chat to customers or to take the time to find out what they were looking for. Besides, any seasonal stuff was merely an add-on for the shop, bought in at the lowest price they could pay, and sold for the highest price possible. It all seemed so impersonal and money-grabbing.

Seren hoped that she and her little travelling Christmas shop weren't viewed the same way.

Daniel held out a mug of steaming coffee and Seren wrapped her hands around it gratefully.

'I think part of it is that the meaning of Christmas has been taken and twisted,' he said, 'and that's one of the reasons I'm not that keen. Listening to all those little ones asking for expensive toys and games, and wondering if their poor parents can afford it...' He sighed, then blew on his coffee and took a sip.

'I see where you're coming from,' she said, 'and I agree with you to a certain extent, but a mid-winter festival of some kind or another has been around for millennia. I was reading somewhere that it was a way to ensure the sun returned and that the longest night was over. Bringing greenery inside to decorate our homes is part of that ancient tradition. Holly, ivy, mistletoe, branches of fir trees, and even the yule log all played a part,' she said.

'Is that why you make wreaths and garlands and so on?'

Seren was thrilled he was taking such an interest, unlike Tobias. But then, leaves and stuff were part and parcel of

Daniel's job. Maybe if she'd rabbited on about spark plugs or gear cogs, Tobias would have been more interested.

'I suppose,' she said. 'But I also like making them, and most of the stuff is free.'

'There is that,' he agreed, wandering over to the last wreath she'd made and bending to examine it. 'You use willow to make the frame?'

'I do. It's sustainable and easy to get hold of, and it can be composted afterwards.'

Daniel turned to face her, and she held her breath when she saw the intensity in his eyes. 'A woman after my own heart.'

Oh, my... He looked like he wanted to gobble her all up.

'How do you make them? Do you just twist them together?' He picked the wreath up, but his attention remained on her and she felt her face grow warm.

'Um, yeah, I can show you if you like?'

'I'd like.'

He was still staring at her intently and the heat in her face travelled down her neck, past her chest and lodged deeper south.

Seren cleared her throat, put her mug down and sat on a stool in front of the bench, then she patted the one next to it. It had a cushion on to raise it up, because the last time she'd babysat Freya she'd kept the little girl occupied by teaching her how to make angels out of cardboard, glitter and glue. Freya had forgotten to take one of them home with her, and Seren moved it out of the way. That child certainly loved pink, she thought, as a shower of pink glitter cascaded over the workbench.

Daniel removed the cushion and perched on the stool, and Seren gave him some thick willow stems, all cut to the same length. They were roughly the same diameter, too, which made for a more even wreath, in her opinion.

'Take three stems,' she instructed, doing the same thing herself so he could follow along. 'Make sure the ends aren't all in the same place otherwise there'll be a weakness there, then twist them together loosely, bending them into a circle as you go.' She leant across to make sure he was doing it right and caught a whiff of his masculine scent. It made her feel rather giddy, and she coughed to cover her reaction.

'Go slow, else you might get a kink in it,' she advised. 'If you use your knee to bend them around, that'll help.' She showed him what she meant and watched as he twisted the stems, making little corrections for him if she could see he was about to go wrong.

At one point their hands touched, and heat surged through her before she quickly snatched her fingers away.

Goodness, if she was like this now, when they were doing the most unsexy thing imaginable, what would she be like when she was relaxed with a couple of glasses of wine inside her? It didn't bear thinking about.

'That's good,' she told him as he held the willow circle up for her to have a look at. 'Use some string to tie the loose ends in, then take another piece of willow and wind that in. If you can, start and finish at a different point to the others, and you can also weave it in the opposite direction. Like this, see?'

She showed him the one she was working on, and he nodded to indicate he understood, then she simply let him get on with it.

By the time she was satisfied with his willow frame, she'd completed two full wreaths and was starting on her third.

'You're so quick,' he said, and she heard the admiration in his voice and she glowed at the compliment.

'I've had lots of practice,' she said, 'more this year than any other. Drat.'

'What is it?'

'I'm going to have to get some more fir branches, as well as holly and mistletoe. I'm just about out.' She could do with some acorns, too.

'Where do you source them from?' Daniel asked, his head bent to his task.

'Anywhere and everywhere. I usually get what I need from the trees in the park, but I'm wary of taking too much from any one place.'

'I can show you where you can get all of those things, if you like.'

'Oh? Where?'

'Neston Wood isn't far from my mum's house.'

'I know it! I haven't been there in ages.'

'I can go there in the morning and see what I can find,' he offered. 'Unless…? Would you like to come with me? It doesn't have to be tomorrow – we can go whenever you're free.'

Seren nearly said that she was free anytime for him, but she thought it might be a bit forward, so instead she said, 'I can do tomorrow morning. I'm at work from two in the afternoon, and most of the day on Wednesday. I have Thursday off, but I've made arrangements to take Dippy to a couple of care homes, to test the water.'

'Dippy?'

Seren giggled. 'The van; that's what I've called it.'

He frowned, then his brow cleared as the penny dropped. 'Nice one. Tomorrow it is, then. Shall I pick you up?'

After a momentary hesitation Seren said, 'OK, but I don't want to put you out.'

His smile when he replied, 'You aren't,' melted her heart and carried her through the hours after he'd left when she was faced with her father's inquisitive looks and his blatant hints as to how her love life was progressing. One thing was sure, she wouldn't be letting either her father or her aunt anywhere near Daniel any time soon, in case they scared him off!

Chapter 15

Seren was waiting outside her house when Daniel arrived to pick her up. To his relief it was a crisp, bright day with not a cloud in the sky, although that did mean it was decidedly chilly. But it also meant it was a fantastic day to go for a winter walk in the woods.

He was glad to see she was wrapped up warm and had a pair of Wellington boots on her feet. Neston Wood was popular with ramblers and dog walkers alike and the paths – such as they were – would be muddy and slippery underfoot.

She gave him a bright smile as she got in the cab, and he was struck anew by how pretty she was. Her cheeks were already rosy from the cold and her eyes sparkled. And she had the most wonderfully long lashes framing those bluebell eyes. He'd love to bring her to the woods in May when those flowers were in full bloom, to see if he was right about their colour.

'All set?' he asked, as she stowed several large bags in the footwell.

'I thought we could put anything we find in these,' she said. 'One bag for holly, one for fir branches, and so on. It'll save me sorting them out later.'

Daniel would happily have helped, but he was also aware she was due at work later, and he guessed it must be hard for her to juggle a full-time job plus trying to get a new business venture off the ground. But doing the two alongside each other was probably the right and sensible thing to do financially.

Neston Wood was only a twenty-minute drive away, and before he knew it he was pulling into the car park at the edge of the trees and wishing the journey had taken longer. He enjoyed chatting about this and that in the warmth of the cabin, her perfume filling the air, and the sound of her ready laughter as he told her a couple of stories about the gardens he'd been to and their owner's odd requests, and in turn she shared stories about some of the odder customers she'd served.

'Ass's milk, I ask you!' she declared, as she finished telling him about a customer who'd read that Cleopatra had bathed in the stuff to keep her looking youthful, and the lady was convinced it would work for her if only she could get her hands on some. 'She had to have been seventy if she was a day,' Seren giggled. 'When I told her we didn't stock any she became quite annoyed.'

'Will you miss it?' he asked, as they got out and he locked the truck.

'Miss what?'

'Working in the supermarket. I'm assuming you'll jack it in if Dippy takes off?'

She fell into step beside him as they walked down the wide trail, dry leaves crunching underfoot and a gentle breeze whispering through the bare branches overhead.

'I honestly don't know what I'm going to do,' she said. 'It started with trying to find a mobile gift shop online that would be willing to pay a visit to the care home, and has ended up with me using all my savings to convert and run one myself. This wasn't what I had in mind when I saw that mobile library.' She bit her lip. 'To be honest, it's got away from me a bit. I should have insisted my dad sold it before I was talked into having all that work done.'

'I'm glad you didn't, because if he had sold it we never would have met,' he told her earnestly and was rewarded by a smile.

She had the loveliest smile, he thought. It lit up her whole face, and he basked in it, feeling warmth spread through his chest and curl around his heart.

'I'm going to get Christmas out of the way and then take stock. Literally,' she giggled. 'It's a full-time job in itself, trying to keep track of what's been sold, who I owe what to, whether they can make me any more and when can I fetch it...'

'Bet it's satisfying, though,' he said. 'You've taken a tired old ice cream van and turned it into a quirky travelling gift shop. Aside from making a profit – which you'll have to do – are you enjoying it?'

'I am. I didn't think I would, but I love being able to tell customers who made the snow globe they're thinking of buying, and how the lady who makes such fab chocolates came up with the flavours. It's so much more satisfying than sitting on a checkout scanning items in.'

'And you seem to enjoy making wreaths and so on. Speaking of which, how does this tree grab you?' Daniel had spied a small juniper which was sporting some marvellous blue berries. 'Or what about this Norway spruce?'

Seren's eyes lit up and she fished a pair of secateurs out of her pocket. 'Other girls carry a lipstick or a purse in their pocket – I've got a lethal weapon. For the poor tree, that is. I do feel rather guilty hacking away at it.'

'You're not most girls,' he told her. 'And I love a decent pair of secateurs. Snap!' Laughing, he brought forth his own pair. 'As long as you don't take too many branches off one tree, the plant will recover. Look at it as pruning,' he suggested. 'Does that make you feel better?'

'Funnily enough, it does. I bet you have to prune all the time.'

'It's part and parcel of gardening, and sometimes it's to make the plant look more pleasing to the eye, and other times it's necessary for the health of the plant. Show me which bits you want, and I'll snip them off for you.'

By the time Seren's bags were full the morning had marched on, and when Daniel's stomach gurgled, she said, 'I think I've got enough. This should last me a couple of weeks, although it will depend on sales.'

Daniel had helped her gather some holly (he'd brought a pair of heavy-duty gloves along for the purpose) and had scaled a tree to pick mistletoe for her.

He'd briefly considered holding it over her head, but thought it might be too soon, even for a jokey Christmas kiss. After all, they hadn't had a single date yet, and scavenging for prickly holly and pointy pine needled branches wasn't up there in the romantic gestures department.

Seren had been pleased with the acorns they'd gathered too, and if she'd thanked him once for bringing her here, she'd thanked him a hundred times.

'Before I take you home, have you got time for a quick bite to eat?' he suggested. 'There's a coffee shop not far from here that does the best paninis ever.'

'Um…' Seren checked the time. 'I'm due at work in two hours.'

'You've got to eat,' he said. 'Going to work on an empty tummy is no good for you.'

'Go on, then,' she said. 'But we'll have to be quick.'

'We will be,' he assured her, crossing his fingers. He'd have a little word with the waitress and let her know they were in a hurry.

Luckily the cafe wasn't busy, and after they'd ordered they easily found a free table. Seren took her coat off and draped it over the back of her chair, then slid into a seat opposite Daniel. 'When is your next Santa outing?' she asked him.

Daniel checked to make sure no one had heard. 'Shh,' he hissed theatrically. 'I don't want any little ones to get the wrong idea.'

'You are so silly,' she giggled, and he felt a surge of pleasure at being able to make her laugh. She had an infectious laugh, and he'd be happy to listen to it all day. In fact, he'd be happy to sit and talk to her all day. It was a pity she had to go to work.

He was jerked out of his thoughts when he felt a nudge on the arm, and he looked around to find his mother and Mrs Williams standing behind him. Both of them had their eyes trained on Seren.

'Fancy seeing you in here,' his mother said. 'Who is this?'

'Hi, Mum; hello Mrs Williams,' he sighed, feeling deflated. He could have done without his mother being here. 'This is Seren. Seren, meet my mum and her next-door neighbour.'

'Pleased to meet you,' Seren said politely, and he wondered what she was thinking.

'I'm Linda,' his mother began, but before she got any further Mrs Williams said, 'Are you Daniel's new girl-friend?'

Seren looked startled, as well she might, Daniel thought.

'It's… um… early days yet,' he stuttered, and was mortified when he heard Seren snigger.

Mrs Williams stared at her. 'I hope you treat him better than that other one. His mother didn't like her at all, and neither did I, from what she told me of her,' she declared.

Daniel wished the ground would open up and swallow him. Then he felt Seren gently kick his ankle, and he risked glancing at her.

Far from taking offence, she was struggling not to laugh, and he felt his tension ease a little.

'Come along Phoebe, let's leave them to eat in peace,' his mother said, catching his eye. 'I'll phone you later, Daniel. Bye, Seren; it was nice to meet you.'

Did he imagine it, or had his mum winked at him?

He was careful to keep his expression blank until his mother's back was turned and then he rolled his eyes. 'Sorry, I didn't expect Mum to be here. She usually pops in on Wednesdays. And I can only apologise for Mrs Williams. She should never have said what she did.'

'Don't be daft – you've already met my dad, and my Aunt Nelly. It's only fair I get to meet your family.'

At that moment their paninis arrived and there was silence for a short while as they both tucked in, although Daniel only made a half-hearted attempt at tackling his. He had been hungry, but seeing his mother and her friend had dimmed his appetite somewhat. He couldn't believe Mrs Williams had asked a question like that, and he was horrified.

'Don't be embarrassed,' Seren said, wiping her mouth with a serviette. 'My dad is the same. I won't let him near a boyfriend of mine, if I can help it.'

'Yes, but you had a double whammy.'

She took a sip of her spiced latte and regarded him with a twinkle in her eye. Daniel squirmed, guessing what she was about to ask.

'Did your last girlfriend treat you badly?'

Yep, that was what he thought she might ask. The last thing he wanted to do was to slag Gina off, and it was a bit too soon to tell Seren all the sordid details, so all he said was, 'You could say that.'

'And your mum didn't like her?' She peeped at him from over the rim of her mug.

'Only because of the way she treated me,' he said. 'It's not as though she'll dislike anyone I'm going out with, just because I'm dating them.'

'Glad to hear it.' Her teasing grin revealed a dimple on each cheek, and he looked away hastily. Seeing them had sent a bolt of longing through him, and he desperately wanted to gather her into his arms.

Control yourself, he commanded silently, willing his libido to calm down and behave. He hadn't even kissed her yet, for goodness' sake!

'Damn, I've just realised the time. I'd better get a move on,' Seren said, jumping to her feet and yanking her coat off the back of the chair.

'Right.' Daniel was abruptly all business. Although he would have liked nothing better than to spend the rest of the day with her, Seren had a job to go to and he didn't want to make her late.

He drove her back as quickly as he dared, all the while sneaking little glances at her out of the corner of his eye. More often than not he caught her doing the same thing, and when their eyes met he gave her a tender, tentative smile, which she returned, making him tingle and setting his pulse racing.

When he turned the truck into her street, Seren said, 'Do you mind taking me straight around the back? I'll shove these bags in the shed and then I must dash.'

Daniel didn't mind at all. 'Would you like me to wait for you to change into your staff uniform and pop you into work?' he offered.

'Aw, that's so sweet of you, but I'm sure you've got things to do. It's only a ten-minute walk,' she added.

He didn't have anything else to do, but he didn't say that, not wanting to push it. He'd made enough progress with her for one day. 'OK. I'll see you Friday?'

'Friday,' she agreed, stuffing the last bag in through the open shed door. Then she hesitated.

Suddenly it felt awkward, and Daniel wondered if she expected to be kissed, or whether he should even try.

He plumped for being honest instead. 'I'd like to kiss you, but I want to do it properly and not rush it.' He let out a breath. 'Besides, I've got a horrible feeling that if I start kissing you I might never stop, so you'd better go inside before I take you in my arms and—'

She stopped his words with a swift kiss on the lips.

Then she dashed off up the path, leaving him staring after her with a stupid grin on his face.

Oh, boy, if that was what a quick brush of her mouth could do to him, imagine how he'd be after a full-blown kiss.

Daniel drove all the way home imagining precisely that, and by the time he arrived at his house he knew one thing – he was smitten, and he couldn't wait to see her again.

Chapter 16

Seren popped a deliciously scented candle and its gorgeous pottery holder into a paper bag and handed it to the old lady she was serving. She, along with many of the residents and quite a few of the staff of Aunt Nelly's care home, were gathered in the lounge where Seren had laid out her wares, and they were examining the items that Seren had brought to sell and exclaiming excitedly.

'My Valerie will be thrilled,' the woman said. 'I always give her money, but I do like her to have a little something to open on Christmas Day. Last year it was slippers.'

Nelly burst out laughing and slapped her thigh. 'Been there, done that, got the thermal vest.'

'I think you mean T-shirt,' Seren said.

'No, it was definitely slippers, wasn't it, Edwin? I'd never dream of buying a strange man a T-shirt.'

'Hey, who are you calling strange?' Edwin protested.

Seren had ferried a selection of things indoors, because many of the residents were too old and frail to stand outside in the cold, so she had done what she'd promised and had brought things to them.

And mighty successful it had been. Most people had bought something, and one old lady had spent a fortune, mostly on Christmas decorations for her room in the home.

'I've got no family to buy for. My son lives in Australia,' the lady had explained earlier, 'and it costs a fortune to post anything over there, so I just give them money. But I've always been a big fan of Christmas. When I moved in here, I got rid of nearly everything, Christmas decorations included. Well, they were all so old, you see? Tatty, most of them. So they went in the bin. But look at all the lovely new ones I've got now. My room will look all cheery and festive when my son Skypes me. He'll be so pleased. He worries about me, you know.'

'I expect he does,' Seren said, surreptitiously popping a divine bauble in the shape of a feathered dove into the bag of items the lady had purchased, and making a mental note to pay her supplier for it later.

Eventually everyone who had wanted to look at her stock had done so, and people were beginning to move away, so Seren thought it was time she packed up as she still had Wheatlands Residential Home to visit before she was done for the day. She didn't have a great deal left in the boxes she'd brought in from the van, and she hoped she'd have enough stock to make a decent show at the next place. At this rate, she'd have to stock up again this evening.

It might be a good idea to let the suppliers know sooner rather than later that she needed more goods off them, so she sat down for a moment to send each one a quick message asking if she could call in on her way home.

Just as she pressed send on the last one, her aunt eased herself down into the seat next to her.

'I thought that went very well,' Nelly said.

'So did I.'

'You can thank me by making me a cup of tea before you go.'

'Thank you for what?' Seren asked, getting up to do as she was told.

'Coming up with the travelling gift shop idea.'

Seren turned to her. 'I think you'll find we both had the idea at the same time.'

'If it makes you feel better to think that…' Nelly cocked an eyebrow at her.

Seren knew there was nothing to be gained by arguing any further, so instead she bent to give her aunt a kiss on the cheek. 'Thank you,' she said graciously, and Nelly beamed at her, her dentures gleaming.

'You're welcome. You might as well have it now as when I'm gone.'

'Pardon?' Seren frowned. What an odd thing to say. It wasn't the first time her aunt had made a comment that was totally out of context, and Seren felt a frisson of unease travel down her spine. Not only that, she recalled that Nelly had been convinced someone was stealing her walking frame. It all added up to a worrying conclusion, and Seren vowed to have a chat with her father about it. Nelly had always been as sharp as a tack, so the possibility of the old lady suffering from dementia didn't bear thinking about.

'Your father tells me you have a young man,' Nelly said as Seren handed her a mug. Nelly took it with both hands and sipped it cautiously. 'Not bad,' she declared. 'What's his name? What's he like? What does he do for a living?'

'Slow down,' Seren chuckled. 'I haven't actually been on a date with him yet, although I am seeing him on Friday. His name is Daniel. You know what he looks like because you've seen him here when he's visited his grandfather, Edwin, and he's a freelance gardener.'

'Ha! Your dad could do with him in your garden,' Nelly chortled. 'Patrick never did like gardening.'

Seren had thought the same thing when Daniel had brought her the ivy cuttings, and she'd also been relieved that it was dark so he hadn't seen it in all its non-glory. He'd seen it on Tuesday though, but she suspected he'd had other things on his mind than her dad's garden. She knew she certainly had. If she closed her eyes, she could still feel the brief brush of her lips on his, and her pulse raced every time she thought of it.

Just at that moment Edwin sauntered back into the room and Nelly pounced on him in glee. 'Did you know that your grandson and my niece are going on a date? Isn't that nice!'

Seren cringed. What was it with the older generation – they all seemed to take an active interest in her love life, and shout about it to the whole world. Then she recalled the way she'd sniggered when Daniel's mother and her neighbour had appeared in the cafe the other day, and decided that karma wasn't a nice person. At least Daniel wasn't here to witness her embarrassment, the way she'd witnessed his.

'You'll make a lovely couple,' Edwin said, scrutinising her. 'He could do with someone like you, and not that awful Gina he was with before. I was glad to see the back of her, I can tell you.'

Gina… so that was the name of the girlfriend who'd treated him badly. Seren filed the name away.

'You've got your future all sorted,' her aunt declared with a self-satisfied smirk. 'The travelling gift shop, a handsome young man… All you need now is your own place. You can't carry on living with your dad forever, you know.'

'I don't intend to, but I used all my savings on doing the conversion for the van. Or I will have done once T&M Conversions send me their invoice.'

'Bugger!' Nelly's hand had slipped when she reached for her mug of tea, and she'd knocked it onto the floor. Flustered, she gave Seren a beseeching look.

Seren hurried to mop up the mess, and by the time she'd finished she really did need to get going.

Giving her aunt a hug and a kiss, and a wave to Edwin, she dashed off, her head full of thoughts of the future.

–

'Deck the Halls' blasted out noisily for the regulation twelve seconds as the van cruised along one of Tinstone's many residential streets. This was the third (or was it the fourth?) housing estate Seren had driven around, and by now she was getting used to curious people looking out of their windows at the sight of the brightly illuminated vehicle trundling along their road.

It was late afternoon and already dark, but she felt rather festive with her flashing antlers on her head and her Christmas jumper underneath a scarlet coat. She even had knitted gloves with snowmen on them, and a scarf to match. As she drove slowly down one street and up another, she loved seeing all the lights on the houses and the lit Christmas trees in the windows. It made her feel all warm and cosy inside, the way she used to feel as a child when a visit from Santa was real and the anticipation made her feel sick with excitement. Her favourite trees were the green ones with multi-coloured lights and an assortment of different baubles. No coordinated display for her; she loved a diverse tree, and had collected the decorations on it over many years, to be lovingly brought out on the second weekend in November, without fail. That was traditionally her and her dad's trimming up weekend, and she looked forward to it every year. Carols playing in the background, a mince pie, and a Baileys liqueur on the go… It was a magical and special time, and it never failed to get her in the mood for the festivities ahead.

The music ceased and Seren parked the van for a few moments, waiting to see if she had any customers.

She hadn't had many people come out of their houses to see what all the fuss was about, and those who had tended to have children with them and a pound coin clutched in their hands. When they realised she wasn't selling ice cream, most of them slunk off, but a few had stayed long enough to have a look at her goods, and one or two had actually bought something.

It was a start, if nothing else, and she hadn't been expecting hordes of people to flood into the street; she understood it was going to be a long, slow process. If it worked at all. She might be better off attending places such as the two care homes she'd visited today and assorted markets.

Hoping someone would come and see what was going on, Seren glanced in the side mirror and spotted two people hurrying out of their house, so she clambered into the back of the van and opened the window.

'Merry Christmas,' she cried as they approached.

'I thought you were the ice cream van,' the older woman said. She was accompanied by a teenage girl, who was only wearing a pair of leggings and a long-sleeved T-shirt, and who must have been frozen.

'It used to be an ice cream van,' Seren explained (for what felt like the hundredth time today) 'but now it sells a wonderful selection of Christmas decorations and unique and unusual gifts.'

The woman eyed her suspiciously. 'Don't you work in that supermarket on Grange Street? Have they got you out selling stuff?'

Seren did a double-take. 'Oh, hello, I didn't recognise you. Yes, that's me.' She laughed lightly. 'As for them having me driving a van, you shop there so you know they don't sell anything as nice as this.' Seren swept her arm around to include all the gorgeous things that were for sale.

'Mum, can I buy the skin care stuff?' The woman's daughter pointed to a pretty box of moisturisers, made from beeswax produced by local bees.

'You've got enough potions and lotions to sink a ship,' her mother replied. 'And by "I" you mean *me*, don't you?'

'Pleeeease? It's for Jodie for Christmas. She always gets me something nice.'

The woman shook her head and got out her purse. 'OK, but this is the last. Your friends are costing me a fortune.' She handed over a twenty-pound note and Seren placed the item in a paper bag decorated with Christmas trees.

'You can use the bag to wrap it,' Seren suggested.

'Good idea,' the girl's mother said, giving her daughter the present to hold. 'It will save wasting yet more wrapping paper. It gets my goat, it does – all that money spent on gift wrap, and all the bother of sellotaping it, only for it to be torn to shreds in a matter of seconds.' She gave her daughter an exasperated look. 'I've got three of them. She's the oldest. They are bankrupting me.'

Seren smiled sympathetically. 'But you wouldn't be without them,' she said, and the woman smiled, the first one to crack her lips since she'd walked up to the window.

'Sometimes I would,' she replied darkly. 'I'd say see you around, but I doubt if I'll see you now that you're no longer working in the shop.'

'Oh, I'm still there. I'll keep a look out for you,' Seren said. 'Bye. Merry Christmas.'

'Yeah, right,' came the muttered reply.

–

'I'm not sure driving around the streets justifies the cost of the petrol I used,' Seren said to her dad later that evening whilst they were having dinner.

'You've got to speculate to accumulate. Anyway, Rome wasn't built in a day. It'll take time for people to get used to the idea, and it'll take time to build a reputation for selling nice, good quality stuff.'

'I suppose you're right.' She hesitated. 'Dad…?'

'Hmm?'

'Do you think Aunt Nelly is OK?'

'What do you mean? You saw her today, didn't you?'

Seren nodded. 'Yes, that's why I'm asking. She seemed… oh, I don't know… not quite with it.'

'In what way?' Patrick stopped eating and put his knife and fork down. Seren could see worry creeping across his face.

'We were discussing who had the idea for the travelling gift shop, when she said something strange.'

'Like what? Come on, Seren, this is like pulling teeth.'

'She said, "You might as well have it now as when I'm gone". What do you think she meant by that?'

Patrick picked his cutlery up once more and stabbed a piece of pasta with his fork. 'No idea,' he replied, 'but it doesn't sound like anything to get your knickers in a twist about.'

'It's not just that – she keeps accusing the other residents of stealing her walker.'

'Yeah, I know.' Her dad sniggered. 'She does it on purpose to wind them up.'

'She *told* you that?'

'Yep.'

'So you don't think there's anything to worry about?'

'Nope.'

'Phew.'

Patrick pointed his fork at her. 'You've got enough to worry about, without looking for additional problems. Your Aunt Nelly has still got all her marbles. I wish she'd give a couple of them to me – I'd forget my head if it wasn't screwed on.'

'I don't think you're the only one,' Seren said, remembering she still needed to phone Tobias tomorrow about the invoice. It was nearly three weeks since she'd picked the van up from T&M Conversions and she was still no nearer to paying her debt.

Briefly she considered the possibility of it being a ploy to get her to go to the garage so he could ask her out again, because she had a feeling he might be unused to women turning him down and that she might be a bit of a novelty for that reason alone. Maybe she'd leave it a week or so – he might do his paperwork at set times of the month – although she did think it was a rather slapdash way to do business, she guessed he must be busy enough that he wasn't living hand to mouth.

She'd give him a ring anyway, just to jog his memory. Although she wondered if Daniel had managed to have a word with Tobias after she'd mentioned it to him.

Daniel... her insides tingled as she thought about their date tomorrow night.

She couldn't wait! This time, she was determined to have a proper kiss, and she had a feeling it was going to be toe-curlingly wonderful.

Chapter 17

'I hope you like Italian,' Daniel said, trying not to gawp as Seren walked down her path. He'd just alighted from the truck and was about to knock on her front door, when she opened it and stepped outside, closing it quickly behind her to keep the heat in.

She was radiant, with her hair flowing over her shoulders and gleaming in the light of the streetlamp, and a shy smile on her lips. A black coat encased her from neck to knee, and she had a pair of black ankle boots on her feet with an eye-wateringly high heel.

She looked sophisticated and elegant, and he wondered what a gorgeous woman like her saw in a man like him. He still had dirt under his fingernails that no amount of scrubbing with a bristle brush could remove, and he was far more at home digging around in the soil than he was sitting in a posh restaurant. And the one he was taking her to was very posh indeed.

He wanted to impress her, but not only that, he wanted to treat her like a princess, and he didn't think a quick impersonal bite in one of the popular pub chains would do it.

Instead, they were going to Liago's, which was one of the best Italian restaurants around. He was aware it was going to cost him an arm and a leg, but he didn't care. He wanted to show her that a date with him didn't have to involve squelching through mud or getting pricked by holly leaves. He wanted to wine and dine her, and kiss her in the candlelight to the sound of violins and cooing doves.

'I *love* Italian,' she declared, standing so close he could smell the lotion she used on her skin, and he had to make a conscious effort not to sweep her into his arms and kiss her senseless.

'Good. Let me help you up.' He opened the passenger door, took her hand and steadied her as she climbed into the cab. Maybe a truck wasn't the best vehicle in which to take a girl on a date, but it was the only one he had, so he hoped she didn't hold that against him. Or compare it to the sleek coupé that Tobias drove.

Dashing around to the other side, his breath clouding above his head, Daniel got in and started the engine. He'd cleaned the cab out especially and had hung a Christmas berry air freshener from the rear-view mirror in the vain hope that the truck would smell less like a manure pile and more like a sedan.

Seren didn't say anything, so he hoped she wasn't too embarrassed at being driven to such a nice place in such a grotty vehicle. Gina had been forever complaining about it, nagging him to buy a little run-around, and to only use the truck for work, but he'd been reluctant, not wanting to dip into the money he'd made from the sale of his house. That was supposed to be for a rainy day, and not for splashing out on something he didn't need.

He must have made some kind of noise, because he came out of his wool gathering to find Seren looking at him curiously. 'I was thinking about Liago's,' he fibbed. 'I've not been there before, but I've heard good things about it.'

'I haven't been there either, although I'm sure it'll be lovely.'

Daniel was relieved when they arrived at the restaurant to see that it was busy, which was always a good sign when it came to restaurants.

'This is nice,' Seren said after a waiter had shown them to their table and handed them both a menu. He took their drinks order – white wine for her, spritzer for Daniel – then left them to peruse the menu.

She hadn't opened hers, but was gazing around the restaurant curiously. 'I like the colour scheme,' she said.

Daniel hadn't noticed; he was too busy staring at Seren, who looked stunning in a slim-fitting, simple red dress that matched her lipstick. It showed off her figure to perfection, and he itched to slide his arms around her trim waist and run his hands over the curve of her hip.

'Daniel?'

He abruptly stopped staring at her and checked out the decor, which consisted of mushroom-coloured walls (although it was difficult to tell the exact shade in the dim lighting), with navy and teal accents, and a hint of grey. When he said that very thing to her, Seren was impressed.

'I use colour a lot in my planting,' he explained, awkwardly. 'I'm not a secret interior designer, or anything. I just know a Michaelmas daisy when I see one.'

'Don't be so modest,' she admonished, and added, 'I bet you can tell a dandelion from a rose, too.' Then she threw her head back and laughed uproariously, ignoring the amused looks from the diners at nearby tables.

Daniel chuckled and went on to tell her a story about how he'd once cut down an old and tatty rosebush because it was blocking the light to some other plants, only to discover it was dearly loved and the owner was heartbroken. 'I was only just starting out,' he said, 'and I wanted to make an impression. I did that, all right. The bloke refused to pay me. I've since learnt to check first before I dig anything up.'

'Oh, dear.' Seren giggled and Daniel laughed along with her.

They were still sniggering when their pasta course arrived, and Daniel guessed they might have continued to giggle if it wasn't for the fact they were both hungry and the food looked and tasted divine.

'What did you order?' Seren asked, her eyes on his plate.

'Penne Genovese – prawns with roasted pistachio, basil and cream. Want to try some?'

She opened her mouth wide like a baby bird, and Daniel scooped up a small forkful and placed it gently in her mouth. Her lips closed around it and when the flavours burst on her tongue she closed her eyes.

'Mmm,' she murmured, and desire poked him in the stomach at the sound. 'Want to have a taste of mine?' she asked, opening her eyes and catching him practically drooling with longing.

'Oh, uh, yeah. Remind me, what have you got?'

'Wild rice with mushrooms and diced sausage in tomato sauce.'

Daniel didn't dare do what she had done and open his mouth for her to deposit a forkful inside, so he took the laden fork from her and fed himself. 'Gosh, that's tasty,' he said, wishing he'd chosen that instead. Actually, he wanted to have a taste of everything on the menu. 'I don't know if I'll be able to manage the second course if I eat all this,' he sighed, indicating his half-full plate regretfully. The portions were huge.

'We've got all evening,' she said, 'so why don't we give it a go. If we're full after this one, we could always have the main course to share. Do you think they'll mind?'

He thought they probably might and if he had been sitting here with anyone other than Seren, he would never have asked the waiter, but ask he did, and the waiter didn't bat an eyelid.

They agreed on the lamb, with a mixed green salad and buttered roast potatoes to accompany it, and when their meal arrived and they began to dig in, Daniel didn't think the evening could be any more romantic. Here he was in a trendy restaurant, sharing a plate of the most delicious food with a gorgeous woman who was so easy to talk to he felt he'd known her all his life. And there were candles and soft music, too.

It felt incredibly intimate to be sharing one dish, and Daniel had difficulty concentrating on the food. He so desperately wanted to kiss her. And more.

Finally, they were done, after sharing yet another course, this time a dessert of tubes of crispy pastry filled with creamy ricotta cheese and smooth, rich chocolate.

He was so stuffed at the end of it, that he didn't think he'd eat again for a whole week. 'How do people manage a starter as well?' he mused. 'Coffee?'

'It'll have to be black,' Seren said. 'Anything more will tip me over the edge from being full, to feeling sick because I've eaten too much.'

'Would you like a digestivo?' their waiter asked, and when Seren heard it was a special Italian liqueur aimed to help digestion, they both decided to have one.

Daniel leant back in his chair, feeling relaxed and happy, as he sipped his drink. He also felt a little drunk – but not on alcohol. He was drunk with desire.

All through dinner he'd kept looking at her delectable lips, imagining how they'd taste when he parted them and found her tongue. Or what it would be like to take her in his arms and feel her curves against his chest. So when she suggested a stroll through town to help their meal go down, he didn't know whether to feel relieved or frustrated. He so desperately wanted to kiss her, but he couldn't decide whether she'd welcome his advances or push him away, but by taking a walk it delayed the point at which he'd find out.

The streets were damp and misty, the wet pavements reflecting the glow from the streetlights and the twinkling Christmas trees in the shop windows. Daniel had a flashback of his parents taking him out on a December night, to dawdle along the high street and admire the decorated shops and the festive windows, and a bolt of the thrill he used to feel at the thought of Christmas and a visit from Santa shot through him and he laughed aloud.

Then he had to explain why he was laughing so Seren didn't think he was a complete idiot.

'I know what you mean,' she said, hooking her arm cosily through his. 'I always feel like that about Christmas. I suppose you could say I'm a big kid at heart, but I adore this time of year. It's so sparkly and fun.'

She was warm tucked up against him, and every time he took a breath her perfume invaded his nostrils until his head swam from the intoxicating scent.

Unable to bear it any longer, he stopped and turned to face her. 'I've had a good time this evening,' he said. 'Do you think you'd like to… would you consider…?' Crumbs this was difficult. 'Can I kiss you?'

Seren pouted and frowned. 'I thought we were meant to be dating?'

'We were – we *are*.'

'So why do you need to ask?' She lifted her chin in an invitation he couldn't refuse.

He took a step towards her and gathered her to him, feeling her melt against him as he drew her into his embrace. Gazing down, his eyes met hers as he bent his head, and he couldn't look away. She captivated him, her dilated pupils holding him prisoner, trapping him with the answering yearning he saw in their depths, and he sensed she wanted this kiss as much as he did.

Slowly, his mouth found hers, and when he kissed her, her eyelids fluttered closed and she let out a soft sigh.

It was all he could do to hold himself back and not ravish her on the spot.

He felt like a teenager again – all hormones and gauche trembling hands – as he reached for the back of her head and buried his fingers in her hair. Her lips parted in response, and his tongue slipped between them, to taste her fully.

He had no idea how long they stood there, lost in each other, savouring their very first kiss, but eventually they resurfaced and Daniel took a shuddering breath as he fought to control his racing heart.

'I could do that all night,' she murmured, and he rested his forehead against hers and said, 'So could I,' meaning it with every cell in his body, but also knowing that he would be unable to stop at kissing.

He wanted all of her, every last centimetre. But it was too soon. He wasn't like Tobias, happy to jump into bed at the drop of a hat, and he didn't think Seren would want that, either. Despite the passion zipping along his veins and the deep-seated longing in his gut, he'd wait until it felt right, and let Seren tell him when she was ready to take things to the next level, especially since they'd only just reached this one.

What an amazing kiss it had been. It had turned him inside out and upside down, and had left him with a pounding heart, a racing pulse and the sensation of being unable to catch his breath.

'When will I see you again?' he asked, not wanting the evening to end, yet knowing that it must.

'There's a song in there, somewhere.'

'Please don't ask me to sing it,' he murmured, his lips against hers once more. 'I don't want you to go off me.'

'That's not going to happen,' she assured him. 'Unless...' She pulled back.

'Unless what?'

'You don't stop talking. Kiss me again.'

Daniel stopped talking and did as he was told.

Chapter 18

'Have I been ice skating? Have I ever!' Seren muttered to herself, as she got ready for her second proper date with Daniel. Ice skating was the one physical thing she was good at. When Daniel had asked her that very question last night when he dropped her home, she had almost jumped for joy. She hadn't been ice skating for years because none of her friends would go with her, all of them too scared of falling over and breaking something, so this was going to be a real treat.

Nicole was the worst for worrying about falling and injuring herself, and Seren used to tease her for being a scaredy-cat, even though she empathised with her friend. Trying to look after a small child if you had a broken arm or leg wouldn't be easy, but Seren had no such responsibilities. Anyway, she was pretty good at skating, even if she did say so herself. Not competition good – but she could do the odd wobbly twirl and propel herself backwards. It might take her a while to find her skating legs again but once she did, she intended to skate circles around Daniel.

Daniel – the very thought of him sent shivers down her back, and she was thrilled she was seeing him again so soon. What could be better than going to a Christmas Winter Wonderland with a gorgeous guy on a Saturday night!

Yesterday would be indelibly written on her heart as their first kiss. The brief peck on the lips that she'd given him after their walk in the woods last Tuesday didn't count. That had been more of a maiden aunt kind of kiss than the full-on clinch they'd enjoyed last night. She *hoped* he'd enjoyed it, because she most definitely had, and she couldn't wait to do it again.

After snogging until her toes had frozen to the pavement, they'd meandered back to the car, arms wrapped around each other. Then he'd driven her home, where they'd shared another passionate embrace in the truck before she'd reluctantly headed inside. She'd briefly wondered whether Daniel had expected her to ask him in, but that wasn't going to happen – not with her dad on full alert. There was no way she had been going to invite Daniel in for coffee (or anything else) when there was the risk of her dad poking his head around the door and asking if they fancied a mug of Horlicks.

She had no intention of inviting him in this evening either, and it was a bit too early in their relationship to go back to his house, because that might suggest she wanted to spend the night with him, and although the thought was immensely appealing, she wasn't quite ready to take such a big step just yet. That wasn't to say she wouldn't after a few more dates…

There, she was finally ready – black leggings tucked into thick woolly socks (no jeans on the ice in case she fell and had to spend the rest of the evening in wet denim), chunky boots, long-sleeved T-shirt underneath one of her many Christmas jumpers, and topped off with her padded jacket and matching hat, scarf and gloves. She might have a Michelin-tyre Man vibe going on, but she'd be warm and cosy for their visit to the town's Winter Wonderland.

Seren squealed with excitement when she heard the unmistakable sound of a truck pulling up outside her house and she shot down the stairs, calling out to her dad that she was off as she sped out of the door.

'Can we go and see Father Christmas?' she asked innocently after she'd got into Daniel's truck and they'd shared a rather nice embrace.

Daniel threw her a dark look. 'Don't even go there. I'm booked to be Santa at the Winter Wonderland next Saturday and for a couple of dates after that.' He pulled a face. 'I'm dreading it.'

She leant across and planted a kiss on his cheek. 'You'll be fine,' she said. 'I wish I could pay you a visit to give you some moral support, but I'll be at work on Saturday.'

'You were in today, weren't you?'

'I was. It was so busy – I'm dreading the next few weeks. Let's not talk about it; I want to enjoy myself this evening.'

Visiting the Winter Wonderland was one of the highlights of Seren's festive calendar and she was determined to wring every last drop of fun out of it. It was going to be even more special this year, with Daniel by her side. In previous years she'd been with friends, and she'd sometimes caught herself envying the couples she'd seen skating serenely around the ice rink holding hands, or the girl whose guy was trying to win her a cuddly toy from one of the stalls in the funfair.

The Winter Wonderland was held in the park, and each year the organisers went out of their way to make it even more magical than the one before. She couldn't wait to immerse herself in all things Christmas, starting with the heavenly aroma of frying onions, doughnuts, the unmistakable spiciness of mulled wine, combined with the smoke of roasting chestnuts. Seren sniffed appreciatively as they joined the throng of people, and she soaked up the atmosphere eagerly.

Although the Winter Wonderland was open from ten in the morning, it didn't truly come into its own until after dark, when everything was lit up and twinkling, and as she gazed around, her hand held tightly in Daniel's, she felt like skipping for joy. Hurdy-gurdy music played from a dozen different rides, the air was filled with the chatter and laughter of many voices, and Christmas songs vied for attention. In the distance she could see the peaked tent of the ice rink, and beyond that thousands of lights danced and twinkled from the Festival of Light illuminations that wove its way through the trees and the flower beds, and around the bandstand to line the small boating lake in the middle.

'Don't you just love Christmas?' she cried, and laughed when Daniel replied, 'I do now.'

'What do you want to do first,' she asked, hopping on the spot with excitement, just like Freya often did.

'I'll let you decide,' he said. 'Just don't ask me to eat anything if you want to go on any of the rides.'

'We'll start with those, shall we? Dodgems? Helter skelter? The big wheel?' She tugged at his hand. 'It'll be fun,' she insisted when she saw his reluctance. 'And don't tell me you don't like heights, because I've seen you up a ladder.'

'Helter skelter? How old are you?' he was chuckling as he said it, allowing her to pull him in the direction of the fair.

'You don't have to be a kid to enjoy fairground rides,' she said. 'Two please.' She handed some money to the man at the bottom of the helter skelter stairs, and he gave her a couple of mats in return.

Seren thrust one at Daniel and cried, 'Race you to the top!' then set off up the steep steps, taking them two at a time until her breathing grew ragged, and her lungs ached. She sensed Daniel directly behind her, and she tried not to collapse into giggles as her legs threatened to fail her.

When she got to the top, she paused for a moment to enjoy the view, but when a hysterically laughing Daniel tried to push her out of the way and claim that he was there first, she plonked her mat down at the top of the slide and poked her tongue out at him.

Then she was off, hanging onto the mat for dear life as she swirled down the slide to fly off the bottom and land in a heap.

Seconds later Daniel came to a halt against her back. 'Oof,' he yelped, setting her off again, and she was laughing so hard that Daniel had to yank her to her feet and pull her out of the way of the next person to come hurtling down the slide.

'That was fun,' he said. 'Not. I've got slide burns on my behind because the mat got away from me.'

'There's an art to it,' she told him, taking his hand again, the welcome warmth of his bare fingers seeping through her gloves. Wanting to feel his skin on hers, she slipped her gloves off and stowed them in her pocket. 'You've got to hold it tight with both hands and scoot forward as far as you can.'

'You've done this before,' he accused, kissing her on the nose.

'I might have. Let's have a go on the dodgems next.'

'Good grief,' she heard him mutter, but he followed her willingly enough, and he even did the steering while she sat in the seat next to him, issuing squealed instructions when she spotted another dodgem car on a collision course with theirs.

'Can we stop now?' Daniel pleaded as they climbed down the steps from the ride. 'I don't think my nerves can stand a go on anything else.'

'Just one more. Please?' She peered at him from under her lashes, giving him puppy dog eyes. She wanted to go on the big wheel, and she knew he'd love it once he got to the top and saw the view.

'Just one more,' he agreed, then blanched when she pointed to the giant wheel, with its swinging metal seats dangling high above the park. 'Is it safe?'

'Perfectly,' she said. 'It wouldn't be allowed to operate if it wasn't.'

'You hear of accidents…' he began darkly. 'I'd hate it if anything happened to you.'

'Aw, that's so sweet.' Seren smiled up at him, then paused when she saw the intensity on his face. He meant what he said, and it gave her a lovely warm feeling inside.

Impulsively, she flung her arms around his neck and pulled his head down to hers. Her questing mouth found his warm lips and for a few delicious moments the noise, sights and smells of the Winter Wonderland faded, and the only thing she was aware of was the taste of him and the heat of his kiss.

Someone bumping into her jostled her back to the present and she reluctantly dragged herself away, and she even resisted the urge to snog him until he begged for mercy as they hung suspended goodness knows how many feet over the park when they ventured onto the big wheel.

She was right though, the view was astounding, and it was well worth the eye-watering price. As he watched the world below revolve and turn, Daniel slung an arm around her shoulders and she had the arresting thought that she never wanted this moment to end.

Hot on its heels was another thought, which made her pause anew – could Daniel be The One? He was everything she wanted in a man: kind, thoughtful, funny, attentive, and hot. Very, very hot. He wasn't in the same league as Tobias (not many men she'd met were) but he was handsome in his own way. His good looks were subtler and more lasting, she thought. She had a feeling Tobias would burn bright for a while before fading like a dimming star, but that Daniel might get even better with age.

Blinking heck! She'd got it bad, hadn't she? So to distract herself, she suggested they take a turn on the ice before getting something to eat.

Daniel, to her surprise, was a decent skater. After an initial wobble before he found his balance and remembered the moves, he glided around the arena, neither flashily fast nor snail-slow, and he even attempted a twirl with her.

Neither of them was Olympic standard but neither of them ended up on their backsides either, and Seren was feeling quite pleased with herself by the time they changed into their shoes and handed their skates back, her legs and ankles aching pleasantly after the unaccustomed exercise.

After purchasing some crepes, they wandered around the array of stalls whilst they ate, Seren eagerly absorbing the atmosphere and feeling incredibly happy to have Daniel at her side. They treated themselves to a mulled wine after they'd finished their snack, the warm spiced drink heating Seren from the inside (not that she needed it after the kiss with Daniel), and she decided that she'd never felt as Christmassy as she did now. The festive spirit was practically shining out of her and she was so happy she felt like climbing to the top of the helter skelter again and proclaiming it for all to hear.

What on earth had got into her?

Whatever it was, it was nice, and she vowed to enjoy it whilst it lasted and make the most of it. All too soon it would be tomorrow morning and she'd be back at work.

Which reminded her… 'Look, there's Santa's grotto. Are you sure you don't want to check it out? You could even offer to give them a hand if they're busy,' she teased.

'Wash your mouth out,' Daniel growled. 'Anyway, why aren't you and your ice cream van here? You could have made a killing.'

'It's not an ice cream van; it's a travelling gift shop, I'll have you know,' she pointed out loftily. 'I wish I could have a pitch here, but I'm working on the days they have spaces.'

'That's a shame. Maybe next year.'

Seren didn't want to think about next year. She was having enough trouble thinking about this one. To be honest, she found it difficult to think at all with Daniel by her side, because the only thing in her head was him. He filled her mind and her senses, and she'd never felt this way about any man before. It was new and exciting, and just a little scary.

‐

'I wouldn't have taken you for a baker,' Seren said to Daniel the following evening. He knew he was probably being overkeen but he hadn't wanted to wait for ages to see her again, so he'd asked her if he could see her today.

His disappointment when she'd told him that she had to work was acute, but she'd said she'd be finished by four o'clock, so would that do?

Would it ever! He'd leapt at the chance. He had been hoping they could have done something or gone somewhere during the day, but even if he only saw her for a couple of hours after she'd finished her shift, it would be better than nothing.

Guessing that she might be tired, he'd offered to cook for her, instead of suggesting they go out, and maybe they could watch a film on TV afterwards – although he was hoping to do less watching and more cuddling.

Before he started on the meal, he was doing a spot of baking, which was why Seren was currently perched on a kitchen chair in his house, a bowl containing flour, sugar and butter on the table in front of her, and she was using her fingers to turn the mixture into the consistency of breadcrumbs.

Daniel kept sneaking glances at her as he worked and thinking how very right she looked in his kitchen. She didn't just look at ease – she belonged there, as though she'd always been there. Which was odd considering he had zero attachment to the house he was renting. It was a place to sleep and to stash his stuff, that was all. His heart lay in the house he'd sold before he'd moved in with Gina. Actually, not the house – it was the garden that had meant the most to him. Over the years, as his love for gardening blossomed and grew, he'd put his heart and soul, his blood and sweat into turning it into a living advertisement for his business. It had hurt him deeply to give it up, and in hindsight he should never have done so. If he'd been thinking straight, he could have rented the house out, but he'd wanted to make a commitment, and in his mind selling his house had showed Gina that he was serious about making their relationship work. The next step would have been marriage, even though he'd realised not long after moving in with her that he didn't love her as much or as deeply as he should have done. But he'd have persevered for Amelia's sake and because he genuinely had feelings for Gina.

But she'd cheated and he'd found out and—

Why was he thinking about the past when the present and hopefully the future was sitting in his kitchen, with a look of intense concentration on her pretty face and rubbing the shortbread mixture with all her might as though her life depended on it?

Meanwhile Daniel was heating butter and syrup together in a pan. 'My mum bakes a lot, so I suppose I picked it up from her. Sort of like osmosis. My favourite bit used to be licking the bowl at the end.'

'Isn't that everyone's favourite part?'

'Don't overwork it,' he advised. 'Rough and crumbly is what we're aiming for. Once you've achieved that, you can bring it all together, like dough.'

'Is this OK?' she asked, showing him the bowl.

'That's great. I take it you don't do much baking?'

'I don't bake at all. Are you any good at cooking proper meals?'

'I'm not bad, although I usually go to my mum's most evenings now that Grandad has moved into the care home.'

'How is he settling in?' she asked.

'He loves it. It seems to have given him a new lease of life. He says it's because he's living with people his own age who can understand references to things like *The Golden Shot*.'

'The what?'

'Exactly. Apparently it was a game show in the early seventies.' He wrinkled his nose. 'Grandad had to explain it to me, but his cronies in the home knew what he was talking about straight away.' He checked the dough she was making. 'OK, roll it out until it's about a centimetre thick, then cut it into fingers. Once you've done that, it's ready to go in the oven. Fancy a glass of wine? Dinner will be half an hour yet.'

'I'd love one, please. What are we having?'

'Shepherd's pie. Sorry it isn't anything more adventurous.'

'I adore shepherd's pie, and anyway, I couldn't face eating à la carte food every day. It's too rich.'

Daniel was relieved, even if she was only saying it to be kind. He had ummed and aahed about inviting her to his house for the evening, hoping she wouldn't think he was aiming to get her into his bed (he was, but not necessarily tonight), but he couldn't go on taking her out every time he wanted to see her. Although she'd insisted on paying her way (except for the meal on Friday because that had been his treat), it was still costing a fortune, and it was money he couldn't afford to throw around. It seemed silly to be doing a job he didn't want to do which was meant to tide him over the winter months, if he was going to spend all his earnings on going out – as nice as the going out had been. He'd thoroughly enjoyed last night at the Winter Wonderland, but it was Seren's company and her kisses he'd enjoyed the most. And he could have her company at his house (he'd been relieved when she'd accepted his invitation to dinner and to cuddle up with a film afterwards) for a fraction of the cost. Plus, not being in public meant he could kiss her as many times as she'd let him.

He was hoping she'd let him kiss her a lot.

With the shortbread biscuits baked, dinner was ready shortly afterwards, and Seren helped him lay the table. He dished up whilst she poured two glasses of water, as she'd driven over in her van and he didn't want to drink wine if she wasn't having any more, then they settled down to eat. To Daniel, it was completely natural her being there, and once again he had the feeling they were meant to be. It was as though he'd known her forever, as though she'd always been in his life, and although it was far too soon to be thinking those thoughts, he realised he was falling in love with her.

As they ate, they chatted about this and that, nothing and everything, but he didn't mention Gina. Seren knew he'd been in a relationship previously, thanks to his mum and Mrs Williams, but she didn't need to know the details and he had no wish to share them with her, so he kept the tone of the conversation light, and the subject quickly arose of when they would be able to see each other again.

Daniel had far fewer commitments compared to Seren, so he was more than happy to work around her.

'Do you like bowling?' he asked. He'd been wondering what they could do on their next date, and he'd seen an advertisement for an activity that he hoped she might enjoy. Of course, they could always go to a wine bar or to the pub, but there was so much going on in the run-up to Christmas, that it seemed a shame to do something they could do any other time of the year. If he budgeted carefully, he should be able to afford it.

'I do, but I haven't been for ages,' she said.

'I was hoping you'd say that. It's not bowling exactly, though… it's a variation on a theme.'

'What is it?' she asked, her face alive with curiosity.

'Wait and see,' he said. 'But you might want to dress up warm.' He got to his feet, collected the plates and took them over to the sink, and was about to run some hot water when Seren pushed him aside.

'Oh, no, you don't,' she said. 'You cooked, so I'll wash.'

He gently pushed her back. 'How about I wash, you dry?'

She narrowed her eyes, but picked up a tea towel and flapped it at him. 'Get on with it – I want to watch the film tonight not tomorrow.'

Daniel did as he was told, and he made a couple of mugs of tea while Seren washed up, then the two of them settled down on the sofa together and tucked into the biscuits they'd made.

'These are quite good,' Seren said in surprise as she bit into one of the shortbread fingers. 'I might give them a go myself, when I find the time. You'll make some woman a good husband,' she continued, then blushed to the roots of her hair. 'I'm, erm, not hinting,' she added hastily.

'I didn't think you were,' he replied, his voice mild, as he removed the mug from her hand and put it on the coffee table. Then he slipped his arms around her and pulled her towards him.

The film could wait – Daniel had more important things on his mind.

Chapter 19

'Before we start, do you fancy some hot buttered rum?'
Daniel asked, and Seren's mouth watered.

She had done as he'd advised and was dressed in a thick
knitted jumper with a snowman on the front, her padded
parker with a fur-lined trim on the hood, a woolly scarf, a
bobble hat and a pair of mittens. She hadn't known what
to expect, but curling wasn't it.

'Ooh, go on then, you've twisted my arm. Only the
one, mind, because I've got work in the morning.'

She'd been on late shift yesterday, and had been able
to have a lie-in – which she'd needed after such a busy
weekend – but she'd been at work at seven this morning
and she was due in early tomorrow, too, so the last thing
she needed was a hangover to go with the tiredness she
knew she'd be facing. And she still had a load more
wreaths to make at some point, although she had no idea
when she was going to fit that in. Plus, she was going
to trawl the streets in Dippy again on her day off on
Thursday. She had a suspicion that evenings might be
better, but for now she'd have to make do with going
out in the van whenever she had some free time. Strictly
speaking, she should be out in it this evening, but the
opportunity to be with Daniel trumped work.

She accompanied him to the makeshift bar, and they
leaned against it to watch the players.

'Two buttered rums,' the guy behind the counter announced, and Seren licked her lips as he placed them on the bar. The drinks were in clear glass mugs and had something poking out of them. 'Cinnamon sticks,' the guy explained, seeing Seren eyeing them.

'Can you eat them?' she asked.

'You can, but they're a bit chewy. They give a lovely flavour to the drink, though. Enjoy.'

Just from the delicious smell Seren was certain she was going to, and when she took a sip, she closed her eyes in bliss. Vanilla, nutmeg, and some other spices she couldn't identify, together with the sweetness of the rum and the richness of the butter, made it one of the nicest drinks she'd had in a long time. Calling it a drink didn't do it justice – it was more like a dessert in a glass, and she devoured hers with enthusiasm, and wondered whether she could risk having another.

'Have you been curling before?' she asked Daniel, licking the last of the rum from her lips.

'Never. But it looks fun.'

'How do you play it?'

'Ah, now, funnily enough, I did some research when I booked. You've got a target down the far end, and the object is to get your stone – the things you bowl with are called stones – nearest to the target. You might have seen it on TV in the Winter Olympics, where it's played on ice, and you get players with what looks like sweeping brushes frantically polishing the ice to get the stones nearer to the target.'

Seren vaguely recalled seeing something similar, and she was relieved to see that this version didn't involve ice or sweeping. It looked like fun though, and she couldn't wait to have a go, her competitive streak coming to the fore.

'I'm going to beat you,' she warned.

'Hah! We'll see! Just because you are better at ice skating than I am, doesn't mean you'll be better at curling. There's a technique to it,' he added, slipping his hand into hers and leading her to their lane, or 'sheet' as it was called.

For someone who professed to never having played the game before, Daniel seemed to know an awful lot about it. When she challenged him, he claimed it was because he enjoyed most sport and had watched curling on the TV several times, and not because he had any prior experience.

Hmm, she thought, a little while later as she was soundly beaten for the second time. And when she managed to lose again on their third game, she threw her hands up in mock despair.

'I give in! You're the curling champion,' she cried.

'I think that's one-all,' he said. 'You were better at skating and I'm better at curling. How are you at karaoke?'

'Dreadful,' she replied cheerfully.

'Good, because so am I. It's still quite early, so how about we have a bit of a sing-song to round the night off?'

'I'm game,' Seren said. She didn't want the night to end, either – she was having far too much fun. And if he could put up with her caterwauling, it was a good test to see whether he was a keeper, she giggled to herself.

To her surprise, he hadn't been joking when he said he couldn't sing. They were currently sitting in a bar which had a sign stating 'Carol-oke here!' Who could resist having a Christmas themed karaoke, and it was just the ticket to top up her festive spirit. It didn't need topping up, because she was already brimming with it, but despite

Daniel doing his best, she had the feeling he still had some way to go before he threw himself wholeheartedly into the holiday season. She knew he thought it was too commercialised and the celebrations started too soon, but she had a feeling there might be another reason for his reticence when it came to all things Christmas. Not knowing what it was, or whether she was right, she put it down to him not feeling comfortable about playing Santa, and pushed it out of her mind.

Who could fail not to feel festive when belting out the words to 'Rockin' Around the Christmas Tree'? It might be karaoke in the bar, but everyone was singing along, no matter who was holding the mic, and both she and Daniel yodelled away until their throats were hoarse and their mouths were dry.

'Can I interest you in a nightcap?' he shouted, his mouth so close that his breath tickled her ear. He was trying to make himself heard over The Weathergirls asking Santa to bring them a man for Christmas.

'I'd love one,' she yelled back, 'but can we go somewhere quieter?' She could hardly hear herself think, and she suspected her ears might be ringing for the rest of the night.

'Good idea!' Daniel helped her into her coat, and she shoved her hat on her head and wrapped her scarf around her neck, as she had a feeling it was going to be chilly outside after the heat of the bar.

She was right, she saw, as their breath steamed over their heads, and she hastily took her gloves out of her pocket and slipped them on.

Realising that Daniel was gloveless, she freed one of her hands and gave the glove to him. 'We can each wear a glove while we hold hands,' she said, 'and the other hand can go in our pockets. That way I can hold your hand without feeling guilty.'

'I don't feel the cold much,' he said. 'I think it's because I work outside all year round and don't wear gloves very often.' But even so, he took the glove she was holding out to him and wriggled his hand into it. Luckily it was stretchy enough to fit.

They strolled across the road, and when they came to an old-fashioned pub advertising darts nights, they went inside. It mightn't be trendy, but at least they could hold a conversation without having to yell.

Seren plumped for an orange juice, hoping to soothe her throat which was starting to get sore from all the singing, and they settled into a little nook near the fire-place, where a log burner was kicking out a fair amount of heat. Fairy lights were draped along the shelves behind the bar and soft Christmas music played.

Shedding her outer garments yet again, she shuffled closer to Daniel and he slipped an arm around her. 'This is nice,' she murmured. 'I could stay here all night.'

'So could I.' He held her tighter and she moulded herself into him, her head on his shoulder.

After the excitement of the evening, the tranquillity was just what she needed, and she was happy to spend the next half an hour snuggled up to him.

Eventually it was time to go, and when he pulled his van up outside her house, she was sorely tempted to ask him in because she didn't want the evening to end.

However, a twitch of the curtains in her dad's bedroom soon persuaded her it wasn't a good idea. He'd be sure to make some excuse to come downstairs, and the last thing she wanted was for him to catch her and Daniel mid-snog.

She had to content herself with a lovely tender kiss in the front of his truck instead.

But what a kiss it was, and it left her wanting more. Much more.

–

This evening Seren fancied 'Jingle Bells' for her tune of choice as she trundled around the streets in Dippy, and the cheerful song made people look out of their windows and come to their doors.

She still wasn't convinced that this was the best way to sell her goods, but she was willing to give it a go. She'd give it a few more shots but she wasn't expecting great things from it; besides, she didn't have anything else to do this evening, so she may as well try to drum up some business. Even if she didn't sell much today, the effort wouldn't be wasted because the more often that people saw her little van, the more accustomed they'd become, and the greater the chance that they'd buy something the next time they saw it. As her dad said, it was all about getting your name out there.

Seren drove into a cul-de-sac and parked at the top end, the jaunty tune still playing, and she noticed the familiar pulling aside of curtains as people peered through their windows, wondering what was going on.

A little boy was standing in the window of the house opposite, gesturing for someone to come and have a look, and she smiled at him, before clambering out of her seat and going into the back of the van in case she did happen to have a customer.

Sliding the window open, she gazed down the street, enjoying the sight of brightly lit Christmas trees and marvelling at the different styles and colours, and the number and variety of decorations. Then there were the additional decorations, such as blow-up reindeer, illumin-ated Santas climbing up ladders, and neon-blue icicles hanging from roofs.

Oh, how she loved this time of year! Everything was so magical and pretty, and she couldn't get enough of it.

'Hi,' she said, spying the little boy she'd seen a moment ago. He was with his mum, and they smiled back at her. 'Are you looking for anything in particular?' she asked.

'My son thought you were Father Christmas, paying him an early visit, and he wouldn't believe me when I said it wasn't and he insisted on coming out and checking.'

Seren leant forward and lowered her voice. Speaking directly to the child, she said, 'I'm not Santa, but I do know him. It was his elves who made all the things you see here.'

'You know Santa?' The child's eyes were round and full of wonder.

'I most certainly do!'

'Will you tell him I'm a good boy?'

'I expect he knows already. He has a naughty list and a good list, and he knows the name of every child on there. Has he been a good boy?' Seren asked his mum.

'Very good. He's doing ever so well in school, aren't you, Nathan?'

Nathan nodded vigorously.

'Hmm…' Seren put a hand on her chin and pretended to think. 'Nathan… Nathan…? Ah, yes, I think I remember Santa mentioning that you are a good boy.'

The child was tongue-tied as he gazed at her solemnly, then he tugged at his mum's arm, pulled her down to him and whispered in her ear.

When the woman straightened up, she was trying not to laugh. 'Nathan wants to know what Santa would like for Christmas, because it's not fair that he doesn't get any presents.'

'Aw, that's so sweet.' Seren beamed at him. 'Santa's present is seeing how happy he makes all the boys and girls,' she said.

She had a heart melting moment when she envisioned Daniel chatting to numerous small children, all of them thinking he was the real deal.

'While we're here, shall we have a quick look?' the woman said, picking the child up and balancing him on her hip so he had a better view, and Seren was thrilled when, after some deliberation, they bought a couple of items.

While they were looking, several other people had emerged from their houses and were also seeing what she had to offer.

A few more sales later, and Seren was starting to enjoy herself. Not everyone bought, some were merely curious, but she knew that word would get around, especially since much of what she stocked was handmade, well-crafted and unusual. It gave her even more hope when, two streets over, an elderly gent told her that he'd heard of her and her little van and was hoping she'd stop by.

She hadn't made a huge profit this evening, but the future of her little business was beginning to look rosy. And it wasn't just Serendipity that was starting to take off – her love life was, too.

For Seren, life was looking very rosy indeed!

—

For Daniel, the past couple of days had dragged, and it wasn't just because he didn't have much in the way of work. It was because he missed Seren. He couldn't seem to hold a thought in his head without it having something to do with her.

Take breakfast this morning, for instance. It was a simple affair of two slices of toast with Marmite, and coffee. But as he tucked into his toast, he wondered whether Seren loved or loathed Marmite, and this thought was quickly followed by wondering what she'd had for breakfast. Which led to him trying to guess what she might be doing right now.

He knew she was at work, because she'd told him she was on earlies this morning, but what exactly was she doing right at this very minute? Was she stacking shelves, on the till, clearing up some split milk that a customer had dropped, or what? And as she was doing it, was she thinking about him?

He hoped she was. He hoped he was as much in her thoughts as she was in his, and he shook his head – crumbs, he had it bad. He was falling for her, as hard and as fast as a coin thrown down a wishing well. All he hoped was that she was as into him as he was into her.

He might not have much work on, but he could make himself busy by pottering in his mum's garden and maybe he'd pop in to see Mrs Williams, too. There was always something he could find to do in a garden, no matter the season, and he had to keep himself busy. It would do no good to mope around all day, dreaming of the next time he could be with Seren.

Although, there was something he could do before he called to see his mum…

Telling himself that it would be better to wait until the hard frost had melted a little this morning before he tackled the dead foliage in his mum's garden, Daniel decided to take a walk first. The temperature had dropped even further as winter's grip intensified, and the air was chilly and dank. He wouldn't be surprised if it snowed soon. It was certainly cold enough for it, and he burrowed deeper into his scarf and coat, as he strode along the pavement.

It would be good to stretch his legs and he could do with a brisk walk to sweep away the cobwebs and clear his head. That his feet led him in the direction of the supermarket where Seren worked was merely a coincidence.

Yeah, right. 'You keep telling yourself that,' he muttered under his breath.

There was no guarantee he'd see her – she might well be out the back – but he popped into the shop anyway, on the off chance.

He must have scooted up and down the aisles several times and was probably in danger of being asked to leave by a security guard because he was behaving so suspiciously, by the time he finally spotted her.

She was lifting bouquets of fresh flowers out of a huge bucket and placing them on a stand, and when he saw her, she was framed by the colourful blooms she held in her hands, and he was struck anew by how pretty she was.

No, not pretty – *beautiful*.

'Hello,' she said warmly, as she saw him heading towards her, and her face lit up with a beaming smile. 'What are you doing here? On your way to visit your grandad?'

Heck, that was a thought – he hadn't been to see Edwin in a couple of days.

'Yeah, that's right.' Daniel decided he would pay him a visit, then he'd pop along to his mum's afterwards. 'I thought I might take him a… um… a bunch of flowers.'

'That's thoughtful of you. Not many people think to buy flowers for men.'

Feeling a bit of a fraud, he winced. 'It was seeing you that gave me the idea,' he admitted.

'Want any help choosing a bunch?'

'Thanks, I can manage. Maybe a plant would be a better option? Anyway,' he gave the array of flowers and potted plants a dismissive wave. 'What I really want is to take you for a coffee. Are you due a break soon?'

Her face fell. 'Sorry, I've just had one.'

'Never mind, it was just a thought. I've got another confession.' He might as well come clean. Even if the lie was a small one, he didn't want any untruths between them. 'I came here just to see you. I hadn't even thought of going to see my grandad.'

'Then it's lucky for Edwin that you called in,' she shot back, but she was smiling, so he knew she was teasing him.

'Seren,' a voice called, and Daniel turned around to see a woman bearing down on them. 'Haven't you finished that, yet? Hurry up,' she carried on without waiting for Seren to answer. 'You've still got the fresh veg to top up. As nice as it is to chat with friends—' the woman sneered the word '—you'd do well to remember you're at work.'

Daniel was about to open his mouth and say something, but Seren caught his eye and gave an almost imperceptible shake of her head.

'Sorry, Pamela, I was just helping this gentleman choose a plant.' Seren turned her attention to him. 'I recommend the money plant – it doesn't grow too big and it's easy to care for.'

'OK, I'll get that,' he said, and picked one up. 'Thanks, you've been incredibly helpful. I don't know the first thing about plants, so I probably would have got the wrong thing.'

Giving Seren's manager an innocent smile, he headed for the till, outwardly calm but inwardly seething. How dare that woman speak to Seren like that! It made his blood boil. He seriously wanted to give Pamela a piece of his mind, but he knew Seren needed the job, because it would be a long time before Serendipity was able to support her.

The knowledge didn't prevent him from wanting to tear into the horrible woman though, and such a wave of protectiveness washed over him that he nearly dropped the plant.

Seren was such a sweet person, his heart ached at the way she was being treated and he vowed he'd do everything he could to ensure no one treated her like that again, if only he was able.

Chapter 20

Daniel couldn't believe how quickly the days were racing by. Yet another weekend would soon be here and Christmas was growing ever nearer.

He'd had a couple more stints as Father Christmas, which was helping to keep the wolf from the door, and the more he played Santa, the easier he was finding it, but today he was thrilled to bits to be able to do what he was trained to do and what he loved doing more than anything else in the world – gardening. Although, if he was honest, working in the garden had been replaced as his top-most-love, by spending time with Seren. He couldn't get enough of her, and she consumed his every waking thought. Talk about smitten!

So it was with a light heart and a spring in his step that he headed off to his job today. The only fly in the ointment as he'd driven towards Mr and Mrs West's house, the elderly couple whose garden he was about to tackle, was spotting Gina and Amelia when he came to a halt at a junction.

Thankfully, neither of them noticed him. He still felt a pang whenever he thought about the little girl, and seeing her hopeful face would have crucified him. It had hurt him dreadfully when he'd cut off all contact with her, and he disliked himself intensely for it, but he'd not had any choice. It wouldn't have been fair on either of them.

Trying to regain his earlier upbeat mood, Daniel pulled up outside the West's house and began uploading some equipment from his truck.

Today's task was clearing leaf-fall from a choked-up pond, and planting various spring bulbs. It was a little late in the season to be putting spring bulbs in the ground, but as Mrs West had explained over the phone, her husband had desperately wanted to do it himself the way he always had done, but he'd been unwell. Having put it off as long as they'd dared, Mrs West had finally persuaded him that unless someone else planted them, there would be no riot of colour in their garden next spring; and they did so love their garden.

'Can I make you a cup of tea before you start?' the old lady asked. She was tiny, only reaching to his armpit, stooped and frail, with a mop of frizzy white hair like a halo, and the bluest eyes he'd ever seen.

'That would be lovely, thanks,' he said. 'I won't come in, though.' He nodded towards his feet, and the scuffed work boots he was wearing. He was also eager to get going. Pond-clearing wasn't his favourite activity as it was usually smelly, slimy and involved getting wet, even though he had thick waterproof gloves for the occasion and a long net.

Mr West was even frailer, bless him, Daniel saw, when he went around the back of the house and noticed the old gent sitting in front of the picture window with a tartan rug spread over his knees and a woebegone expression on his face.

'Would your husband like to point out what he wants me to plant where?' Daniel asked, after he'd quickly slurped his tea and Mrs West had opened an old coal shed to show him where the bulbs were being stored.

Many of them were already starting to sprout. Daffodils, crocuses, tulips, grape hyacinths and fritillaria, all needed to be planted.

Conscious of the old man's baleful gaze, and understanding that Mr West might be feeling resentful that the tasks he usually performed himself were having to be done by a stranger, Daniel tried to involve him as much as possible. And when he wasn't looking, Daniel also took it upon himself to tidy up the edges of the borders and do a bit of discreet pruning. That rosebush could do with chopping back, for a start: a good prune now would ensure more vigorous growth in the spring, followed by healthier and more abundant blooms.

He hoped Mr West would be in a position to do his own pruning and planting next year, but for now Daniel would do whatever he could to help. After all, one day it might be Daniel himself watching another, younger man, working in his own garden, and feeling resentful about it.

Seeing Mr and Mrs West together, and how she lovingly tucked the rug around her husband's knees, Daniel hoped he'd be like that when he was their age – still in love. And he was beginning to hope he might have found the very person he wanted to grow old with.

–

Seren wasn't rolling in money, but she had made a modest profit from her travelling Christmas van sales this week and she knew what she was going to do with it – treat Daniel to an evening out. He'd taken her curling last weekend, and then onto that karaoke bar, so it was only fair she did something nice for him. And, as he'd pointed out, it was a shame not to fully indulge in all the wonderful about a Christmas pudding? Consisting of gin, brandy and Amaretto, along with orange, lemon and cinnamon, it sounded incredibly luxurious. Then there was the scrumptious-sounding White Christmas martini, which had Malibu, marshmallows and maraschino cherries in it.

Ooh, she was spoilt for choice! Deciding to order two different drinks for her and Daniel, on the premise that they could each have a taste of the other's concoction, she carried the cocktails carefully back to their bench, inhaling the mouth-watering smell. Seren didn't usually drink anything more exotic than wine or sometimes cider on a hot summer afternoon, but Christmas was an exception. Aunt Nelly always insisted she have a glass of sherry with her, her dad loved his eggnog so of course she had to have a taste of that, and how could she resist mulled wine? But these cocktails took festive drinks to a whole new level.

'Mmm,' she murmured, sipping at her straw, the taste of gin and marzipan busting on her tongue.

Her drink was quite strong though, so she'd have to be careful not to have too many, else she'd be squiffy in no time. It was probably a good thing for her sobriety, if not her pocket, that they were so expensive.

'Enjoying your night out?' a voice said, and Seren looked up to see the familiar face of one of her customers staring down at her. Seren didn't know her name, but the woman had been shopping at the supermarket for years, plus she'd also bought something from Dippy.

'You've got to have some time off now and again,' Seren told her with a smile.

'Oh, I agree! As I expect you well know, if we're not careful us women will run ourselves ragged at this time of year!' The woman laughed. 'At any time of year, actually.

I've got a partner and three kids, so I could do with a break once in a while.' She frowned as the man waved to her. 'I'd better be off; his nibs wants some of that hog roast. He hasn't had any tea yet, so he's starving!'

Seren watched her go, thinking she might like some hog roast in a minute, too. There was also a pizza oven, and she quite fancied a slice or two of that as well, but she didn't want to come across as a greedy little pocket, as Aunt Nelly liked to say. Though what was so greedy about a pocket, Seren couldn't work out. Her old aunt was full of odd sayings, and they often made her smile.

'Aunt Nelly would love this,' Seren said, feeling a small measure of guilt that she hadn't visited her in a while, but she'd been so busy, and when she wasn't working or manning the van, she was seeing Daniel. There were only so many hours in the day.

'Grandad is quite partial to a bit of roast pork,' Daniel said. 'I don't know what he'd think of this, though.' He held up his cocktail.

'Nelly would try every single one, then go back for more,' Seren laughed. 'Not sure she'd appreciate the music.'

'Do you think she's happy, living in the care home?' Daniel asked, his expression turning sombre.

'Yes, she is,' she declared firmly. 'I know you're still worrying about whether your grandad has made the right decision, but I think he has. Every time I've seen him, he's been having a great time, joining in with this, that and the other.'

'You've got a point,' he said. 'It can't have been much fun for him stuck at home on his own all day with Mum at work. I wasn't living there, either, so...' He shrugged. 'I recently did some work for this old couple, clearing their see Aunt Nelly on the way back from the market, to let her know how it had gone.

'Not a lot. I'm doing a Santa gig at the Winter Wonderland this coming week and for a couple of days the week after, but that's it. I just wish I could find some more gardening work, but it's a bit thin on the ground right now.'

'It's not long until Christmas and once the new year is out of the way, people are bound to start thinking about DIY and their gardens.'

'That's true. It's the same every year, so you'd think I'd be used to it by now. Each spring and summer I have more work than I can shake a stick at, then come the winter, nada.'

'You do make a cute Father Christmas,' she teased.

'Cute?' His voice was flat. 'I prefer ruggedly handsome, myself.'

'That, too,' she said. 'But I didn't want to say so in case you got big-headed.' She lifted her chin, inviting him to kiss her, and as his lips joined with hers, she murmured, 'Did I say sexy?' then she giggled at his sharp intake of breath.

'Woman, you'll be the death of me,' he growled in return, before crushing her to him and stopping any further words with his mouth.

Even as she lost herself in the wonderful sensations flooding through her, her mind continued to dwell on what he'd said earlier – that she was the best thing to have happened to him – because she had a feeling he might be the best thing that had happened to her, too.

Chapter 21

There was nothing more reminiscent of childhood than a Christmas panto, Seren decided as she clasped Freya's hand tightly in her own and guided her through the throng. The pair of them were going to the theatre to see Aladdin, and Freya was beside herself with excitement and brimming with energy.

But first, they were off to get a burger and fries. Nicole didn't let Freya have much in the way of fast food, but she usually allowed it on occasions like these. Besides, Nicole wasn't here to see it.

The three of them had intended to go to the panto together but Nicole hadn't felt well this evening. Aaron, her other half, was working so either Seren and Freya went on their own, or Freya would miss out on the treat and no one wanted that.

Freya hung onto Seren's hand as she skipped along at her side, and now and again she'd play a truncated version of hopscotch on the flagstones.

'Can I have popcorn?' Freya asked.

'Let's see what's there, shall we?' Seren cautioned. She hadn't been to the theatre since last Christmas when she'd accompanied Nicole and her daughter to see Dick Whittington, and she couldn't for the life of her remember whether the theatre sold popcorn, or whether it was more up-market refreshments. She knew they had a bar, so maybe she could ply Freya with a bag of crisps and a glass of something fizzy instead.

'Will Dame be there?' Freya asked, her face turned up to Seren's. Her nose was pink from the cold and her eyes were bright in the light from the streetlamps and the shop windows.

'Dame who?'

'You *know*,' Freya said, hopping up and down and tugging at her arm. '*Dame*. She was there last time and Mummy says she's always there. But she's not really she. She's him.'

Seren frowned, then her face cleared as she understood what the little girl was referring to. 'Do you mean the Pantomime Dame?'

'Yes! Pantomine Dame.'

'Panto*mime*,' Seren corrected.

'Whatever.' Freya danced sideways and pulled a face at herself in the window of a card shop. 'I look like a monkey.'

'That's because you *are* a monkey,' Seren said. 'And did you just "whatever" me?'

Freya giggled and Seren swung her up into her arms. The little girl's legs clamped around her waist and her arms circled her neck.

'See what I mean? Monkey.' Seren nuzzled her face into the child's neck and blew a raspberry. She growled into her ear, 'I'm a big lion and I'm going to eat you all up.'

'No, God–Mummy!' Freya squealed, and Seren's heart melted. Freya had taken to calling her that ever since Nicole had explained to her that Seren was her godmother. It was too adorable for words.

'Roaaarr!' Seren cried, nibbling the little girl's neck and pretending to bite her.

Freya was laughing so hard she slipped from Seren's grasp and slid to the ground, landing on Seren's toe.

'Ow! I was wrong. You're not a monkey – you're a hefty efelump. I don't think efelumps should have burgers, and they definitely don't like fries.'

'Aww.' Freya bounced on the spot like an excitable puppy and Seren was about to chase her down the pavement when she became aware she was being stared at.

'Seren?' Tobias was standing in front of them, his head cocked to the side.

'Oh, hi,' Seren said, reaching out for Freya's hood and grabbing hold of it to make sure the child didn't run off. 'I'm glad I bumped into you. I meant to ask you about my invoice.'

'Oh, er, right. Haven't you had it?' Tobias glanced at Freya who was trying to squirm out of Seren's grasp.

When the little girl saw him staring, she quietened down immediately and shuffled closer to Seren.

'No, that's why I'm asking,' Seren said.

'I see. I believe I posted it a few days ago. If you haven't had it yet, I expect it's because of the Christmas post.'

'You could email it?'

'Why don't you wait a couple of days. If it hasn't arrived by then, give me a shout.'

'I left you a message, but you didn't get back to me.'

'Yeah, sorry about that. I… er…'

Freya tugged on Seren's arm. 'Can we go? I'm starving.'

'You're always starving,' Seren said. 'Sorry, what were you saying?' she said to Tobias.

Tobias blinked. 'Oh, I was about to ask you how the van was running. Any problems?'

'None at all. She's running like a dream – although now I've said that something is bound to go wrong. I should have knocked on wood.' She tapped Freya gently on the head. 'Touch wood.'

'God-Mummy! Stop! I'm not a tree—'

'I have to go. Got a date,' Tobias said abruptly, interrupting her.

Seren smiled, unsurprised. She suspected guys like Tobias always had dates. 'OK, bye. I'll keep an eye out for that invoice,' she called after him and he walked away.

'You do that.' He waved a hand in the air without looking at her and she watched him stride off.

'Who was that man?' Freya glared at his retreating back.

'He's the man who turned the ice cream van into a Christmas van,' Seren told her.

'Is he your boyfriend?'

'No, my little sugar plum, he's not my boyfriend. My boyfriend is Santa Claus.'

Freya's eyes were huge. 'Is he?'

'Yes. I can take you to see him, if you want.'

'At the North Pole?'

'No, silly, that's too far away and it's really, really cold. It's so cold there, that your nose would turn blue and fall off. And then how would you smell?'

'I don't know,' Freya said, touching the tip of her upturned nose with a mittened finger.

'Awful!' Seren tittered.

Freya scrunched her face up. 'I don't get it,' she said, so Seren explained the joke.

'I've got one,' Freya said after she'd stopped giggling. 'What do you call a fish with no eye?'

'I don't know, what do you call a fish with no eye?'

'Fsh.' Freya squealed with laughter, and Seren joined in, a flood of love for the child threatening to overwhelm her. Freya might not be hers, but she loved her as fiercely as though she were.

'Come on, missy, Let's get you fed,' Seren said, pushing open the door of the fast-food restaurant and letting Freya go ahead of her.

'Will you really take me to see Father Christmas? And is he really your boyfriend?'

'I will, unless your mummy and daddy want to take you instead, and he definitely is my boyfriend,' Seren said.

She hoped Nicole would say yes, because she had a feeling Daniel would adore Freya, and she couldn't wait to show him off, even if it was to a five-year-old!

-

Seren couldn't stop humming the Wishy-Washy song. It had been stuck in her head on autoplay ever since the audience had been encouraged to sing along to it last night. It was so annoyingly catchy that she hadn't been able to rid herself of it, despite the noise of the market as everyone set up their stalls and the tunes blasting out of one of the open shop doorways behind her.

Dippy was more or less ready and, after watching several of the stallholders having to unload trestle tables and display stands, plus boxes and crates of assorted goods, Seren was relieved that all she needed to do was to unroll the awning and open the window and she would be able to start serving. Of course, she did a few other things as well, which mainly consisted of hanging up the samples of wreaths, garlands and table decorations (she'd carefully put the new ones she'd made in bags and had labelled them meticulously so she knew which ones were which), and the final touch was to don her flashing antlers and grab a coffee.

Which was when her smugness backfired on her.

She was at this market on her own today. It was held every Thursday in a small town an hour's drive from Tinstone and was renowned for its farmers' market. She wouldn't normally have bothered to drive quite so far, but today there was an additional feature of a craft fair, and as it was her day off, she'd been unable to pass up the opportunity.

But no one had been able to accompany her – and by no one, she meant her dad or Nicole. Her dad was at work and so was Nicole, having been asked to do an extra shift because someone was ill, so Seren was winging it on her own. Unfortunately, she hadn't realised just how alone she was going to feel.

She knew she'd quickly get into the swing of things as soon as she started chatting to customers, but for now even the simple act of nipping off for a cup of coffee would be fraught with anxiety as she didn't want to risk leaving the van unattended. Goodness knows what she was going to do when she needed the loo.

Pushing that disconcerting worry out of her mind for the time being, she grabbed the float, checked that there was no one taking any particular interest in Dippy, and dashed towards the nearest cafe and darted inside.

Thankfully there wasn't a queue, and she was in and out again with her coffee in a matter of minutes. She knew she wouldn't be able to do that again, so she was grateful her dad had made her a sandwich to bring with her. Maybe she should invest in a flask?

When her phone buzzed and she saw she had a message from Daniel, wishing her good luck for today, she was filled with warmth that he was thinking about her.

She was thinking about him, too. He was constantly in her thoughts, a heady backdrop to whatever she was doing, and she couldn't wait to see him again, to feel his arms around her, and his lips on hers.

It wasn't only the physical things that she loved about him, it was how he made her feel. He had an air of dependability, and she felt secure that he wouldn't mess with her emotions. Which was a good thing, because each time she was with him she knew she was falling for him more and more.

Neither of them had mentioned the 'L' word, but she hoped it was only a matter of time. Time was what they had plenty of, so there was no point in rushing it. They'd only met less than a couple of months ago, and they were already spending as much time together as they possibly could, which wasn't easy with her work schedule and her Dippy schedule, but she'd managed to see him nearly every day for a week.

Her phone buzzed again.

Thinking of you x, she read.

Her fingers flew over the keys.

> Thinking of you, too xxx

> Wish I was there.

So do I!! I don't think I like being at a market on my own.

You don't have to be.

???

I could drive to you, if you want me to?

You'd do that for me?

I'd do anything for you.

Seren took her eyes off the phone and stared into space. Wow, what a heart stopping thing to say. If he meant it the way she'd taken it, of course. Which he probably didn't. It was just a phrase.

Do you mean that? You'd come here?

I'll be with you in an hour. Is there anything you need?

Just you.

Seren took a shaky breath. 'Falling' for him indeed? She'd already fallen. She was in way over her head, and she hadn't realised it until now. But instead of making her feel anxious or scared, she felt empowered and energised. She fizzed and tingled with excitement and felt on top of the world.

Was this love?

She hoped it might be...

–

'I think I prefer this to being Santa Claus,' Daniel said, after handing several bags of assorted winter greenery to a lady who had seventeen people coming to Christmas lunch and was looking for decorations that the kids couldn't break. He'd been extolling the virtues of the ivy Seren had used for the table decorations she'd made and had even suggested that the lady could pot the ends in some soil after Christmas and they'd probably take root.

'Surely not,' Seren teased. 'You make a fetching Father Christmas. I think it's the beard.'

'You like beards, do you?' he teased. 'Long, silky ones? I can grow one, if you want. What about some bushy eyebrows to go with it?'

He stood behind her and slid his arms around her waist, pulling her gently into him. His chest was solid against her back and she snuggled in deeper as he nuzzled his face into the crook of her neck. The feel of his lips on the delicate skin there sent shivers of delight along her nerves and she shuddered with pleasure, wanting to turn around to kiss him.

However, this was neither the time nor the place.

'That's right, wrap her up and keep her warm,' an old gent said, peering up at them through Dippy's side window. 'I used to cuddle my Bertha like that.' His voice wobbled and his rheumy eyes filled up. 'She went last winter.'

Seren stepped forward and leant on the counter, bending down to speak to him. 'I'm so sorry. How long were you married?'

'Eh? We weren't married.' He used a grubby hankie to wipe his eyes. 'Bertha was my dog. A ruddy great big Irish Wolfhound. They don't live long, you know. She was only eight when she went. I've got a Sheltie now, but it's not the same. I love her to bits, but I can't cuddle her like I did Bertha.'

'Ah, I see.' Seren was lost for words, and she could feel Daniel trying to control his laughter. 'There's nothing like the love of a dog,' she said, fishing around desperately for something to say.

The old man wrinkled his face. 'Yes, there is – the love of a good man. You want to keep hold of him. He's looking at you like he's won the lottery.' He nodded at Daniel, and it was Seren's turn to try not to laugh.

'I can't stay here yakking all day,' the gent said. 'I've got to get home; there's snow forecast and I don't want to get caught in it.'

'It'll only be a few flurries,' Seren said. She'd checked the weather forecast last night and again this morning, hoping it wasn't going to rain, and she'd been thrilled when she saw they were due to have the odd snow shower. A smattering was what the telly had said, and she thought how Christmassy and seasonal the market would look if there were snowflakes in the air. It would certainly add to the festive atmosphere and would hopefully increase sales as people got in the mood for the big day.

Seren loved snow, especially when it was falling, and even as she was thinking about it, she saw a lone flake drift idly down from the heavens.

'Ooh, look, it's started snowing already,' she said, her eyes alight with wonder.

The solitary flake disappeared as soon as it touched the ground, melting instantly, and Seren thought that if it continued to snow and melt like this, they would have the best of both worlds – flakes falling but without any build-up underfoot to put potential customers off.

When she heard the first line of the Shakin' Stevens song, 'Merry Christmas Everyone', being played by someone with a sense of humour, she clapped delightedly. This market was turning out to be the best one yet. Not only was she selling loads, and the atmosphere was one of Christmas anticipation, but it was also snowing and she had the most gorgeous man by her side. One who, the old man had said, looked at her as though he'd won the lottery.

Seren had a feeling this Christmas was going to be the best one ever, and she couldn't wait to share it with the man she was falling in love with.

Chapter 22

Seren peered anxiously out of Dippy's windscreen, the wipers working double time to clear snow from the glass. It was a blizzard out there, and she could hardly see more than a few metres ahead. The only thing stopping her from panicking was the steady red glow of the tail lights of Daniel's truck. He was leading the way, claiming that his truck was better in the snow than a former ice cream van.

Seren thought he might have a point.

Every so often he'd brake, and she had to resist the urge to slam her own brakes on. It was better to slow down gently than run the risk of bumping into the back of him. If that happened, she was in no doubt that Dippy would come off worse, and Seren didn't want to damage her.

Daniel slowed down again but this time he pulled over to the side of the road.

Seren followed suit, wondering what the problem was. Apart from driving snow and slippery roads, that is.

She saw him get out of his truck, a shadowy figure in her headlights, blurred by the flakes on the windscreen, and she wound her window down as he approached.

'What's wrong?' she asked.

'I think you ought to leave the van here and get in my truck. It's too dangerous.'

'How much further until we reach Tinstone?'

'At least twenty miles.' He pulled his hood up higher and shuffled around so the wind was at his back. Although he'd only stepped out of his truck a minute ago, his shoulders were already coated with a fine layer of the white stuff.

'Is that all? We've been driving for nearly an hour.' Seren was starting to worry. If an hour's drive had only got them seven miles... 'Will we go any faster in the truck?'

Daniel pursed his lips. 'No. And I don't think it's a good idea to go much further. We could end up getting stuck. If you leave the van here, we can come back for it tomorrow, in the daylight and when they've had a chance to clear the roads.' He wiped a gloved hand across his wet face.

'So what do you suggest we do?' A flicker of panic licked at her mind, like a flame curling around a log.

'According to my satnav there's a village up ahead with a pub, and I've had a quick look on my phone and it says they serve hot meals and have rooms available. Let's hope they're not fully booked, because I don't fancy spending the night in the truck.'

Seren regarded him with concern, noticing the tightness around his eyes and mouth. For the first time since they'd hastily packed Dippy up as the twirling flakes had turned first into a flurry, then into a blizzard, she realised he was more worried about the situation than he'd let on.

'OK, let me grab the takings.' Seren switched the engine off and hauled herself out of the driver's seat and into the back of the van, quickly checking that everything was secure. There wasn't much else she could do, so after having a swift look around, she picked up the cash tin and got out.

Immediately the wind hit her, dashing fat white flakes into her face, and she staggered.

Daniel grabbed hold of her, pulling her close. Seren leant into him, garnering strength from his solidity as he walked her around the passenger side. The snow was already ankle-deep and drifting in places, the road ahead merging with the verges. The hedges lining either side of the road at least gave some indication of where the road was, and Seren was relieved she was no longer behind the wheel – she didn't think her nerves could stand it.

Walking gingerly, thankful that her fur-lined boots protected her feet from the worst of the cold, she clung to Daniel as he opened the door to the truck and helped her climb inside.

Brushing the snow from her shoulders, she realised her lashes were wet with flakes (or tears), and she used her scarf to wipe her face as Daniel started the engine.

'OK?' he asked, and she nodded, too choked up to speak. If he hadn't been here, she didn't know what she would have done, because immediately as the truck pulled off she could sense how grippier its bigger tyres were on the slippery road, and how much more substantial a vehicle it was compared to Dippy.

Poor Dippy, she was designed for sunshine and hot tarmac, not for blizzards and ankle-deep snow.

'I'm so glad you came,' she said to Daniel, as she gazed at the rapidly obscured van in the wing mirror. They'd only gone a short distance and already Dippy was barely visible. 'I'd have been stuck, otherwise.' She shuddered at the thought of spending the night in the van.

'If I hadn't been here, you wouldn't have attempted to drive home,' he pointed out.

True… They'd made the decision together to risk the journey, but if she had been on her own, she would have found a B&B and wouldn't have dared set foot on the road.

'Who knew it would come down so fast?' she said. 'One minute there were a few odd flakes, the next it was a whiteout.'

Daniel was concentrating hard, leaning forward, his eyes glued to the winding ribbon of smooth snow between the hedges, which Seren hoped was the road. 'You looked very cute with your tongue stuck out. What do snowflakes taste like?' he asked.

'Didn't you catch snow on your tongue when you were a kid?' She realised he was trying to distract her, but she wasn't fooled – she could tell that he was getting more worried by the second. But she played along anyway, grateful for the attempt at normality.

'I don't think so,' he said.

'They taste of winter,' she said. 'And childhood.'

He was about to say something else when the truck's headlights illuminated a sign and he let out a sigh of relief. 'We're here. The pub should be just around the… There it is!'

'The White Hart,' she read, seeing the yellow glow of lights through the pub's windows spilling into the darkness.

Except, it wasn't totally dark. The sky was that strange shade of greyish yellow it got when it was laden with snow, and the white stuff on the ground meant that it would have been possible to see where you were going even without the streetlights.

As Seren got stiffly out of the truck and stretched her tension-taut limbs, she saw that the flakes were coming down less heavily than earlier.

'Don't even think it,' Daniel said, taking her hand and pulling her towards the pub's entrance. 'Even if it stops completely, the roads will still be blocked.'

'I suppose you're right,' she said. 'It's just that I've got work tomorrow.'

'They'll have to do without you,' Daniel said as they stepped inside a small porch.

Warmth and a delicious smell of food hit her, and Seren felt herself relax a little. Even if the pub didn't have any rooms for the night, at least they could have a decent meal. They'd worry about being turned out onto the street later. For now, all she wanted to do was to warm up, have a sip of brandy (purely for medicinal purposes) and take a gander at the menu.

Daniel had other ideas. 'Excuse me, do you have two rooms available for tonight?' He was speaking to a middle-aged woman behind the bar who was pulling a pint of creamy dark ale.

She placed it in front of a man who looked as though he'd been there for a while, judging by the colour in his cheeks and the bleariness of his eyes.

'Cheers,' the bloke said, lifting his pint and taking a deep swallow.

The barmaid frowned. 'I'll have to roll him home at this rate, and it's not seven o'clock yet. What's it like out there? Still snowing?'

'I think it's easing off a little.'

'Got caught in it, did you?'

'Just a bit. I think we're stuck here for the night, if you can put us up?'

The woman pulled a face. 'I dunno. We stopped letting rooms out over a year ago. Too much hassle.'

Daniel blew out his cheeks. 'Is there anywhere else in the village?'

'Not that I know of.'

'OK, thanks anyway. We'll just have to make the best of sleeping in the truck.' Daniel put his arm around Seren and murmured, 'We'll be fine. I'll keep the engine running, so we should be warm enough.'

'You can't sleep in a truck,' the barmaid said. 'You'll freeze to death. Let me see what I can do. We knocked most of the bedrooms into one to make a function room, and the one we didn't is full of spare tables and stuff. Wait here.'

She went to walk away, but before she did Daniel asked, 'Can we have a look at the menu?'

She gave him two, then disappeared through a doorway, so Seren made her way to a table by a log burner. She intended to absorb all the warmth she could while she could, before they were turfed out at the end of the evening.

Taking her layers off, she sat down and stretched out her feet to the fire to toast her toes, then she checked out her surroundings.

The pub was a lovely olde-worlde, flag-stoned, wooden-beamed affair, with stone walls and tapestry style soft furnishings. The bar was dark polished wood and behind it an impressive selection of bottles glittered, the light of several table lamps reflecting off them. The place looked clean and welcoming, and if the smells from the kitchen were any indication, the food would hopefully be tasty and filling. Seren had the feeling they were going to need a substantial meal inside them if they were to get through the night without freezing to death.

Daniel still looked worried, even though he was doing his best not to show it, and it was that which troubled her more than anything.

'What do you fancy?' he asked, his eyes on the menu. 'I think I'll go for the steak and ale pie.'

'Make that two,' Seren said. 'And chips. It's got to be chips.'

'Wine?'

'Better not.' It was tempting to have a glass, but if she was going to be in such close proximity to Daniel all night she wanted to keep a clear head.

Daniel had just got to his feet and was about to go to the bar to order, when the landlady approached.

'I've had a word with my husband,' she said, 'and we can't in all conscience let you sleep in your van tonight. Did you say you wanted two rooms? If so, one of you can have the spare room, and the other can sleep in our son's room. He's phoned to say he's staying at his girlfriend's house. It's a bit of a tip – I usually just shut the door on it, to be honest – but I can put some clean sheets on the bed and give it a quick tidy. Is that OK?'

'Thank you, that's very kind—' Daniel began, but Seren interrupted.

'We don't need two rooms,' she said quietly. 'We don't want to put you out.'

She was looking at the landlady, not at Daniel but she could see his reaction out of the corner of her eye. Shock, hope, desire… they all flashed across his face.

'You don't have to do this,' he said. 'You can take the spare room and I'll—'

'I want to.' Seren was firm.

'Ahem.' The landlady cleared her throat. 'So it's just the one room, is it? And will you be wanting breakfast? I can do you a full English. You'll probably be needing it.' Her smile was warm and knowing.

Seren blushed – she certainly hoped so.

'Are you sure about this?' Daniel asked after the landlady had taken their order, along with a promise to find them a couple of toothbrushes and some toiletries.

Her tummy fizzed in anticipation and her appetite abruptly fled, to be replaced by a different kind of hunger. It might be unorthodox, but it felt right: romantic, even. Trapped by a snowfall, seeking shelter for the night, thrown together and giving in to their attraction to one another...

'I've never been so sure about anything in my life,' she said.

His gaze bored into hers and she shivered at its intensity. All she wanted to do was to drag him upstairs and ravish him.

'Here you go,' the landlady said, putting their drinks on the table. 'As soon as you're ready I'll show you to your room. Goodness, this is just like the old days. I've missed saying that.'

She pottered off and the spell was broken. For the moment, at least.

'I'm just going to wash my hands,' Daniel said, getting to his feet.

Seren watched him walk away, admiring his broad shoulders, his trim waist, and long legs, and not for the first time she wondered what he'd look like without any clothes on.

She was going to find out later...

Taking a deep breath, she rooted around in her bag for her phone, and called her father, noting that she had hardly any charge on her phone, although if she was quick, she'd probably have enough to call work in the morning.

'I've been worried,' her dad said as soon as she told him where she was and that she'd be staying the night (but not that she'd be spending it in Daniel's arms). 'Are you sure you're going to be all right on your own?'

'I'll be fine. I'll let you know what's happening in the morning. Could you do me a favour? I was supposed to be visiting Aunt Nelly this evening, can you let her know I won't be there? Although she probably wouldn't be expecting me what with all the snow.'

'It's not been too bad here. Just a covering on the pavements and the roads are mostly clear. I'll pop in and see her instead, on my way to skittles.'

'Thanks, Dad. Give her a kiss from me and tell her I love her.' Seren noticed Daniel had returned to the table. 'Got to go. Love you.'

She met Daniel's eye and blushed. Putting her phone away, she wondered how she was going to face her dad tomorrow after spending the night with this gorgeous man.

But when Daniel reached across the table and took her hand, she found she didn't care. The only thing on her mind was Daniel.

–

Daniel suspected that if he grinned any wider his face might turn inside out. But he couldn't help it; he was so happy this morning that he could burst.

'Come here,' he said, holding his hand out to Seren, who had just got out of bed.

'I thought I'd have a quick shower.'

'After,' he insisted.

'After what?' she teased, catching her bottom lip between her teeth and smiling at him provocatively from under her sweeping lashes.

God, she was gorgeous. He couldn't get enough of her. Nor she of him, if last night had been anything to go by. They'd hardly slept a wink, yet he felt as fresh and as alert as if he'd had a solid eight hours.

She ignored his hand and walked across to the window, pulling the curtain aside. It was early, only just seven-thirty and still dark. 'It's pretty,' she said, peering outside.

'It most certainly is.'

'You can't see from— Oh.' She blushed when she realised he was referring to her and not the scenery beyond the window.

'Will you please come back to bed?' His voice was husky with desire and when he saw the answering flame in Seren's eyes, he groaned. 'What are you doing to me, woman?'

Seren slipped back into bed and as her searching hands found what she was hunting for, she murmured, 'This…' She nibbled his earlobe. 'And this… and this. Eek!'

Daniel pounced, and for a while neither of them said anything because there was no need for words, but when Seren's tummy rumbled as she snuggled against him under the covers afterwards, he knew it was time to make a move if they wanted any breakfast. He guessed she was as hungry as he was, so he reluctantly slid his arm out from underneath her and got out of bed.

'I think I'll have a quick shower,' he said.

'Fancy some company?'

'Not if I want to eat this morning. Can I take a rain check? I quite fancy seeing you all sudsy and bubbly.'

Seren sighed. 'I'm due at work in an hour, so I'd better give them a ring. Pamela isn't going to be happy.'

'It can't be helped,' he said. 'No one knew it was going to snow so much.'

'I suppose, although Pamela's not going to see it that way, especially since my dad said there was only a light dusting at home. She's not going to believe me.'

Daniel left her to her phone call while he had a shower, and by the time he'd finished she was sitting on the bed with a cross expression on her face.

'What's up?' he asked.

'Pamela. She practically accused me of lying. I feel like taking a photo and sending it to her.'

'You should.' He posed naked. 'You can tell her this is the reason why you can't go to work.' He waved an arm down the length of his body, and she giggled as he hoped she would.

'Stuff her,' she said. 'I feel guilty that I'm not at work when I should be because everyone else will have to take up the slack, but I'm not responsible for the weather, and I'm hardly ever off. I can't remember the last time I had a day off sick.' She stood up and lifted her chin. 'I'll just jump in the shower, then we can go down for breakfast.'

Daniel dressed, wishing he had a change of clothes, then he messaged his mum to tell her where he was. He'd turned his phone off last night, partly to conserve the battery and partly because he didn't want any interruptions, and when he switched it on again he saw he had a missed call from Miss Carruthers at Fernlea Manor.

He'd phone her back later. Right now the only thing he wanted to concentrate on was Seren and spending the rest of the day with her. Work could wait.

Breakfast was a cheerful affair, with Sally Prescott, the landlady, making a fuss of them, asking if they'd slept well (her knowing smile made Seren blush again, which Daniel thought was delightful) and plying them with more food than they could possibly eat.

'The main road is clear,' she told them when she brought them more toast, 'but the road through the village is still blocked. My husband said it should be clear by lunchtime, and you're welcome to stay until it is.'

Daniel looked at Seren, who shrugged. 'It's not as though we can go anywhere,' she said. 'Thank you so much for putting us up. What do we owe you?'

'Nothing.'

Daniel cocked his head to the side. 'You must let us pay you. For breakfast, at least. There's enough food here to feed an army.'

'It's my pleasure,' she said. 'If the B&B part of the pub was still a business, it would be a different matter. But it isn't. I was simply helping out a couple of people caught in the snow. Anyone would have done the same.'

'Not anyone,' Daniel argued. 'Look, take my card.' He removed his wallet from his pocket and handed the woman a business card. 'When you need the pub garden seeing to, give me a call. I owe you a favour, so let me repay it.'

Sally smiled. 'I'll do that. Now, eat up. More tea or coffee? Or how about another slice of bacon?'

Seren blanched and when Sally was out of earshot she said, 'If I eat any more, I think I might explode.'

'How about we go for a stroll in the snow and walk it off?'

'Great idea!'

'And you can help me dig the truck out,' he added, laughing when she pouted at him. 'I've got a couple of shovels in the back. I know how to show a lady a good time.'

Seren inched closer and whispered, 'You most certainly do,' then giggled when she saw heat steal into his face, reddening his cheeks.

'Minx,' he replied. 'I'm glad I wasn't a disappointment.'

'Actually, I am a bit disappointed,' she said, and his heart dropped until she added, 'I'm disappointed that we have to go home. Another night here would be fabulous.'

Wouldn't it just, he thought, then blushed again as images of last night (and this morning) surged through his mind. God, he would love to take her back to bed and… But no, that wouldn't do at all, not when their landlady was expecting them to leave as soon as they were able. And he did need to dig the truck out, as he'd noticed a decent drift had formed around the front wheels. He could probably drive it out as it was if he was careful, and he might have done so if he'd been on his own, but with Seren in the vehicle he didn't want to risk an accident, no matter how minor it might turn out to be.

He felt so protective of her, that if he could have driven both vehicles home to save her having to negotiate such treacherous conditions, he would have. But there was nothing for it – she'd have to drive hers and he'd have to drive his if they wanted to get home today.

First, though, they had to wait for the snowplough to do its work, and until then they might as well have some fun.

As soon as breakfast was over, the two of them togged up and ventured outside. In contrast to yesterday, the sky was a brilliant blue with not a cloud in it, and the low sunlight sparkled and shimmered on the snow. Already Daniel could see that it was beginning to melt, and the steady drip and gurgle provided the backdrop to the sounds the shovels made as they rasped against the tarmac.

Birds flitted from tree to tree, uttering the occasional tweet or twitter, but the rest of their little corner of the world was muffled and quiet.

Until, that is, Daniel was hit in the back of the neck by something cold and wet, and realised Seren had hurled a snowball at him.

'Right,' he growled, bending down to scoop up a handful of the white stuff and fashion it into a sphere. 'You asked for it.'

But before he could throw it, she'd flung another one at him, this time hitting him in the chest, before she ran away, slipping and skidding, squealing loudly as he chased after her.

By the time their snowball fight ended, both of them were breathless, damp and in dire need of a cup of something hot, so they retreated inside to dry off and warm up, and await the arrival of the snowplough.

'Thank you so much for putting us up,' Seren said to Sally later, when they were about to leave to fetch her van. 'We had a lovely time.' She even managed to say the words without any hint of double entendre, which Daniel wouldn't have been able to. As it was, he was forced to turn his childish snigger into a cough, earning himself a sharp look from Seren and a smirking one from Sally.

'Grow up,' Seren said, when they were outside.

'Says the woman who shoved a handful of snow down the back of my neck,' he retorted, and when he caught her eye, the pair of them collapsed in hysterics.

'I've had such a good time,' Seren said, when she could speak again. 'It was so romantic.'

'It was,' he agreed. 'Any regrets?'

'None whatsoever.' She sounded adamant, so he had to take her word for it.

It had felt so right, so perfect, making love to her. He'd never felt so connected to another person, and he simply knew she was the woman he wanted to spend the rest of his life with.

Chapter 23

Darn it, Daniel had meant to give Miss Carruthers a call yesterday, but his mind had been too full of Seren that he'd completely forgotten. He'd been shattered, too. After he'd dropped her off at her house, he'd gone home and had only intended to have a nap to recharge his batteries, but the darkness outside and his extreme state of tiredness had conspired to make him fall into such a deep sleep he hadn't woken until this morning.

Flustered, he'd shot out of bed, knowing he had to be somewhere. When he remembered he was supposed to be playing Santa at the Winter Wonderland, and realised he was going to be late if he didn't hurry, he groaned in frustration. The last thing he wanted to do today was to listen to loads of children telling him what they wanted for Christmas, but in the absence of any other work and because he was committed to this particular job, he had no choice. He was consoled by the knowledge that Seren would also be at work, so seeing her today wouldn't be an option anyway, as much as he would have liked to.

However, he was seeing her tomorrow – they were going to the cinema and he was hoping they would sit in the back row and canoodle like a pair of teenagers – so hopefully that would sustain him through the next few hours. Plus, he was meeting Tobias for a pint after work, so he was looking forward to that, too. He hadn't had a drink with a mate for ages, and a catch-up would be nice. It felt a little strange to think that Tobias had dated Seren before him, but they hadn't even kissed, so he didn't feel too bad about it. Besides, knowing Tobias, he'd have got through at least another two or three women since he'd taken Seren out, so it wasn't as though Daniel was stepping on Tobias's toes.

It might have been Seren's influence, or it might have been that he was getting used to being Santa, but halfway through the morning Daniel realised he was enjoying himself. Seren was right, there *was* something magical and uplifting about seeing the joy and wonder on the faces of the little ones. Their total and unwavering belief was heart-warming and rather endearing, and he could feel himself mellow and begin to enjoy the experience for the first time.

Maybe being Santa wasn't so bad if it brought so much joy to so many small children, he thought, as a little girl gave him the biggest smile and the jauntiest wave of the day so far, as she skipped out of the grotto, holding her present in one hand and her father's hand in the other.

Abruptly a pang caught him in the chest, and he wondered what Amelia was doing. He tried not to think about her too much, because doing so only made his heart ache. Last year, her giddy excitement had made Christmas so wonderful, and he'd loved seeing her glowing little face and her wide eyes as she hurtled downstairs on Christmas morning, skidding to a disbelieving halt when she'd spotted her previously empty stocking now bulging with presents. And he'd never forget her excited squeal of 'He's been! He's been!'

How he missed her. He'd never thought he could get so attached to a child who wasn't his, and it still hurt to think he'd never see her again.

Daniel glanced at the queue as he waited for the next child to be brought to see him and he almost fell off his plush gold chair in shock. He was missing Amelia so much, he was seeing her face superimposed on a girl of a similar age and the same hair colour who was—

Wait a sec – the woman standing by her side was Gina. Which meant he wasn't hallucinating, and that the little girl really *was* Amelia.

His heart simultaneously leapt for joy and plunged to the toes of his big, black boots.

It was a most disconcerting and uncomfortable feeling.

Blinking away an unexpected sting of tears, he tried to concentrate on the boy who had just been shown in, but it was difficult when his mind was focused on Amelia.

For the briefest of moments he considered saying he was unwell and beating a hasty retreat, but he couldn't be that cruel to the children who were lined up waiting to see him.

Instead, he took a calming breath, and waited with a dry mouth and a lump in his throat for Amelia's turn.

'Santa, this is Amelia and she's seven,' his elf for the day informed him, propelling the child and her mother forward.

Amelia was looking cute in a pink dress and with her hair in pigtails. They were messy and he remembered how she used to beg him to do her plaits for her because her mother didn't do them right, and his chest tightened in pain.

Gina also looked good, but then she usually did. She was an attractive woman and knew how to make the best of herself. Today she was dressed in brown suede boots with a matching handbag, and a long white coat. Her dark, almost black hair was piled on top of her head with tendrils curling around her face, she wore red lipstick, and her brown eyes were outlined with kohl. She was a head-turner, but pretty is as pretty does, as Edwin once said, and Daniel would have been mighty glad he had ended their relationship if it wasn't for her daughter.

Gina was scrutinising him sharply, but Daniel ignored her, keeping his attention firmly on the child standing by his knee, who didn't appear to have recognised him.

'Hello, Amelia, what would you like Santa to bring you?' Daniel asked gruffly, trying to disguise his voice. At seven, she still firmly believed in Father Christmas and Daniel would hate for her to guess it was him she was talking to and risk her being disillusioned (worst case scenario) or confused (better, but still not ideal). He didn't care a jot if Gina recognised him (she did, he knew she did), but it was imperative that Amelia didn't.

Amelia hung her head and swung her arms, and Daniel couldn't decide whether she was shy or if something else was making her reticent.

'Didn't you say you wanted the Lego Ice Palace?' Gina prompted, her eyes continuing to scan Daniel's face.

'No.' Amelia whispered.

'Speak up, Santa can't hear you, can you Santa?' Gina inched closer and Daniel lowered his head, trying to hide his eyes, which was probably the most telltale part of him.

'Amelia, you said you wanted to see Santa,' Gina said, and Daniel could tell she was losing patience.

'You're not real,' Amelia announced abruptly, looking up at Daniel from underneath her lashes, and for a second Daniel thought he'd been rumbled.

But Amelia didn't look as though she knew it was him. She might just be testing the theory because of something she'd heard in school or seen on the TV.

'Are *you* real?' he countered.

She nodded and stared at the floor.

'If you are real, then I must be real, too.' He'd been advised not to lie outright and claim to be the real Santa when asked the question, and he'd been given a couple of pointers on how to deal with it, should it come up, which it did surprisingly often.

'If you are real, you'll bring my daddy back,' Amelia said, and Daniel flinched as though he'd been struck.

'Amelia, your daddy doesn't want to come back,' Gina said. 'He doesn't love us any more.' She was examining him keenly, and Daniel realised she wasn't fooled. Gina had known from the start that it was him under the Santa disguise. She grasped her daughter's arm. 'If you're not going to tell Santa what you want, then there's no point in you being here.'

The elf handed Daniel a present for him to give to Amelia, but the child backed away, so Gina snatched it out of his hands, muttering, 'I might as well get something for my money.'

Then they were gone, leaving Daniel shaken and upset.

Fancy telling little Amelia that he didn't love her, because he didn't doubt that the daddy Amelia had referred to was *him* – that was what she'd started to call him before he'd discovered Gina in the arms of the child's biological father.

Never again, he vowed silently. Never again would he become involved with a woman who was also a mother – because he didn't think he could face breaking another child's heart. Or his own.

'What are you smiling about?' Nicole tapped Seren on the shoulder, making her jump.

'Nothing…' Seren had been daydreaming about Daniel when she should have been concentrating on her job. Pamela would have her guts for garters if she caught her slacking.

'Don't give me that. How did yesterday go? And why are you blushing?' Nicole persisted.

Seren lowered her head to the ticket machine and tried to compose her face into a less smug expression, as she continued pricing up some clementines.

'Seren…' Nicole warned. 'I won't go away until you tell me what's going on.'

'You know there was a bit of snow on Thursday?'

'Yeah, so?' Nicole frowned.

'There was loads at the market I was at. It came down really fast and I couldn't get home.'

Nicole gasped. 'That's awful! What did you do?'

'I tried to get back and got stuck just outside a village about twenty miles away, so I stayed the night in a pub.' She paused dramatically, then added, 'With Daniel.'

Nicole's squeal made Seren wince, and she hurriedly looked around to make sure no one was keeping tabs on her. She'd seen Pamela briefly as she came in, but not since, and Seren was staying out of her way. The less she saw of her manager, the better.

'You didn't!' Nicole said, lowering her voice in response to Seren's shushing. 'How was it?'

'Wonderful,' Seren replied, dreamily.

'I'm so pleased for you.' She gave Seren a quick hug, and as she did so, she whispered, 'I want all the details.'

'Oh, no, I'm not telling,' Seren said, pulling away and scanning the bar code on a six-pack of yoghurts.

'Spoilsport. You do know that although Aaron and I live together, with him working all hours I have no love life, so I live vicariously through you.'

'Ha! That's a laugh, I don't have one either.'

'Until now,' Nicole pointed out and Seren grinned.

'He's so lovely,' she sighed. 'And it was so romantic. I'll give you a ring later and we can have a catch-up.'

'Not seeing lover-boy tonight?'

'I'm working until ten, so he's going out with a friend.' Seren checked the time, disappointed to see she still had another three hours to go until she finished her shift. 'Will that be too late?'

'Nah, I'll still be up. Aaron is off to work soon, so I thought I'd pop out for a bottle of wine and some crisps while I had the chance. I left him reading Freya yet another bedtime story. She's so wound up about Christmas it's taking ages to get her off to sleep, so I told him he can take a turn while I came out for some light relief.'

'You call coming to the supermarket on a Saturday evening "light relief"?' Seren was incredulous.

'It is when you've been forced to read the same story four times in a row. Your goddaughter is a tyrant.'

A movement at the end of the aisle caught Seren's eye and she saw Pamela heading purposefully towards her. 'Oops, you'd better scarper. Pamela's on the warpath.'

'Seren, I need a word with you. In my office,' Pamela snapped.

Nicole sent Seren a sympathetic look, while putting two fingers up to the woman behind her back.

Seren tried not to laugh. Nicole was so naughty – which was where Freya got it from. She gave her friend a little wave, then turned to follow Pamela's retreating back. No doubt she was in for a telling off about yesterday. Seren would just have to bite her lip and let Pamela get it out of her system. After all, there was nothing her manager could do about it. Being snowed in and unable to get to work was hardly a sackable offence.

'Take a seat,' Pamela instructed, as she closed the door behind Seren, her expression grim.

Seren sat, unaccountably nervous.

'I've had some disturbing news,' Pamela began, then paused.

'Oh?' Seren noticed a smudge of mascara below the woman's brow, and she looked at her mouth instead. Pamela's lips were a thin line and her jaw was tense.

'Contrary to popular belief, I'm a fair person. I wouldn't ask anyone to do anything I'm not prepared to do myself. Which is why I refused the offer of HR to sit in on this meeting.'

'HR?' Seren floundered. 'Why would they want to sit in on a meeting about me missing a day's work because of bad weather?'

'That's not what this is about. This is a preliminary meeting to inform you that you are being suspended for gross misconduct. There will be a formal hearing to which you will be invited, and you can bring your union rep, or a friend, or a colleague if you wish. HR will be present at that, as will I.'

Seren's mouth hung open as she tried to take it in, then she closed it, and swallowed nervously, her mouth dry, tears pricking her eyes. 'What did I do?'

She honestly couldn't think of any reason why she would be accused of gross misconduct. She hadn't stolen anything, not threatened anyone, heck, she'd not even had bad words with anyone. She wasn't under the influence of anything – paracetamol for a headache didn't count – and neither had she refused to do anything asked of her, or breached health and safety regulations as far as she knew.

'There are two reasons. One of them is the setting up of a competing business, and the other is bringing the organisation into serious disrepute. Do you, or do you not, operate a mobile gift van?'

'A travelling gift shop. Yes.'

'And do you deny telling one of our valued customers that "they" – meaning this supermarket – doesn't sell anything as nice as the items you sell?'

'Yes, but—'

'Then I'm afraid I have no choice but to suspend you. Without pay. With it being only ten days to Christmas I highly doubt there will be a hearing until the new year. I'm sorry, Seren, but you leave me no choice. Please make sure you remove any personal items from your locker, and I'll need your staff badge. HR will be in touch in due course. Do you have any questions?'

Seren's mind was empty. She seemed to have lost the ability to think.

Mindlessly, she unpinned her badge and placed it on the table, then took the key fob which gave her access to the staff areas out of her pocket and put that on the table too. An image of a cop handing over his badge and his gun popped into her mind, and she felt like laughing.

She felt like crying, too, and if she opened her mouth to ask a question she didn't know which sound might come out of it.

Without saying a word, she got numbly to her feet and walked to the door. Pausing to look over her shoulder as she put her hand on the handle, she felt she should say something in her defence, but she couldn't. Because what Pamela had said was true – she had done what she'd been accused of and there was no point in denying it.

She kept her head down as she went into the mercifully empty staff room and cleared her locker. Leaving the key in it, she put on her coat, her scarf and her hat, then made her dazed way onto the shop floor and went outside, ignoring the curious glances of her co-workers. They'd find out what had happened soon enough.

Blinking back tears, she forced herself to put one foot in front of the other as she walked slowly home.

Too ashamed – no one in her family had ever been sacked before – she fleetingly considered phoning Daniel, but she was too upset to speak to him.

It was going to be bad enough telling her father when she got home.

She knew she should never have listened to him and Aunt Nelly. She should have insisted her father put the ice cream van up for sale the minute she'd got it home. But no, she'd become swept up in his enthusiasm and had done something she shouldn't have done – she'd spent all her savings on having the blasted thing renovated. And she hadn't even paid for the work Tobias had done yet!

She wanted to wail at her own stupidity, but she had to get home first before she broke down.

What an absolute fiasco – no savings, no job, and little prospect of getting another since the company was hardly likely to give her a glowing reference. They probably wouldn't give her a reference at all.

There was only one good thing to come out of all this, one light in the darkness that her life had suddenly become, and that was Daniel. Because if her dad hadn't bought the van, and if she hadn't taken it to Tobias to be converted, then she never would have met Daniel.

Falling in love with him *was* the best thing to have ever happened to her.

Chapter 24

'They can't do that,' Seren's father said, a look of horror on his face after Seren finished telling him what had happened, her voice a monotone.

He'd been out when she'd arrived home and immediately the front door had slammed shut behind her, she'd rushed upstairs, thrown herself on her bed and had burst into noisy tears.

Now all she felt was drained and disheartened.

Patrick put his arms around her and she snuggled into him, smelling his familiar aftershave, the one he always wore. It never failed to make her feel safe and secure, and she knew that whatever happened she had a roof over her head and a father who loved her.

'They can do that, Dad, and they did. Pamela would have made sure she did it by the book, and with HR involved...' She trailed off.

'What did Daniel say?'

'I haven't spoken to him.' Seren didn't want to speak to him just yet. She felt too raw, too emotional to explain it again, even though she knew he would be supportive and sympathetic. 'Everything had been going so well,' she sniffed, tears threatening to fall again, despite having cried bucket loads earlier.

'I know, my love, I know.' Her dad stroked her hair, holding her close, the way he'd done when she was little and had fallen over or someone had upset her. 'It'll be all right.'

'It won't.' She was adamant. 'It'll be impossible to get another job without a reference.'

'Do you need another job?' He leant back a little and wiped her cheek with his thumb.

'Of course I do. What am I going to live on?'

'Aside from the fact that you live here and I won't see you go short of money, you've got the van.'

'Ah, yes, the van; the source of all my troubles. If it wasn't for that van, I'd still have a job.'

'A job you don't like,' her dad observed.

'That's beside the point. A job is a job, and now I've not got one. I should have known it would end in tears.'

'I'm sorry, I should never have agreed— Should never have bought it for you. I blame myself.'

Seren sighed heavily. 'I could always have said I didn't want it. And I would have done if I'd known the trouble it would cause, but hindsight is a wonderful thing. You're not to blame.'

'Neither are you. I've got a good mind to go down there and give that Pamela a piece of my mind.'

'It won't do any good, Dad. If anything, it'll make things worse. I'll just have to suck it up and hope I find something else soon and that my new employer won't ask for a reference.'

'You don't need to look for anything just yet,' her father persisted. 'You've got the van, and it could give you a nice little income if you work at it. Look at it this way, you losing your job means you've got more time to grow your business. January might be a slow month, but you can spend the time looking into other markets, like weddings and baby showers.'

Despite herself, Seren smiled. 'What do you know about baby showers?'

'I've read about them.' He kissed the tip of her nose. 'Let's have a nice cup of tea, shall we?'

Seren followed him into the kitchen like a lost puppy. 'The van was only meant to be for Christmas,' she said.

Patrick shot her an astonished look. 'Did you think your—' He stopped and shook his head '—that I spent all that money buying you a van, for you to only use it at Christmas?'

'Yes, no... What I thought was, that I'd do the Christmas thing, then you could sell it on.'

'Don't you think the same principle applies during the rest of the year? People don't just buy gifts at Christmas.'

'I know, but I've got a full-time job already and—' She bit her lip and amended, '*Had* a full-time job.' Tears threatened again and she blinked hard. Crumbs, she was such a mess. The only thing that wasn't a mess was her love life. And her relationship with her dad. Everything else was all to pot, as Aunt Nelly liked to say.

'What will Aunt Nelly think?' Seren said. 'She'll be so disappointed in me.'

Patrick looked shocked. 'I don't think she'll be disappointed at all,' he said slowly. 'She never thought that supermarket was the right place for you. That's why—' He hesitated.

'Why, what?'

Her dad frowned and screwed up his face, but he didn't say anything further and Seren guessed he didn't want to hurt her feelings.

'Never mind,' she said, letting him off the hook, and she caught the expression of relief on his face. 'I'm not looking forward to telling her, but I suppose I'll have to. I'll go visit her soon.'

Patrick handed her a steaming mug. 'Drink that, you'll feel better.'

Seren didn't think so. A cup of tea was nice, but it wasn't going to magic away the last few hours. She was still facing the sack for gross misconduct.

She shuddered when she considered those words. In her mind they were associated with things like theft, or sexual harassment, or bullying: not for having a little hobby on the side.

But *was* it a hobby? In all honesty, she didn't know. For her to have spent the kind of money it took to convert the van into what she wanted, it definitely wasn't a hobby, but at the time she thought she'd have the luxury of a secure job to fund it. And she had to admit, it was doing well so far. She hadn't made anywhere near enough profit to make any dent in replacing what she'd shelled out for the renovation, but at least she *was* making a profit. Even with having to cut short the market on Thursday (a warm glow engulfed her at the memory), she'd still made a decent amount of money.

Maybe her dad was right in that she did now have the time to devote to it, although it was a bit late for this Christmas, considering it was already the fifteenth of December and there was only one more shopping weekend to go until the big day. If she worked fast, though, she might be able to arrange to visit a couple more care homes and even a market or two.

Feeling a little more positive, she sent Daniel a quick message saying she was thinking of him. There was no point in phoning him now because he was meeting Tobias for a drink. She'd tell him all about it tomorrow, and by then she'd hopefully have a plan for her travelling gift shop, which would take her beyond Christmas and into the new year.

–

It was the end of a long day and Daniel had never felt so relieved in his life to be able to rid himself of the blasted Santa suit and walk to the pub. He was due to play Santa at the mall again next Saturday, so he'd left his outfit there because he had nothing else lined up between now and then, which saved Tobias from spotting it and giving him a ribbing.

Daniel was early, so he got a round in, took the drinks to a free table and checked his messages while he waited, smiling to himself when he saw one from Seren, saying she was missing him. He was missing her too, and he pinged the same message back along with a red heart emoji. Neither of them had said the 'L' word yet, but he thought it was only a matter of time and, after the night they'd spent together, telling her he loved her was more of a formality, because he was pretty sure she'd guessed how he felt. And, as she still wanted to be with him, he hoped she felt the same way.

He'd downed half of his drink and was thinking he'd better take it easy because he didn't want to have a hangover tomorrow, when Tobias showed up.

'Ta, mate,' his friend said, taking a deep draught, then wiping his mouth with the back of his hand. 'I needed that. I've had a shit day.'

'I know the feeling.'

'What's up?'

'I'll tell you in a minute, but before I forget, do you remember that conversion you did on the ice cream van?

For a woman called Seren?' He thought he'd best come clean and tell Tobias he was seeing Seren, and he hoped it wouldn't lead to any awkwardness between them.

'How could I forget?'

'Yeah, she is lovely, isn't she?'

Tobias said, 'I thought so. Simple lines, elegantly done. What about it?'

It took Daniel a second to realise Tobias was referring to the van and not Seren. 'I've been seeing Seren. As in, we're dating.'

'You dark horse! Good for you, mate.'

'Anyway, she asked me to remind you she hadn't had an invoice from you. That's not like you – you're usually on the ball when it comes to getting paid. Are you being charitable in your old age?'

'Not bloody likely! The bill's been paid, mate. I wouldn't have let her take the van out of the garage if it hadn't.'

'But I'm sure she said—'

'There's a story behind this.' Tobias leant forward, his forearms on his thighs. 'You were there when I got that call from that chap saying he wanted an ice cream van converted? That was Seren's dad. He bought it for her without telling her first.'

Daniel nodded – he knew all this. 'So?'

'It wasn't *him* who bought it. It was her aunt. Or *his* aunt… Anyway, it was some relative of hers who bought it. She paid for the work to be done, too. But Seren isn't supposed to know.'

'Why not?' Daniel was taken aback.

'Some old-fashioned idea about not handing it to her on a plate. That if Seren thinks she has to pay for it herself, she'll appreciate it more.'

Daniel could see the logic in that, but it put him in a difficult position and he wished Tobias hadn't told him. How was he going to keep it secret from Seren? He'd told her he was seeing Tobias this evening – she was bound to want to know if he'd remembered to ask him about the money she owed him. Or thought she owed him.

'I had a job trying to keep a straight face when I saw her the other day and she asked me about it,' Tobias continued. 'It's a good thing she had her kid with her; the kid kept saying she was hungry and distracting her. If it wasn't for that, I might have given the game away. I told her it was in the post.' He slapped his thigh and cried, 'Ha! That old chestnut – but it's usually the cheque's in the post, not the blimmin' invoice.'

Daniel froze; his mind had gone blank when he'd heard the words 'her kid'.

Tobias downed the rest of his drink. 'Are you OK, mate? You look a bit pale. What you need is another pint. Same again?'

Wordlessly Daniel handed him his empty glass. He had a feeling one pint wasn't going to be enough. A pub's worth of pints mightn't be enough.

Maybe he'd misheard…?

Praying he was mistaken, he waited impatiently for Tobias to come back from the bar, and as soon as he was within earshot Daniel said, 'Are you sure about Seren having a child?'

'I'm not blind and I'm not deaf. She definitely had a kid with her. A girl. She called Seren mummy.' Tobias shuddered. Daniel knew he wasn't too keen on children and avoided them at all costs. 'Didn't you know? Aw, sorry, mate. I shouldn't have said anything. I know how much Gina's kid meant to you, but it didn't occur to me that—'

'How old?' Daniel broke in, woodenly.

Tobias shrugged. 'No idea. About this high.' He held his hand up to his hip before he sat down and took a sip of his fresh pint.

Quite young, then. 'Four, five, six?' Daniel hazarded a guess.

'There or thereabouts.'

Daniel screwed up his face. Did it matter how old Seren's daughter was? The fact was that she had one and she hadn't thought fit to tell him.

Suddenly everything fell into place: on several occasions when he'd either picked her up or dropped her off he'd got the impression he was being watched. Then there was that cardboard angel he'd noticed on the workbench in her shed when she'd shown him how to make a wreath, that had clearly been made by a child, and Seren had shoved it to the side when she'd realised he'd noticed it.

And what about the phone call she'd made from the pub when they were snowed in? Was that only two days ago? Suddenly it felt like a lifetime. As he'd returned to the table she'd ended the call, but not before he'd heard her say, 'Give her a kiss from me and tell her I love her.' She must have been talking about her daughter.

Not only that, but she'd never once invited him back to her place. It hadn't occurred to him to think it odd because they'd always been out, or they'd gone to his. On looking back, it did seem a little strange, but he hadn't thought so at the time – they'd only just reached the kissing stage – and if he'd thought about it at all, he'd have concluded that Seren might think that if she invited him to her house it might give him the impression that she wanted to take their relationship to the next level.

He snorted. They'd done that all right. Several times. And it had been marvellous and wonderful, and…

Unable to believe he'd been so stupid, he inhaled slowly and closed his eyes, leaning his head on the back of the padded bench and wishing he could turn the clock back.

When he opened them again, it was to see Tobias at the bar chatting to two young women, and a sharp stab of envy lanced him in the chest.

Why couldn't he be more like Tobias – playing the field without a care in the world, and not bothering who he hurt in the process.

But that wasn't him, that wasn't who he was.

Even as he knew he'd have to end it with Seren, his heart bled. He understood the reasons why she hadn't introduced him to her daughter – or he could guess – and he didn't blame her. If he had a child, he would want to be careful who he let into his or her life, and he'd also want to be certain that person was going to stick around. But for Seren not to *tell* him?

If she had, he would have walked away— Maybe she'd suspected that he would? Had the very same thing happened to her in the past? Not every man wanted to have a ready-made family. How many men had shied away from her on learning that she had a child, without even bothering to get to know her?

To his shame, he realised he was in that category, but not because he disliked children or wouldn't consider raising another man's child – if he hadn't become involved with Gina, then he would happily continue to date Seren knowing she had a daughter.

But not now. Not after what Amelia had gone through. Was *still* going through.

He couldn't do that again, and especially not after today.

He wanted to be angry at Seren for deceiving him but he couldn't, even though it might make dealing with it easier. Because no matter which way he cut it, his heart was breaking. He'd fallen passionately in love with her, and now he had to end it.

It was going to be the hardest thing he'd ever had to do.

Chapter 25

Daniel didn't want to wake up, but his phone was insisting he did. For a second, he considered ignoring it but when he checked the time and saw it was only eight o'clock a feeling of dread came over him. No one rang anyone this early on a Sunday morning unless it was bad news, and his first thought was for his grandad.

Trepidation making him clumsy, he snatched the phone off the bedside table and squinted at the number. It looked vaguely familiar, but it wasn't his mum or the care home – it was Miss Carruthers.

Sinking back onto his pillow, relief making him feel slightly weak (or was that due to the lack of sleep last night?) he croaked, 'Hello?'

'Is that Daniel Oakland?' The woman's voice was clipped, and she sounded cross.

'It is.'

'That's not the way to greet people. I could have been a customer. The last thing I want to do is to have to ask you who you are when you pick up the phone.'

'Sorry, Miss Carruthers.'

'You neglected to call me. I left a message.'

'Sorry,' he repeated. She had the effect of making him want to apologise for simply being alive. 'I've been busy.'

'Nonsense! You should never be too busy to answer your phone to a client. That's not the way to do business.'

'Sorry,' he said, for the third time.

'So you should be. Now, listen carefully: I have recommended you to someone of whom I think very highly, who is in need of a permanent gardener. Highfields House – have you heard of it?'

Dumbly Daniel nodded, before realising Miss Carruthers couldn't see him. 'Yes, I have.'

'Then you'll know what an excellent opportunity this is. Mr John, the head gardener, will phone you tomorrow. Please be polite. That is all. Goodbye.'

Daniel continued to hold the phone to his ear for several seconds, then he slowly lowered it, his mind reeling.

What had just happened? *Highfields House?* Gosh.

He should feel pleased, elated even, but all he felt was numb. His thoughts were too full of Seren and the way she had deceived him, to think about anything else.

OK, maybe deceived was too strong a word, but she had kept an incredibly significant and important piece of information about herself from him, and he knew he was being a heel to even think about ending their relationship just because she was a single mother, but for his own sake and sanity he didn't have any choice.

It was better to end it now, rather than have things progress to the point where her daughter became attached to him, only for the child to get hurt if everything fell apart.

Logically, he knew that Seren wasn't Gina, but after seeing his ex and Amelia yesterday and hearing the little girl say those words that cut him to the quick, there was no way he could even think of continuing to date Seren.

He might have fallen in love with her and she him (he hoped for her sake he was wrong about that because the last thing he wanted was to hurt her) but cutting Seren out of his life was for the best, no matter how much pain it caused him.

Last night had been horrendous. He'd made his excuses, leaving Tobias in the pub happily chatting up one or both of the young women, and he'd made his slow way home, his heart breaking.

If he'd realised Seren had a child, he would never have asked her out, and he blamed himself for not checking. But asking a question like that was hardly the done thing, and if he was honest, it hadn't even occurred to him – he'd assumed she would have mentioned a child at some point, and especially before they'd spent the night together. But she hadn't said a word. Not even a hint.

He'd lain awake most of the night, dwelling on how he was going to break the news to her that he didn't want to see her again. What would he say? 'Sorry Seren, but I don't want a relationship with you because you're a mother'? What kind of a man did that make him? Not a very nice one, clearly.

He'd have to give her some other reason, one that didn't make her feel awful about her being a single parent, one that didn't knock her confidence, and one that didn't make him out to be the worst of the worst.

Suddenly it came to him – *Highfields!* The place was a few hours drive away and it would be impossible to commute to it from Tinstone; it was the perfect reason to break off a relationship.

Daniel got out of bed, knowing he wouldn't be able to go back to sleep, despite having had only an hour and a half rest. After tossing and turning all night, his thoughts churning and his heart aching, sleep had finally been a blessed relief and he dearly wished he could sink back into its oblivion, but he knew he wouldn't.

He may as well get up and get on with his day. He was supposed to be taking Seren to the cinema this evening, with a bite to eat first. He'd pick her up as arranged and he'd tell her over dinner that it was over. It wasn't ideal and he felt sick thinking about it, but it was better than ending their relationship over the phone. She deserved to be told face to face, no matter how much he didn't want to do it. He was dreading seeing her reaction, knowing he was causing her pain, and if she accused him of dumping her as soon as he'd got into her knickers, then so be it.

–

'Not seeing your lady friend today?' Edwin asked when Daniel arrived to pick him up from the care home to take him to Linda's for lunch.

'She's working. We're going out to dinner this evening.'

'You don't sound very happy about it,' his grandad said, astutely.

'Sorry, I've got a lot on my mind.' Daniel didn't feel like confiding in either his grandad or his mum, although knowing how he felt about Amelia, they were probably the only people who would truly understand where he was coming from.

'Like what?' his grandad asked.

'I'll tell you over lunch.' Ever since he'd moved out of Gina's house and into the one he was currently renting, he'd made a point of having Sunday lunch with his mum and Edwin. Now that Edwin had gone to live in the care home, it seemed even more important the three of them continued to have at least one meal together.

How long that could continue once he'd told them his news about Highfields was another matter.

'Our Daniel has got something on his mind,' Edwin said to Linda, taking his usual seat at the small dining room table.

'Oh?' Linda turned her attention away from the green beans she was ladling onto Edwin's plate and looked at Daniel.

'I might have a job,' he said. 'Miss Carruthers has put in a good word for me with the head gardener at Highfields House.'

'What kind of a job?' His mother was surveying him intently.

'A permanent, salaried job.'

'Is that what you want?'

'It beats playing Santa Claus every Christmas. A place that big needs attention all year round,' Daniel said.

'Have you heard of Highfields House?' Linda asked Edwin, and Edwin shook his head.

'It's a stately home with one of the most impressive gardens in Britain,' Daniel explained. 'It would be an honour to work there. I haven't spoken to them yet though, so they might not give it to me. They've only got Miss Carruthers' word to go on.'

'Don't underestimate her. She's as formidable as Phoebe. They know each other from boarding school and their families go way back. Phoebe was telling me that Minty Carruthers was rumoured to have had an affair with one of the royals.'

'Really? Which one?'

'She wouldn't say, but all you need to know is that very often when it comes to getting positions in those types of places it's not what you know, but *who* you know. And Minty is well connected.'

'What kind of a name is Minty?' Edwin asked, helping himself to a fluffy Yorkshire pudding.

'Apparently, it's short for Arimenta,' Linda said.

'Good Lord, fancy saddling a child with that,' Edwin said, tucking into his lunch. 'I suppose shortening it to Minty is better than shortening it to Ari — sounds like Harry with the "h" missing.'

Daniel's thoughts flew to Amelia, and he wondered whether she or her friends would shorten her name in the future and if so what they would shorten it to, and it sent an ache through his chest to think he'd never know.

'What's the catch?' his mum asked, sitting down to enjoy her own plate of food.

'It's two hundred miles away,' Daniel said.

His mother put her fork down with a clatter. 'I see.' She looked downcast for the briefest of moments before her expression cleared, and he knew she was trying to be pleased for him.

Daniel continued brightly, 'The head gardener, a guy called Mr John, is going to phone me tomorrow, so hopefully he'll invite me down for an interview before Christmas. If I get it, it'll be nice to know I have a job to go to in the new year. I love being my own boss, but I can't be dealing with the lack of work during the winter months.'

'That's a shame. You've worked so hard to get your business off the ground,' Linda said.

'It's not enough, Mum.'

'I can see that. But you don't have to be Santa next year — I'm sure there are plenty of other seasonal jobs around in the run-up to Christmas.'

'Let him make his own mind up, Linda,' Edwin said. 'He's got to do what feels right for him, same as I had to. You didn't want me to move into the care home, but I'm happy there; so you have to let him sort his own life out.' His grandfather had one more thing to say, though. 'What about your young lady? I thought you were sweet on her, especially after the other night.'

'What other night?' Daniel asked; there was no way his grandad could know about that. Daniel hadn't told anyone he'd spent the night in a pub in the middle of nowhere with Seren because of the weather.

'That night you got stuck in the snow,' Edwin said.

'How do you know about that?'

'Nelly's nephew, your young lady's dad, told Nelly that Seren had got caught in a snowstorm the other night.'

'So?' Daniel was conscious of his mother's probing stare and he tried to ignore it.

'I might be old, but I'm not daft,' his grandad declared. 'Your mother told me you'd gone haring off to give your young lady a hand because she was on her own. It stands to reason you were with her when it started to snow. So I put two and two together.'

Dear God, was nothing private? 'And came up with the grand sum of mind your own business,' Daniel said, more sharply than he'd intended. 'She's not my young lady. Not any longer.'

'I knew there was something wrong. I could tell by your face. You can't fool me, Danny-boy.' Edwin shovelled a forkful of peas into his mouth and chewed noisily.

Linda put a hand on Daniel's arm. 'I'm sorry,' she said. 'I hope you're not too upset.'

'Not at all,' he lied, his heart constricting with the pain of what he had to do later. 'It's for the best. I'll be moving away and even if she didn't have a job here, she's got a young daughter and I doubt she'd want to uproot her. Besides, it's not serious – we haven't known each other very long.'

Edwin frowned. 'Are you sure? Nelly hasn't mentioned anything about Seren having a child.'

'I'm sure. Tobias saw Seren and her daughter in town the other night.'

Linda shot him a doubtful look. 'Why do I get the feeling you're not telling me everything? You might as well tell me now as later, because you know I'll get it out of you eventually.'

Daniel pressed his lips together – his mother had always been able to see straight through him. 'If you really want to know, my relationship with Seren isn't going to work out anyway, because she's got a kid, and I can't and I won't get involved with another woman who has children. Not after Amelia.' He blinked rapidly, but carried on, 'Gina brought Amelia to see Father Christmas yesterday, and do you know what Amelia asked for?' He swallowed, his throat raw with the ache of it. 'When Santa asked her what she wanted for Christmas, she said she wanted him to bring her daddy back. Me!' He jabbed himself in the chest. 'She meant *me*. I'm her daddy.' He drew in a shaky breath and let it out slowly. 'I *was* her daddy. I'm not any more.'

His mother let out a sob and dabbed at her eyes. 'Oh, Daniel, you must do what you think is best. I just want you to be happy,' she said, and Daniel bit his lip.

'So do I, Mum. So do I.'

–

Seren couldn't wait to tell Daniel her news. She'd been stewing over it since she'd left the supermarket yesterday and had been itching to tell him, but she wanted to do it face to face and not via a message, because she knew she'd be upset and she wanted to have his arms around her and tell her it would be all right, that it would all work out in the end. She briefly considered asking him to pop over, but she knew he was going to his mum's for lunch, and she didn't want to intrude on his family time, especially since she was going out for a bite to eat and the cinema with him later.

However, she knew something wasn't right as soon as she got into his truck and leant towards him for a kiss, because he turned his head a fraction, so instead of their lips connecting, her mouth landed on his cheek just above his jaw.

'Are you OK?' she asked, disquiet teasing at the edges of her mind as she wondered what could have possibly happened for him not to meet her eye. His jaw was clenched and his knuckles were white as they gripped the steering wheel.

'Fine,' he said. 'You?'

'Not really.' She pushed the faint alarm to the back of her mind. If he said he was fine, she had to believe him. 'I've got something to tell you.'

The glance he threw her was fleeting. 'I thought you might.'

She blinked, puzzled. He couldn't possibly have heard about her being sent home from work in disgrace. Unless…? Perhaps he'd called into the shop, expecting to find her there, only to be told she was suspended. But if that was the case, why wasn't he being more supportive?

'If you already know, I don't need to explain,' she said shortly, tears pricking at the back of her eyes.

'I've got something to tell you, too,' he said, his eyes on the road as he indicated to pull out onto the bypass. The cinema was in an out-of-town complex, as was the fast-food place they were intending to eat at.

Abruptly, he swerved into a layby, and Seren grabbed the edge of her seat for balance as she swayed to the side.

'I can't do this,' he said, coming to an abrupt stop. 'I'm sorry Seren, but this isn't going to work, me and you.' He was still staring straight ahead and refusing to look at her, and her stomach roiled in dread.

'What do you mean?' Her voice was a whisper.

'I've got another job.' His Adam's apple bobbed as he swallowed and she noticed his fingers tightening on the wheel even further, his white knuckles in stark relief to the black sleeves of his jacket.

'That's good, isn't it?' she said, trying to work out how him having another job could have anything to do with things not working out between them.

'It's two hundred miles away.'

'Oh.' So that was it. She looked up at the ceiling of the cab, willing herself not to cry.

They sat in silence for several long, awkward seconds.

'What does this mean for us?' she asked eventually, the tears she had tried so hard to hold back, trickling down her cheeks – because she knew the answer to her question. It was obvious from the expression on his face and the way he was behaving. He was ending it, and her heart was breaking.

'There can't be any us,' he said quietly.

Seren shook her head, refusing to believe what he was telling her. 'It's not too far,' she said. 'I can drive to you,

you can drive to me, we could meet halfway. Please don't throw what we have away. At least give it a chance. *Please.*' She hated to beg, but he was tearing her apart and she couldn't bear the pain.

'It won't work,' he insisted. 'It's too far.'

'It isn't. We can *make* it work.'

'No, we can't.' He turned his face away, staring at nothing on the opposite side of the street.

Seren was openly sobbing, tears dripping onto her coat, her voice thick with emotion. 'I thought we had something special? *Look at me.* Look me in the eye and tell me you didn't feel it, because I know you did.'

He slowly moved his head, his expression blank, his eyes hooded, and an awful thought occurred to her.

'You didn't feel anything for me at all, did you? God, I've been such a fool.' Her chin wobbled and she screwed up her face.

He'd obviously been out for one thing and one thing only – and she'd given it to him the night they'd been stranded by the snow. She let out a cry of despair and sniffed loudly, swiping at the tears on her face, as she fought to control herself. 'Take me home, please.'

Wordlessly Daniel put the truck in gear and turned it around.

Seren endured the short drive in silence, and when the vehicle came to a stop outside her house, she didn't look at him or say anything. She simply got out and stumbled onto the pavement.

The whine of the truck's window going down made her hesitate, but only for a second. Nothing he could say would annul the hurt he'd caused her, or make her feel better. It was clear he hadn't felt the same way about her as she had about him.

'Seren, I—'

'Don't. Just don't,' she called over her shoulder, and when she heard him drive away she made her slow, aching way up the front path and fell into the arms of the only man she could trust.

–

'I've been such a fool,' Seren said later the same evening. 'I never should have spent the night with him.'

Her dad flinched.

'Sorry, I know I shouldn't discuss my love life with you, but that's the truth of it.' She blew her nose noisily, and Patrick nudged the box of tissues closer to her.

She was sitting on one side of the sofa, clutching a cushion to her chest for comfort, and her dad was sitting on the other, the front of his shirt still bearing the splodges of mascara from where she'd sobbed into his chest.

'If I hadn't, I wouldn't have fallen so deeply, or be so hurt,' she added.

'I want to give him a damn good talking to,' Patrick said, his face tight. 'How dare he mess you about like this.'

Seren let out a shaky breath. 'It won't do any good, Dad, but thank you for the offer. What hurts more than anything is not knowing if he already knew about this job before we spent the night together.'

Patrick slapped his palm on the arm of the sofa. 'The little git. I could do time for him, I really could. I hate seeing you so upset.'

She gave a bitter laugh. 'I'm not too keen on it, either.' Blowing out her cheeks, she shook her head. 'What an awful weekend: first I get the sack – don't try to be nice about it, Dad, because we both know the hearing is only a formality – and then my boyfriend dumps me. What did I do to deserve this?'

'Come here.' Her dad shuffled closer and held out his arms, and she sank into them, the familiar solidity and sense of love and safety she always felt when her dad gave her a cuddle enveloping her. His support meant everything, and she didn't know what she'd do without it. Even if he couldn't make her feel better or take away the pain of Daniel's rejection, at least he was there for her, to provide hugs and a shoulder to cry on.

'It will be OK, you know,' he said, after she withdrew to wipe her eyes and blow her poor, sore nose yet again. 'You'll move on from this and one day it'll be a distant memory. When you've got a fleet of travelling gift shops to your name and you're happily married to the love of your life, you won't give this a second thought.'

Bless him, he was trying so hard to make her feel better, to give her hope for the future, but she couldn't shake the awful suspicion that the travelling shop business was a damp squib, and that she had already met the love of her life. Met him, loved him and lost him.

For once she wasn't looking forward to Christmas.

All in all, Seren thought, the next few days were going to be the worst of her life and she just wished she could go to sleep this evening and not wake up until all the festive madness was over.

Bah flipping humbug.

Chapter 26

Daniel should be excited about today, but he wasn't. Working somewhere as prestigious as Highfields House was a dream come true, but right now it didn't feel that way.

He was driving up the motorway, carrying with him a deep sadness in his heart and an ache in his soul that he hadn't been able to shift since Sunday, and which he guessed wasn't going to go away any time soon, even if Mr John offered him the job. Because his heart and head were trapped in the events of two days ago when he'd told Seren it was all over between them, and he'd had to watch her heart breaking in front of him and hear the anguish in her voice as she pleaded for him to give their love a chance.

When she'd accused him of never having had any feelings for her, he'd nearly given in to the pain in his own heart and begged her to forgive him for hurting her.

He loved her. Nothing was going to alter that. But he couldn't be with her, not when she'd kept such a vital piece of information from him.

The satnav informed him robotically that he should leave the motorway at the next junction, so he moved into the inside lane, his foot wavering on the pedal until he realised he was slowing down prematurely, so he sped up again.

His reluctance was telling. He didn't want to go for this interview. He didn't want the job, even though he would have given his right arm for a chance at it not so long ago.

Today it was as though all enthusiasm for life had been sucked out of him, leaving only empty despair, and it was his own fault.

For the past thirty-five hours and seventeen minutes, the only thing on his mind had been Seren and the way he'd treated her.

It was unforgivable.

He'd hardly slept for thinking about her. He'd not eaten more than a single piece of toast, and he'd had to force that down, and he'd never felt so miserable in his life.

He was missing her, goddammit. More than he'd thought possible. His arms ached to hold her, his lips yearned for her kiss, and his eyes burned to see her.

What a mess he'd made of it, and all because he'd allowed his bad experience with Gina to influence him. Seren was nothing like Gina, and the more he thought about it (and he'd done nothing *but* think about it), the less he was able to blame Seren for being cautious when it came to her daughter and a new boyfriend. The most significant thing was that she'd finally been about to tell him that she had a child, but he'd got in with what he wanted to say before she'd had a chance. He'd been so focused on his stupid vow to never again go out with a woman who had children, that he'd let it blind him.

He was in love with her, and he didn't care whether she had ten kids or none. It was Seren he wanted, and if that meant accepting her daughter and loving the child like he would his own, then so be it.

But he'd blown it.

There was no going back. Whether he was offered this job or not, how, in all conscience, could he go crawling back to Seren with his tail between his legs after the way he'd behaved? He'd let her believe this job was more important to him than she was, and he could hardly come clean and admit he'd dumped her because she had a child. If she didn't already hate him, she soon would when she knew what a jerk he was.

Which led Daniel right back to why he was on the way to an interview for a job he was fairly sure he didn't want. Putting Seren aside (yeah, he'd done that all right), even though this might be a dream job, he'd been his own boss for so long that he honestly didn't know whether he would be able to work under anyone again. Mr John had informed him on the phone that he'd be one of three other gardeners, plus there was an army of volunteers. He'd be one of many, being told what to do and when. No autonomy. No captain of his own ship.

If Highfields House was closer to home and he was the sole gardener, he'd jump at the chance, but as things stood…

Feeling even more of a heel because he knew he'd be going into this interview with no intention of taking the job should he be offered it and was therefore wasting everyone's time, as soon as he was off the motorway he found a suitable place to pull over.

'Hello, is that Mr John? It's Daniel Oakland here. Sorry to mess you about, but I've changed my mind about the interview. I was halfway to Highfields when I realised it's not for me.'

'Well, now, that is a pity. Miss Carruthers gave you a glowing recommendation.'

'I know, and I feel rather awful about it, but I don't want to waste your time. Maybe I'll pay a visit to your garden another time? I'd love to see it.'

'It's almost eleven o'clock. When you say you're halfway here, where exactly are you?'

'Um…' Daniel checked his satnav. 'About five minutes away.'

'Why don't you come now, and take a look. You've driven all this way, so it seems a shame to drive all the way back without having a tour of the garden.'

'That would be lovely! Thank you.'

What a nice chap, Daniel thought as he headed towards Highfields, feeling a little better about things. This was one thing he hadn't made a hash of, and although he fully expected Miss Carruthers to phone him and give him a piece of her mind, he'd take it on the chin. Mrs Williams would probably give him what for as well, but her bark had always been worse than her bite and once he explained how he felt, he knew she'd come round. Besides, what would she do without him to do her gardening for her? He chuckled out loud as he thought of her having to get her own hands dirty by doing her own weeding, and the sound surprised him. He was still feeling incredibly low, but not as bad as he'd felt when he'd set off this morning.

If only he could put things right with Seren… But that wasn't going to happen, so he tried not to think about her for the next two hours. Having a guided tour of Highfields by the head gardener was a once-in-a-lifetime opportunity, and he didn't want to waste it.

Despite his best intentions and although he found the gardens amazing and Mr John incredibly informative, Daniel could feel Seren's presence in the back of his mind and he knew it would be a very long time indeed before he got over her.

If he got over her at all.

–

With the day looming emptily before her, Seren decided to try to get herself out of the fug she was in by paying Aunt Nelly a visit. She hadn't seen the old lady for a while, mainly because firstly she'd been too busy, then since being sent home from work on Saturday she had been too ashamed. She'd spent all of yesterday lounging around the house feeling incredibly sorry for herself, and wishing Christmas was out of the way so she'd have a date for her meeting with HR. Once she'd attended that, she'd know for certain where she stood. Seren had a fair idea already, but until she was officially informed that she was being sacked for gross misconduct, she harboured the faint hope she'd have a reprieve.

In between obsessing over how her relationship with Daniel had gone so very wrong and wondering what he was doing now and whether he had given her any thought at all since he'd dumped her, she tried to decide what to do about the van. The sensible thing would be to sell it – hopefully for a high enough price so she and her dad could recoup the money they'd spent on it. Then she could at least replenish her depleted savings. Which weren't as depleted as they should have been because she still hadn't received Tobias's invoice, but once she'd paid him what she owed him her bank account would be empty.

She felt she didn't have any choice other than to persuade her dad to sell Dippy: she needed the money because it might be all she'd have to live on for quite some time if she failed to get another job quickly.

It was ironic, considering she'd spent most of Sunday (before Daniel had dropped his bombshell) on the internet, sending off emails to various organisers inquiring whether they had any slots for a stall in their market, and she'd even sent one to the organisers of the Winter Wonderland after her dad had persuaded her that being sacked might be the best thing to happen to her, career-wise. But her heart wasn't in it anymore. Daniel dumping her had been a blow to her heart, her confidence, and her belief in herself.

Not only that, whenever she set eyes on the blasted van, she'd always be reminded of him. She'd never forget him (no one forgot their first true love) but she didn't need the memory of him thrust into her face each time she looked out of the living room window and saw the van parked in the street.

With a sigh, she realised she'd have to contact all her lovely suppliers and—

Damn it! If she pulled out of the final event she was booked in for tomorrow, she'd be letting them down. They'd trusted her with their stock and had given it to her in good faith, and she felt an obligation to do the best she could for them – which meant manning her travelling gift shop for one last time.

Dragging her feet, Seren walked into the foyer of Aunt Nelly's care home and pressed the buzzer, giving the receptionist a wave as she waited for her to unlock the door.

'Nelly is in the day room,' she told Seren. 'Having a read. The mobile library came yesterday, and she's had her nose in a book ever since. Talking about mobile whatnots, your gift shop was a roaring success and many of the residents have asked if you'll be visiting us again in the new year. Cissy wants to buy a couple of little wedding things for her granddaughter's nuptials, and Dot has three birthdays, one after the other.'

'Oh, I'm... I haven't decided yet,' Seren said, caught on the hop. 'I'll let you know.'

'Brilliant. Thanks.'

Seren scuttled off, wishing she'd never set eyes on the blimmin' mobile library. If it hadn't appeared when it had, Seren would never have thought about a travelling shop and she wouldn't be in the mess she was in now.

Spotting Nelly huddled in a corner with an open book held up to her face, Seren went over to her and gave the old lady a kiss on the cheek.

'Seren, my darling girl, how lovely to see you. Fetch us a cuppa, then come and sit down.' Nelly closed the book and put it on a nearby table.

Seren blinked when she saw the title – *Effective Business Practices for Entrepreneurs*. She'd been expecting a whodunnit, or one of those medical romances her aunt loved so much.

'What on earth are you reading that for?' she asked.

'For you. So I know what I'm talking about when you ask for my help. Get the tea, there's a good girl, before I die of thirst. I might not want to be on this earth any longer, but I'd prefer to go quietly in my sleep and not because my great-niece couldn't be bothered to bring me a cuppa.'

Seren muttered 'For goodness' sake,' under her breath, but went to do as she was asked.

'I heard that,' Nelly called after her.

When Seren returned with the drinks, Nelly was on her feet and peering out of the window, holding onto the sill as her head turned this way and that. 'Where's the van?'

'Outside the house.'

'What's it doing there? You're not going to sell much if you leave it at home. Frequency and recency are important, my book says, if you want to build your brand. You've got to drive it; let people get used to seeing it around.'

'I don't want people to get used to seeing it. I want Dad to sell it. I've got one more market to attend, then that's it; no more van.'

'It's not just a travelling *Christmas* gift shop,' Nelly said, shuffling slowly back to her chair and letting Seren help her into it. Seren moved the walker out of the way, earning herself a sharp look. 'Make sure you put it where I can see it,' her aunt snapped, 'otherwise someone will filch it. They'll steal anything they can get their hands on. Someone nicked my glasses the other day.'

'Dad said you thought they'd been stolen but when he asked about them, the duty manager told him you'd left them in the dining room.'

Nelly scowled at her. 'Pass me my tea.'

Seren obliged, then straightened her shoulders as she prepared to share her news, but Nelly got in first by saying, 'You can't sell the van. I won't let you.'

Keeping her tone as gentle as she could, Seren said, 'I know I don't technically own it, but Dad bought the van for *me*. He'll sell it if I ask him to.'

'*He* didn't buy it. *I* did. And I'm not selling.'

Seren opened her mouth. Closed it. Then opened it again, but no words came out.

'Stop that, you look like a guppy. It's not a look you want to cultivate.'

Seren cleared her throat and tried again. 'I'm not sure I heard you right: I could have sworn you said *you* bought the van.'

'That's because I did. I told your father about my idea and when he found it on that Bay thing on the computer, I gave him the money to buy it. For *you*. But I thought you might get cold feet, so I told him he had to put my name on the papers.'

'The logbook?'

'I don't know what book it is, but it's got my name on it. Not yours, not your father's, *mine*. So there.'

Seren's initial reaction was shock, but as her aunt's words began to sink in, the shock began to turn to anger. She'd been manipulated by an old lady who had scant idea how tough it was out there, and who had tricked Seren into spending a fortune on having the ice cream van converted into a mobile shop that she was now refusing to sell, so Seren couldn't recoup the money she'd wasted turning it into a travelling gift shop.

'Before you say anything you might regret, think about your future,' Nelly added calmly.

'That's what I *am* thinking about,' Seren retorted through gritted teeth. 'I've just lost my job because of that stupid van, and all my savings, and the man I love.'

Nelly stared at her over the rim of her mug, then slowly placed it on the table with an age-spotted gnarled hand. 'You'd better start at the beginning,' she said.

So Seren did.

–

'Can they do that?' Nelly asked, when Seren finished telling her about the gross misconduct charge hanging over her head.

'They can and they did. They're well within their rights, apparently.'

Nelly screwed her face up. 'It's their loss. You're a good little worker.'

'I'm also in competition with them and I more or less said they sold rubbish, so I don't think they would agree with you.' She rubbed her hands across her face, feeling weary to her bones, and so sad she could curl up in a ball for the next six months and pretend the rest of the world didn't exist.

'If they do sack you, I think it's the best thing that's ever happened to you. You were wasted there, and they didn't appreciate you.'

'Really?' Seren sent her a despairing look. 'You do realise I won't get a reference, and without a reference I'll find it hard to get another job.'

'Why would you need another job? You've already got one.'

Seren was about to argue when she understood what her aunt was referring to. 'If you're talking about that van...' she warned.

'I am. That's your job. Your father tells me it's going well.'

'It is. It was.'

'So why on earth would you want to go back to a place where you are just a number and they couldn't care less about you? Being your own boss must be so much more rewarding, and you've done the hard bit. Your van is up and running, so all you've got to do is to go out there and sell stuff.'

'That's easy for you to say,' Seren muttered. Her aunt didn't have a clue what it was like nowadays. Competition was tough, and although Seren wasn't scared of hard work, she was scared of failing.

'Is it?' Nelly asked, eyeing her critically. 'Are you thinking that I don't know what I'm talking about because I'm old? Because I haven't worked for over thirty years? You might be right but what have you got to lose? Give your travelling gift shop your best shot – if, after say six months, you're not making enough of a profit to pay yourself a wage, then I'll agree to sell it.'

'What am I supposed to live on whilst I'm giving it my best shot?'

Nelly snorted. 'There's something else you need to know, so listen up.'

Seren froze. Oh, God, please don't let Aunt Nelly be ill, she prayed. She might be shrunken and frail, have trembling hands and not be able to walk far, but that was down to old age. Her aunt had hardly suffered a day's ill health in her life, and Seren had an urge to shove her fingers in her ears so she didn't have to hear any more bad news, because she didn't think she could bear it.

'You haven't lost your savings,' Nelly said.

It took Seren a second or two to divert her racing thoughts away from more disastrous news and onto the subject of her depleted bank account. 'Pardon?'

'*I said*, you haven't lost your savings. *I* paid for the work on the van. You don't owe the garage a penny.'

For the second time in as many minutes, Seren was speechless.

'Now, stop looking like a cat that can't find its kittens and sort yourself out. Moping about isn't going to help. You need to have more get up and go.' Nelly huffed. 'You youngsters don't know how good you've got it. When I was a girl I was never lucky enough to have a van handed me on a plate. I had to work hard for every penny. I'd have jumped at the chance to have my very own business.'

Seren knew her aunt had a point, but her heart wasn't in it. She felt too miserable and down to put the amount of energy into the van that she knew she'd have to in order to make a success of it.

Nelly was looking at her shrewdly. 'Have a think about what I said about giving it six months and don't make any hasty decisions. Isn't that right Edwin?'

'Eh?' The old gent had made the mistake of poking his head into the day room, and Nelly pounced on him.

'I was telling my niece that she shouldn't make any hasty decisions. She wants to sell the travelling shop.'

'After all the work you've put into it?' Edwin said, walking into the room. 'It would be a shame.' He lowered himself carefully into a chair. 'Sometimes you have to take a risk. Look at Daniel – he's gone for an interview for a new job today.' Scratching his chin, Edwin pressed his lips together. 'It's a pity about you two, though; I thought you made a lovely couple, but if it's not to be, then it's not to be.'

The last thing Seren wanted was to discuss her failed relationship with Daniel's grandfather, so all she did was smile sadly and say, 'These things happen.'

'What things?' Nelly snapped.

'My Daniel and your Seren have split up,' Edwin said.

'Why?' Nelly glared at her.

'As I said, these things happen,' Seren repeated. 'Can we talk about something else, please?'

The three of them sat in silence, then Edwin asked, 'How is your daughter, Seren? Nelly, you didn't tell me you had a great-great-niece.'

'That's because I don't,' Nelly said.

'Oh? I was under the impression Seren had a little girl.' Edwin glanced from Nelly to Seren and back again.

Seren was shaking her head. 'No kids. Not yet. I've got to find the right man first.' She'd thought she'd already found him, but evidently he hadn't felt the same.

Nelly looked baffled. 'What made you think Seren had a daughter?' she asked.

'Daniel said Tobias told him.' Edwin had a peculiar expression on his face.

Where on earth did Tobias get that idea from? She'd not given him the impression she had children, unless he thought she was so fuddy-duddy that she must be a mummy, which was an insult both to her and to mothers everywhere. Look at Nicole – she was as far from fuddy-duddy as a woman could get. She was funny and outgoing, gorgeous and sexy, and—

Seren slapped a hand to her forehead as she remembered who had been with her when she'd last met Tobias. 'I bet it was when I took Freya to the pantomime. Freya is my best friend's daughter. Nicole, her mum, was supposed to come with us, but she didn't feel well, so I took Freya on my own.' Seren smiled: it had been a fun evening. 'I'm her godmother, and since Nicole explained to her what that meant, she's taken to calling me God-Mummy. It's so cute. I think she must have called me that, and Tobias jumped to the wrong conclusion.'

Edwin was staring at her so intently that it made Seren wonder if she had a huge spot on the end of her nose.

'What did Daniel say when he ended it?' Edwin asked, and Seren blanched.

What a personal thing to ask someone you hardly knew. She felt rude not answering though, and it was hardly a secret, so she replied, 'He told me it was because of this new job.'

'I thought as much,' Edwin said. 'And I know why. A few months ago, Daniel was living with a woman called Gina. Did he tell you about her?'

Seren inclined her head. 'He did mention her, but he didn't go into any details.'

'Did he tell you she has a child, a seven-year-old daughter named Amelia?'

'No.' Where was Edwin going with this, she wondered.

He scratched at his whiskers again and his expression was pained. 'It's not my place to say anything – Daniel should be telling you this – but he hasn't told you the full story, and it does have a bearing on why he ended things with you.'

She felt a little awkward, but her curiosity got the better of her. 'Go on…'

'He and Gina lived together for two years; he was virtually a father to that child. She called him Daddy, and he thought the world of her. But… I'm not sure he felt the same way about her mother, and I'm damned sure Gina didn't feel the same way about him. She cheated on him with Amelia's biological father. When Daniel found out, he ended it. It hurt him to walk away from Amelia, but he said he couldn't stay in the relationship any longer. If Amelia had been his or if he'd adopted her, it would have been a different matter, but to all intents and purposes he thought Gina and Amelia's real dad were getting back together, and it would have been wrong of him to stand in the way.'

Seren's heart squeezed as she imagined what Daniel must have gone through.

Edwin wasn't finished. 'That's not all,' he said. 'It didn't work out between Gina and her ex. Gina begged Daniel to take her back, but Daniel couldn't trust her again, so he refused. She used Amelia to try to get to him. Amelia was devastated at him leaving, you see...'

Seren choked back a sob. 'Poor Daniel.' Tears gathered in the corner of her eyes and trickled down her cheeks. Even Nelly's eyes were full.

'Daniel vowed to never again get involved with a woman who had children, because he didn't want another child to go through what Amelia had gone through.' Edwin paused, then continued, 'He didn't want his heart broken all over again, either. He loved that child as though she was his own, you see.'

Seren saw.

She understood where he was coming from, and what he must have thought when he was informed she had a child. But what she couldn't understand was why he hadn't spoken to her about it. He could have asked her outright about Freya and she would have told him the little girl wasn't hers. It would have saved them both a great deal of pain.

Unless...

...he wasn't at all upset about their breakup.

Slowly Seren rose to her feet and picked up her coat. 'Thank you for telling me,' she said. 'I appreciate it, but it doesn't make any difference. Next time you see him, please tell him I wish him well in his new job.'

She managed to walk away with her head high and fought not to break down again; whether or not she had a child was irrelevant – Daniel had a new life and there was no room in it for her.

Chapter 27

Daniel should have been buzzing as a result of the fantastic guided tour around the amazing gardens at Highfields House earlier today, but he wasn't. He was sitting on his couch, staring at a TV he hadn't bothered to switch on and feeling incredibly sorry for himself.

What was Seren doing now, he wondered? Was she at work? Out with her travelling shop? Or sitting at home and wondering what *he* was doing?

He thought about her smiles, the love in her eyes when she looked at him, the kisses that sent him weak with longing, her soft sigh of pleasure when he—

Crossly, he blew out his cheeks and told himself to stop wallowing.

What was done, was done. There was no going back, even if he now recognised that he loved her and that her status as a mother didn't matter. He'd made a complete hash of everything, and he was paying the price.

Unfortunately, so was she – no matter how hard he tried, he couldn't rid himself of the image of her sobbing in his truck and pleading with him to give their relationship a chance. Whenever he closed his eyes, it flashed in front of him. It broke his heart to think she was so upset, and that he was the one responsible for that.

A knock on the front door made him jump, and he leapt to his feet, hope threatening to rise up and wash over him; before common sense kicked in and he realised it wasn't going to be Seren.

He considered ignoring it, but the knock came again, louder and more forceful, so he trailed into the hall, his feet dragging, intending to tell whichever political candidate it was to go away.

However, when he opened the door and saw his mum and grandad, he was flummoxed. 'What are you doing here?'

'That's a fine way to greet your mother. We're here to see you, if that's OK? Can we come in?'

'Sorry, um, yeah, of course.' He opened the door wider and moved forward to help his grandad shuffle slowly up the single step, and held onto Edwin's arm to steady him as he crossed the threshold.

'Tea?' he asked, wondering what on earth they were doing here. He'd brought his mum and grandad to see the house when he'd first moved in, to satisfy their curiosity, but neither of them had set foot inside since.

He showed them into the kitchen and lowered Edwin onto the hard wooden bench in the corner. His mum took her coat off and sat on the other side, scooting over to allow Daniel to sit down once he'd made the tea.

He filled the kettle and while he waited for it to boil, he said, 'It's lovely to see you, but if you don't mind me asking, what are you doing here? You never come to me, I always come to you.'

'We're concerned about you,' his mum replied.

'Worried enough to drag Grandad halfway across town in the cold and the dark?'

'Yes, actually.'

He didn't miss the exchange of glances between them, and a worm of worry coiled in his stomach.

With the tea made, he sat down next to his mum and eyed her cautiously. 'Well?' he asked.

His mum didn't answer. Instead she said, 'How was your trip to Highfields? Did you get the job?'

'I didn't go for it.'

'Why not, son?' Edwin asked.

Daniel shrugged. 'A number of reasons. I had a good look round and the gardens are stunning.' He could hear how wistful he sounded, and he cleared his throat. 'It would have been perfect if it wasn't so far away and having a boss to report to. But you haven't come here to ask me about the job. You could have done that over the phone. What is it? What's wrong?'

His stomach knotted in fear. Was it his grandad? His mum? He couldn't bear it if either of them was ill. He knew Edwin had Parkinson's Disease, but he'd done enough reading up on it to know that his grandad was unlikely to suddenly deteriorate. Therefore it had to be something else, and for the pair of them to arrive on his doorstep unannounced meant it had to be seriously bad news.

His mum must have seen the worry on his face because she stroked the top of his arm and said, 'Nothing's wrong, but your grandad has some news – something he found out today – and he wanted to tell you before you did anything you might regret, such as giving notice on this place.'

'What news, Grandad? What's going on?'

'It's about Seren.'

Daniel got to his feet and headed to the door, his heart thumping wildly, praying nothing had happened to her. 'Is she hurt? Has she been in an accident?'

'Sit down, son, she's fine,' Edwin patted the seat beside him, and Daniel slowly sank onto it. 'She came to visit Nelly earlier and she was a bit upset.'

Daniel stared at the floor, not daring to look up in case his pain showed on his face. He'd been such a fool. But why come here to talk to him about Seren?

Edwin continued, 'She told Nelly she was going to sell the van.' He snorted. 'You'll never guess – it wasn't her father who bought her that ice cream van, it was Nelly. And she also paid to have it converted.'

'Dad, that's not important right now,' Linda reminded him.

'Sorry, love, you're right.'

Daniel was confused. 'Why was she upset? I'd be dead chuffed if someone bought me a van and paid to have work done on it.'

'She's been sacked,' Edwin said. 'Because of the van. They claimed it's gross misconduct, something to do with a conflict of interest and her telling a customer that she said the stuff she was selling was of better quality than the goods in the supermarket she works in.'

'Did she tell you this?'

'Nelly did, after Seren left.'

If Daniel hadn't felt awful before, he most certainly did now. He'd dumped her, and then she'd been sacked. 'She must be at her wits' end,' he said, his chest tightening as he thought of how terrible she must be feeling. 'To lose her job just before Christmas is the pits, and with a little girl to support, too.'

'Dad, for goodness' sake, tell him!' Linda cried.

'That's the thing, that's what I wanted to tell you,' Edwin said. 'Seren doesn't have a child.' He sat back smugly. 'Your friend got it wrong.'

Daniel gawped at him, his mouth open, his eyes wide, not certain he'd heard properly. 'Are you sure?'

'She told me so herself. The little girl Tobias saw her with was her friend's. The child calls Seren God-Mummy because Seren is her godmother. Tobias must have thought he heard the girl call her Mummy.'

Daniel slumped back in his chair, and nausea washed over him as the news sank in. He'd been an idiot, a total wally. If only he hadn't acted so hastily. If only he had checked for himself. If only he'd not made such a stupid vow. If only...

He swallowed down a lump in his throat, and there was an ache in his heart so fierce he thought it might shatter into a thousand pieces. 'Thanks, Grandad, I appreciate you telling me this. But...' He swallowed again. 'It's too late. She probably hates me, and even if she doesn't, when I tell her the reason I broke up with her she'll definitely hate me.'

'I already told her.' Edwin had the grace to look sheepish. 'I thought she deserved to know.'

Daniel blinked hard, tears gathering in his eyes, and he shook his head in despair. God, what must she think of him? 'What did she say?'

'Not a lot,' Edwin admitted. 'Did I do the right thing?'

'I don't know.'

'She did say one thing,' Edwin added after a pause. 'She said to tell you she wishes you well in your new job.' He paused again. 'But you haven't got a new job, have you?'

Numbly Daniel shook his head.

'In that case, shouldn't you tell her that?'

'What's the point?' Daniel asked.

'Love is the point, son. *Love.*'

Seren seriously wasn't in the mood for making Christmas decorations. She was sitting in the shed, her fingers freezing and her heart sore. Or was her heart freezing and her fingers sore? Both, probably. She felt cold inside and out, and all of her hurt. Not so much a physical ache, but an ache deep in her soul.

She was only out here in an attempt to use up the rest of the greenery so she didn't have to throw it away. She was supposed to be taking her van to a Christmas tree farm tomorrow, and although she desperately didn't want to go, she felt obliged to shift as much of her suppliers' stock as she could by the end of the day so she could ease her conscience that she'd done her best by them. As for her own stuff, she'd leave it until nearer lunchtime before discounting all the wreaths, garlands, and assorted table decorations she'd so lovingly made.

The farm held a Christmas tree sale every year which was usually well attended, so she was hoping for a good turnout. She was also hoping that those people who preferred real trees would also prefer fresh garlands and not the fake variety, which was why she was using up the last of her supplies. If she didn't manage to get rid of everything she'd made, she'd donate whatever was left to any residential homes and shelters willing to take them off her hands.

'I've brought you a mug of hot chocolate,' her dad said, poking his head around the door and letting in a blast of icy air.

He wore a worried expression, as well he might. Seren hadn't forgiven him for letting her believe *he'd* bought the ice cream van, when it had been Aunt Nelly's doing all along. And letting her believe she'd spent all her savings on such a crazy idea as a travelling gift shop, had been downright cruel.

'Thanks,' she said. 'Put it over there, please.'

'Seren, I know you are cross with me—'

'Cross is an understatement.' She looked away. 'OK, so I mightn't have used up all my savings on that stupid van, but I have lost my job. And let's don't forget that if it wasn't for Dippy, I wouldn't be sitting here with my heart broken because I would never have met Daniel.'

Her father perched on the stool next to her and picked up a pair of pliers, turning them over in his hands, studying them. 'Pretend for one minute that you'd never met Daniel, how do you think you'd feel about the van? Would you still feel like giving it up?'

Seren wrapped her hands around the hot mug, letting its warmth seep into her, and she took a sip. She might still be annoyed with her dad, but it was a reasonable question.

'Possibly. I'm not sure. I might have felt a little more positive about it.' She thought back to Sunday when she'd spent most of the day on the internet, searching for venues that might have a vacancy for a little travelling gift shop, before Daniel had dropped his bombshell and blown her heart apart. 'I probably would continue with it,' she admitted, reluctantly.

'Like your aunt said, why don't you give it a go for a few months? I know your heart's not in it, but in time it might be, and it would be a shame to jack it in without giving it a fair crack of the whip. You were doing quite well, weren't you?'

'Better than I expected,' she admitted grudgingly, deciding she might as well forgive her dad and have a proper conversation with him. After all, he'd only done what he thought was best for her, and he couldn't have foreseen that it would cost her her job. Neither was it his fault that she'd had her heart broken.

'So, you might make a go of it, if you tried?' he persisted.

'I might. I hadn't thought much past Christmas.'

'A travelling shop is for life, not just for Christmas,' he'd joked, but she failed to crack a smile. 'Sorry.'

'It's OK.'

He gestured to the mound of ivy. 'Can I do anything to help?'

'Not really. I can't do much more as I'm nearly out of willow branches.'

Patrick rose and went over to a shelving unit, rooting around noisily. He returned to the workbench and set a handful of things down. 'Are these any good?'

Seren saw three circular hoops that she remembered her mum using when she went through her cross-stitch embroidery phase. All of them had broken screws, but the lightweight wooden hoops themselves were still service-able. Her dad had also found a couple of picture frames whose glass had long since been put in the bin.

'Maybe,' she said, her imagination firing, and she felt a tiny jolt of creativity surge through her. It didn't dispel her misery, but it was welcome nevertheless, as a way to focus on something other than Daniel. 'Thanks, Dad.'

'I'll leave you to it,' he said, squeezing her shoulder. 'It's going to be OK, Seren, you'll get through this.'

Seren wasn't so sure. This was the first time she'd experienced the pain of a broken heart, and the way she felt right now, she didn't intend to ever expose herself to the risk of it getting broken again.

Engrossed in weaving tufty branches of pine-scented fir around the smaller of the rectangular frames, she barely registered the sound of the shed door opening again.

Without looking up, she said, 'Put it over there, Dad,' assuming her father had brought her another hot drink to keep her going. She knew he was concerned about her because she'd been living on little more than tea and the occasional digestive biscuit, her appetite having given up the ghost for the time being, so he plied her with drinks on a regular basis, making sure she at least stayed hydrated.

'Seren.'

The oh-so-familiar voice stopped her in her tracks, and she stiffened at the sound of it.

Slowly she put the frame down and turned around.

Daniel was standing uncertainly in the open doorway, letting the heat out and the cold late-afternoon air in.

'Daniel.' Her tone was expressionless, but her heart was beating uncomfortably fast and she felt she couldn't catch her breath.

'Can I speak to you?'

'You'd better come in.' She shivered, but it wasn't just from the chill.

He sidled in, closing the door gently behind him, but made no move to come any nearer.

Seren wrapped her arms around her middle and waited for him to explain why he was there.

'I came to...' He stopped. 'I wanted to...' Another pause, followed by a small self-conscious laugh. 'This isn't easy.'

Seren waited. Him telling her he was dumping her because he was moving two hundred miles away hadn't been easy for her to hear. Neither had it been easy to discover he would have finished with her anyway because of a child she didn't have. If he thought *he* had it hard, he ought to try *her* shoes on for size.

'I love you,' he said.

Seren tried to draw a breath, but the air was too thick. Putting both hands on the worktop, she thought she might faint, and she lowered her head, turning away from him, praying she wouldn't pass out.

He loved her. He'd just said so.

But it didn't change anything.

Or did it?

She managed to suck some oxygen into her beleaguered lungs, and when she could finally speak she discovered she didn't know what to say.

'I didn't take the job,' Daniel said, into the lengthening silence. 'I went there with the intention of taking it, but... I love you. I know it's too late, but I wanted to tell you.'

'Freya isn't mine.'

'I know. My grandad told me.'

'You should have asked me.' She looked up, meeting his gaze.

'Yes, I should. I am so, so sorry.'

'Would it have made any difference? Or was Freya just an excuse?'

'I wouldn't be here if it was.' He hung his head. 'What I did, how I treated you, it was inexcusable.'

Seren huffed. You can say that again, she thought, but even as she thought it, her tummy turned over. Dare she hope?

'Can you forgive me?' He peeped out from underneath his lashes, and she noticed they were wet. Was he crying?

'I don't know.' She forced the words out through a throat full of glass shards.

His response was little more than a whisper. 'I understand.' He turned to leave.

'Wait. Don't go.' Was she about to do the stupidest thing in her life – or the best thing? She thought back to what Aunt Nelly had said about giving her business her best shot, and about how she was seriously considering doing that very thing. If she could take a chance on a travelling Christmas gift shop, surely she could take a chance on Daniel.

What did she have to lose?

Her heart, that's what.

But she'd lost that already. It was firmly in Daniel's possession. The question was, did she have the courage to trust him with it?

He was watching her, his face damp, anguish in his eyes. There was pleading too, and suddenly she understood that he was hurting as much as she. Ending their relationship had been as hard for him to do, as it was for her to hear. He'd done it not because he didn't care for her, but because he cared so deeply about someone else – a child. Admittedly one that wasn't hers, but if his decision to walk away had been because he didn't want to risk another child getting hurt, it could be seen as admirable. In a roundabout way.

He'd come back to tell her he loved her and ask for her forgiveness. But there was one thing she wanted to know…

'If I forgive you, what then?' she asked. 'Do you see us getting back together?'

'That's what I'm praying for. I'd like us to start over; because, Seren, my love, I had a good long look at my life without you in it, and I didn't like it one bit.' He caught his bottom lip between his teeth and shook his head then said, 'I love you, please believe me.'

She did believe him. 'I love you, too,' she said softly. 'I have one condition. Two actually. The first is that for this to work we've got to be open with each other. If something is bothering you, you must promise you'll talk to me about it.' She looked at him expectantly, her pulse loud in her ears, her insides somersaulting.

'I promise. What's the other?'

'That you come to the Christmas Tree Farm with me tomorrow and help me with Dippy, because I've got an awful lot of garlands and wreaths to sell.'

Daniel briefly closed his eyes and when he opened them again he was smiling softly. 'I'm going to be there anyway,' he said. 'I'm Santa.'

'Of course you are.' Their paths had crossed so many times during the past few weeks that there was an inevitability about it. They wouldn't have been able to escape each other if they'd wanted to. Fate was pushing them together, whether they liked it or not.

Thankfully, Seren wasn't complaining.

'Seren…' Daniel strode across the shed and swept her into his arms. His voice was low and hoarse, and the hunger in it made her head swim and her heart race, but before his head bent to hers and his mouth found her lips, he stroked a thumb across her cheek, wiping away the tears that had spilled over. 'I promise I'll never hurt you again,' he vowed.

As he kissed her, Seren found she believed that, too.

Chapter 28

'I've got something for you,' Daniel said, when Seren arrived at his house ridiculously early the following morning to pick him up to go to the Christmas Tree Farm.

He had his hands behind his back and she could see tufts of foliage poking out around him.

'What is it?' she asked.

'Ta da!' With a flourish, he presented her with a misshapen wreath.

'It's lovely,' she said, taking it from him. It was decorated with lots of greenery and some rather pretty white flowers, and she inhaled their sweet scent with pleasure. 'What are they?'

'These are *helleborus niger*, also known as Christmas rose.' He pointed to several wide-open flowers with bright yellow stamens, which didn't look like any rose she'd ever seen before. 'And these here…' He touched the petals of another white flower, with longer yellow stamens '…are *lonicera fragrantissima*, winter honeysuckle. I grew them myself. I made the wreath myself, too.'

He was so proud of it, Seren was touched by his thoughtfulness. It didn't matter that it was an odd shape, the fact that he'd made it and hadn't just grabbed a bunch of supermarket flowers, meant the world to her.

'I haven't quite perfected the shape yet – the bottom of the heart is easy enough, but the rounded bits at the top are more difficult to get right.'

Seren examined it, thinking *so that's what it's supposed to be – a heart-shaped wreath.* 'You've not done too bad a job,' she said, giving him a kiss.

It was a few minutes before they were able to carry on the conversation.

'I thought you could maybe make some for Valentine's Day,' Daniel said. 'I think they'd go down a storm, with red roses obviously, not white ones. Although you could use white ones for weddings. What do you think?'

Seren thought it was a marvellous idea, but they had today to get through first and loads of fresh greenery to sell before she could turn her mind to the new year and beyond. 'Get in,' she told him, returning to Dippy and climbing into the driver's seat.

She was glad Daniel was with her, because the farm was off the beaten track and down a narrow lane and she didn't think she would have found it on her own. Making a mental note to invest in a satnav after Christmas, she parked the van and began to set up, while Daniel went off to find the grotto in which he was to spend the next few hours.

Seren blew him a kiss and he pretended to catch it, clutching his hand to his chest with a blissful expression on his face. Abruptly he became solemn, and even from this distance she could see the sincerity in his eyes as he mouthed, 'I love you.'

Smiling to herself, Seren marvelled at how her world had turned upside down in twenty-four hours. This time yesterday, she'd had to drag herself out of bed and force her reluctant body to go through the motions of pretending to be a functioning human being, when all she'd wanted to do was to hide under the duvet and sob into her pillow.

But she'd made the effort to visit Aunt Nelly, and now here she was with a job (of sorts – if it panned out), her savings intact and in the loving arms of her boyfriend.

Not only that, but she also couldn't wait for Christmas, because she'd be spending the biggest part of it with Daniel. Which reminded her... she intended to pay Santa a visit later, sit on his knee and tell him what she wanted for Christmas.

–

It was only going to be a short day because by four in the afternoon it would be too dark to wander around a Christmas Tree farm, so Daniel didn't mind only having a short comfort break to wolf a sandwich down and have a hot drink.

He'd gone from dreading today (having to be happy and joyful when he felt anything but, would have been a nightmare) to having a thoroughly good time.

He put it down to being in love and knowing that his love was returned.

His grandad had been right – love *was* the point. He was so grateful to Edwin for making him see that he needed to make things right with Seren.

And he'd certainly done that – although kissing for hours in a draughty shed hadn't been the most comfortable of experiences, it had been the most magical. Eventually though, the cold had driven them indoors, where Patrick had plied them with hot toddies and mince pies, until Daniel thought it best to head home.

He'd longed to spend the night with her again, to show her just how much he loved her, but it was enough for now that they were back together, and he'd gone home on a cloud of sheer bliss, his soul light and his heart singing.

His heart almost stopped when his mobile rang just as he'd finished his last bite of cheese and pickle on sourdough and he hurried to answer it, his pulse thrumming in his veins. He could have sworn he'd turned it off before he'd entered the grotto.

'Hello?'

'What have I told you about answering your phone in such a manner? It simply won't do. If you answer your phone like that when you're working for me, I won't be very impressed.'

'Miss Carruthers. Hello,' he repeated.

'This is she. I'm most disappointed in you. I went to all that trouble to recommend you to Highfields and you turned them down.'

'They didn't actually offer me the job,' Daniel began, wondering how quickly he could get rid of her; he was due back from his break in a few minutes.

'Mr John would have, if you'd been interested,' she declared.

That was nice to know.

'So I'll have you instead,' Miss Carruthers finished.

'What?' Daniel had no idea what she was talking about. She wasn't making any sense.

'Stop being so dim. And don't say what. Say *pardon*.'

'What?'

'Give me strength! You should say pardon or excuse me. Not what.'

'Eh?'

'I give up. What was I saying? Oh, yes, the job. I expect you here on the second of January at eight a.m. on the dot. Don't be late.'

'Late for what?' He had absolutely no idea what she was on about, and he briefly wondered if she was having a funny turn.

Her sigh nearly burst his eardrums, it was so loud. 'Don't make me regret giving you the job.'

'I'm sorry, Miss Carruthers, but what job are you talking about?'

'Gardener, of course.'

'For who?'

'It's *whom*, not *who*. For me. Who else would it be for?'

Daniel didn't have the foggiest. 'Work for you, you mean? In Fernlea Manor?'

'Good grief. Handsome is as handsome does. You might be nice to look at, but you're a bit dim. Yes, Fernlea Manor. We're going to open the gardens to the public in the summer, so you'd better get a move on. I'm willing to pay the same wages as Highfields, and you'll get twenty-five days holiday a year. No more, no less. I trust that's acceptable?'

'Very. Yes. Thank you.' Crumbs. Daniel turned his phone off and sagged against the back of his chair.

He'd got a job. Gosh.

As the news sank in, he was about to reach for his phone again to tell Seren, when he realised he should have been in the grotto five minutes ago.

Speaking to Seren would have to wait – he had magic to dispense.

–

'Someone looks happy,' Nicole said, appearing at Dippy's window later that afternoon. She had her partner, Aaron, and Freya in tow. 'You'd better tell me the news. It's to do with Daniel, I take it?'

Seren beamed broadly. 'We're back together.' She squeaked with joy and clapped her hands, earning herself a quizzical look from Aaron and a wide-eyed one from Freya.

'I thought he was moving away because he'd got a new job?' Nicole said.

'He decided not to go for it in the end. He said he realised how much he loved me and he didn't want to leave Tinstone.' It was mostly the truth, and Nicole didn't need to know all of it.

'I'm so pleased for you.' Nicole held her arms out, and Seren leant through the window to give her a quick hug. 'We're taking Freya to see Santa, then we're going to choose a tree. We've decided on a real one this year. Wish me luck.'

'Huh?'

'I just know I'll spend the next two weeks vacuuming up pine needles and cursing under my breath. So whilst I'm at it, I may as well buy a garland for the fireplace and a wreath for the door.'

'You're not paying a penny,' Seren said. 'I don't want your money.'

'In that case, let me give you a hand after Madam Freya has told Santa what she wants. You could probably do with a break.'

Seren agreed – and she knew what she was going to do when she had one.

Stroking reindeer wasn't what she'd had in mind, but when Nicole returned, Freya demanded Seren take her to see the reindeer. Again.

'We had to drag her away by her pigtails,' Nicole said. 'She was doing her best to try to ride one.'

'Rudolph isn't there,' Freya said. 'The deers have all got black noses. I asked Santa where he was and he said he'd left him at the North Pole to rest.' The little girl frowned and wrinkled her nose. 'How can he be tired, God-Mummy? He's not flown anywhere yet.'

Seren swapped places with Nicole, who clambered aboard Dippy. 'I expect he's been practising his flying, so that's what is making him tired. He has a lot of ground to cover on Christmas Eve.'

'He's not on the ground. He flies.'

Seren stifled a laugh. 'It's a figure of speech.'

'How can Santa get to everyone's house? Is he magic?'

'I think he might be.'

'How does he deliver presents if my house hasn't got a chimney?'

Seren shot Nicole a 'help-me' look, but all Nicole said was, 'Good luck with that.'

'Did you ask Santa?'

Freya shook her head. 'I wanted to, but Mummy said other children also wanted to speak to Santa, and I should give them a turn. The deers are over there.' She tugged Seren's hand, pulling her towards a small enclosure containing three placid reindeer who were contentedly chewing on a bale of hay.

It was getting dark rapidly now, and most people were heading off home, their trees chosen. Seren intended to pack up soon and head off too, and her toes curled in anticipation. She was going to drop the van off at her house, then go to Daniel's.

She didn't expect to emerge until tomorrow, and the thought of spending the night in his arms was incredibly intoxicating.

With a squeal that made Seren jump, Freya broke free of her hand and launched herself at a rather jolly rotund gentleman in a red suit with a white beard.

'Santa!' Freya yelled, her little arms around Daniel's pillow-enlarged waist.

'Santa,' Seren said, her voice soft and full of love. 'I think you've already met Freya.'

'You're the little girl who wanted to know where Rudolf was,' Daniel said, as Freya let go of him, suddenly shy.

Seren took hold of her hand in a firm grip.

'Why don't they have horns?' Freya asked, her attention switching to the reindeer in the pen.

'They're called antlers,' Daniel said. 'These ones don't have antlers because they've dropped off.'

Seren's eyes widened and she waited for him to elaborate, whilst keeping a firm hold on Freya who was attempting to squeeze through the bars so she could get closer to the animals.

'Do you know why they dropped off?' he asked Freya.

'No…?' Freya reached out to stroke the antler-less head of the nearest reindeer.

'Because that's where all the flying dust is stored, and once it's used up the antlers drop off to let Santa know that he has to use another reindeer if he wants to fly somewhere.'

'Is that why you didn't bring Rudolph with you?'

'Exactly! I don't want to use up all Rudolph's flying dust before Christmas Eve, because I wouldn't be able to visit every boy and girl if he did.'

'Nice one,' Seren said, filled with admiration.

'You don't have to visit every boy and girl,' Freya said. 'Some of them have been naughty.'

'Ah, but I still leave them something, and do you know what it is?'

'No?'

'A lump of coal.'

'I don't like coal.' Freya's little nose wrinkled again. 'God–Mummy, what is coal?'

'A lump of dirty black rock,' Seren explained.

'Ew.'

Seren met Daniel's gaze. 'Thank you. That was awesome. She's cute, isn't she?' Seren was as proud of Freya as if she were her own child.

Daniel smiled at the little girl, and Seren's heart melted at the tenderness she saw in his face. Some day he'd be a fantastic father, but for now he was turning out to be quite a good boyfriend.

'Freya, you remember me telling you that Santa is my boyfriend? Do you mind if I give him a kiss?'

And when Freya shook her head to indicate that she didn't mind, Seren leant forward and kissed her very own Father Christmas.

This Christmas was promising to be the very best yet, thanks to a scruffy little ice cream van that had magicked itself into a cosy travelling Christmas gift shop.

But, as her dad said, a travelling gift shop wasn't just for Christmas!

Acknowledgements

Thank you to my husband for his unwavering support, and for insisting I take time away from the computer now and again – I always feel more energised after the break. My mum also deserves a huge thank you – she knows why. And I must mention my daughter, because she'd be upset if I didn't.

Emily at Canelo has my undying gratitude for working her magic to turn my rough and sometimes incomprehensible scribblings into a proper story, as do the rest of the pixies and elves at Canelo who have helped make this book come alive.

But most of all, thank you, lovely reader – I hope you still believe in the magic of Christmas xxx